WHEN ALL MY
DREAMS COME TRUE

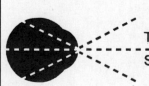

This Large Print Book carries the
Seal of Approval of N.A.V.H.

WHEN ALL MY DREAMS COME TRUE

JANELLE MOWERY

THORNDIKE PRESS
A part of Gale, Cengage Learning

GALE
CENGAGE Learning·

Detroit • New York • San Francisco • New Haven, Conn • Waterville, Maine • London

GALE
CENGAGE Learning™

Copyright © 2011 by Janelle Mowery.
Colorado Runaway Series #1.
Thorndike Press, a part of Gale, Cengage Learning.

LIBRARY OF CONGRESS CATALOGING-IN-PUBLICATION DATA

When all my dreams come true / by Janelle Mowery.
      p. cm. — (Thorndike Press large print Christian romance) (Colorado runaway series ; bk. 1)
    ISBN-13: 978-1-4104-3711-2 (hardcover)
    ISBN-10: 1-4104-3711-6 (hardcover)
      1. Ranchers—Fiction. 2. Ranch life—Fiction. 3. Large type books.
    PS3613.O92W47 2011b
    813'.6—dc22   2011003362

Published in 2011 by arrangement with Harvest House Publishers.

Printed in the United States of America
1 2 3 4 5 6 7 15 14 13 12 11

*To my Lord and Savior, Jesus Christ,
the author and perfecter of faith,
who endured the cross for all.*

*And to Rodney, my one true love,
who shows me how to find joy
in each day.*

ACKNOWLEDGMENTS

My deepest thanks to those who played a part in helping me with this story: Tammy Ayers, Marcia Gruver, Elizabeth Ludwig, Rachel Moon, Rod Morris, Sandra Robbins, MerriDee Shumski, and Nancy Toback.

A special thanks to Harvest House Publishers, who believed in me and this story and took me into their loving family.

And finally, to my agent, Sandra Bishop. Your hard work and dedication deserve much more than a simple thank you. I'm honored to be working with you.

ONE

Colorado Territory 1872

I'll be dead in a minute. Maybe less.

Bobbie McIntyre spurred her horse. "Faster, Mack. Hurry." She peeked over her shoulder, saw the man's gun poised at her back. Her heart thudded harder than the beat of Mack's hooves.

"Go, Mack!" The wind swallowed her plea.

The bandit was gaining ground fast. She leaned lower over the saddle. The cold mountain air blurred her vision and whistled past her ears. Mack's chest heaved and sweat streamed down his neck. He stumbled, then righted again.

She veered left toward the boulders, pulled her pistol from her holster, then turned in the saddle and aimed.

Something slammed into her back. Her gun blasted before it slipped from her grasp. She hit the ground, knocking the breath from her. A heavy weight pressed her down, then rolled off her. She lay dazed.

What happened?

The click of a gun hammer set fire to panic. She scooped up a fistful of soil and stones, pushed to her knees . . . and stared into the steel barrel of a pistol. The dirt in her hand trickled through her fingers to the ground.

She peered around for her own gun and faced another barrel. Two men. At least that answered her question of what threw her from the saddle. The second man must've been hiding behind the boulder she'd planned to use for protection. She stilled while her mind scrambled for a way out of her mess.

The tall, scruffy man grinned. "Well, looky here, Jace. We chased a man and caught us a gal."

Jace? Could this be Jace Kincaid?

The man named Jace shook his head. "Doesn't matter. An outlaw is an outlaw be it male or female."

The tall man snorted. "Outlaw? This slip of a woman?"

"Well, look at her. She's sure not dressed like a girl."

Bobbie grabbed her hat out of the dirt, resisting the urge to fling it at Jace, and

10

shoved it on her head as she stood. "I don't know who you expected to find, but I ain't her. And I sure ain't no outlaw."

The tremor in her voice didn't make her sound as ominous and convincing as she'd hoped.

"Get her horse, Grant," Jace said. "Let's head on back."

"So we're not gonna hang her?"

Bobbie felt the blood drain from her face. "Hang? For what? Look, I'm —"

Jace swung his pistol toward her again. "Stay quiet, miss. You're already in trouble for prowling around on land that isn't yours."

"This is the Double K, ain't it?"

He scratched his forehead with his thumb. "Yes."

"And you're Jace Kincaid?"

Jace squinted and cocked his head. "Right again. But then, I'd expect you'd know that, what with all you've been up to."

"I ain't been up to nothing." She glared at him, brushing dirt and dead grass from her coat sleeves.

Jace took a deep breath and stood straighter, making him appear even more threatening. By the look of him, he could wrestle a steer and lasso a calf at the same time.

11

"Why'd you chase me, anyway?" she said. "I wasn't prowling. I was on my way to meet you."

"Likely story." He motioned to the horses. "Mount up. The next man you meet will be the sheriff."

Bobbie scowled and took several angry breaths through her nose. "Fine. Maybe he'll listen to me."

Grant lifted the strap on her saddlebags.

"Hold on there, that's private," Bobbie said.

He smirked. "Not anymore."

A gun barrel to her back kept her from taking more than a step. She raised her arms. "Those are my things."

Jace moved beside her. "Leave it be, Grant."

"I only plan to look."

"I said quit."

The tone of Jace's voice would've halted a stampede. Grant stepped back, hands poised in surrender, though a trace of a smile still pulled at his lips.

"Let's mount up," Jace said.

Bobbie looked around for her pistol, and Jace pushed the barrel into her back. "Get moving."

"I want my gun."

Grant pulled it from his waistband and

12

handed it to Jace. "You mean this?"

Jace holstered his pistol and then pointed her gun at her nose. "Mount up."

She headed toward Mack.

"Hold it."

Jace's growl halted her in her tracks. He tucked her gun into his belt, jerked a piece of rope from his saddle, and tied her hands in front, then moved past her and yanked her rifle from the scabbard.

"Now you can get on."

Hoofbeats pounded toward them, and Jace turned to look.

"Great. Hank Willet and his two henchmen. Just what I need."

The lead man astride a dappled horse reined to a stop in front of them and gave Bobbie the once-over. Long gray hair sprawled from under his fine black hat, and his leathery face showed the number of winters spent in the brutal mountain wind. He leaned his forearms on the horn of his fancy saddle as if he had all day.

"Kincaid."

Jace pulled his gloves from his coat pocket. "What can I do for you, Hank?"

Hank bumped his hat up with his thumb, and a smile twitched at the corners of his mouth. "Heard some gunshots. Thought you might need help. I always figured a ranch like this was too much for a boy."

Jace smacked his gloves against his thigh. "I've been doing just fine without you, Hank."

"That's not what I've heard. At the rate your herd is dropping, you'll be out of the cattle business by summer."

"They aren't dropping from lack of care. Someone's been stealing them."

One corner of Hank's mouth pulled back in a sneer. "Call it what you want, boy. The fact remains that you're in over your head." Hank eyed the rope on Bobbie's wrists. "Who's your friend?"

"She's not a friend."

"Obviously. Having trouble with your women now?" Hank snorted and slapped his leg. "You sure know how to pick 'em." He tipped his hat. "I'll leave you boys to your fun."

He nudged his mount into a gallop and departed with the two other men the way he came.

The scowl on Jace's face deepened with the glare he pinned on her. He grasped her arm and led her toward Mack. Before she could climb onto the saddle, he spun her around to face him.

"I've got to admit that you don't fit the type of person I figure could be callous enough to steal another man's cattle." He crossed his arms and narrowed his eyes as he leaned toward her. "But sometimes it's the innocent-looking people who need watching the most. So I have to ask, just what's your business here?"

"I have a note for you."

"Is that right?" He took a step closer. "Let's see it."

"It's in my coat pocket." With a nod of her head, she indicated the pocket on the right side of her jacket.

Jace reached carefully into her pocket and found the piece of paper, which he took out, unfolded, and began to read. While he read, she watched his face. His eyes widened as they traced the lines scrawled over the page and then narrowed when he glanced up.

"You're Bobbie McIntyre?

She licked her dry lips. "Yes."

"From Roy Simms's ranch?"

"Uh-huh."

His gaze hardened.

"Is that a problem?"

The muscles along his jaw jumped like a horse with a burr under its saddle. He crushed the letter in his fist and shook his head. "You bet there's a problem. I was expecting a man."

TWO

Unbelievable.

Early this morning, Jace had told Grant his day couldn't get any worse. But proof of his error stood in front of him in the form of a female with defiance flaring in her eyes. He'd learned his lesson. A comment like that would only set him up for something worse.

So now what? In his note, Roy praised Bobbie as an excellent worker, all but daring him to allow her to prove herself. He might do just that. He'd deal with Roy later. In the meantime . . .

"Give me your hands."

She narrowed her eyes and didn't move.

For the first time that day, Jace's mood lightened. Who wouldn't be cautious after being treated like a criminal? He reached for the rope. "I'd like to untie you."

"Whoa." Grant put out his hand. "You sure about this? How do you know she's who the note says she is?"

"There's an easy way to find out." He looked the girl in her eyes. "What's the name of Roy's wife?" At her irritated sigh, he crossed his arms. "The quicker you answer — correctly — the quicker you get freed."

Nostrils flaring and lips tight, she raised her chin. "Maggie."

"And the name of his youngest daughter?"

"He doesn't have a daughter."

"Who's his foreman?"

This time tears appeared, and she bit down on her bottom lip. "It was Robert McIntyre." She blinked and drew a deep breath. "Now it's Tim Hughes."

For the first time, the McIntyre name struck a chord. "Robert was your father."

Her chin dropped to her chest.

He shuffled his feet, scuffing the dirt into a tiny dust cloud. "I'm sorry for your loss."

She didn't look up but nodded her acknowledgment.

He lifted her hands and untied the rope. "Let's go."

The brim of her hat raised just enough to let him see the moisture in her eyes. "You're going to hire me?"

The irritation from earlier returned. "I didn't say that, but there's no way I'm going to leave you out here alone. Roy said in the note you were a good worker . . . that I'd be surprised at your abilities."

No response. At least she wasn't a girl who'd talk the legs off a wagon team.

"You carried both pistol and rifle. Do you know how to use them?"

The slightest twitch moved the corner of her mouth. "Give them back, and I'll show you."

Not the response he expected. He pulled her pistol from his belt and her rifle from his scabbard. With only a slight hesitation, he handed her the weapons.

She holstered her pistol and checked the ammunition in the rifle. "Pick a target."

As Jace glanced around to find an impossible shot, Grant slowly shuffled to a place behind them, putting some distance between him and this girl. Jace was inclined to do the same, but he stood his ground.

He spotted what he wanted. "There's a knot in the tree standing off to the left of that largest boulder. See it?"

She squinted at the tiny target, then cast him a frown. He squelched a smile.

Seconds later, she snapped the barrel closed with a click, hefted the rifle to her shoulder, and squeezed off a shot. What used to be the knot was now a light-colored spot where the bullet splintered the trunk. A low whistle from Grant put voice to Jace's amazement.

"How'd you learn to shoot like that?"

"Daddy wanted to be sure I could defend myself. Didn't work out so well today, though, did it?" She shoved the rifle into its scabbard. "So, do I get the job?"

Jace headed for his horse. "Time to get home."

He climbed onto his saddle and waited for Grant and Bobbie to do the same.

A gunshot blasted to the west. Two more followed in quick succession. Jace looked at Grant. Without a word, they raced in the direction of the trouble. Bobbie rode hard alongside them.

They rounded the curve of a cliff and came upon Hank Willett and his two men hiding behind some boulders. One of the men sat propped against the rock with blood oozing from his shoulder.

Hank waved his gun at them. "Get down before you get your fool heads blown off."

They dismounted and dashed for cover. Jace scooted close to get a better look at the bullet wound. The man would live, but he'd hurt awhile. "What happened?"

"What does it look like? We got shot at." Hank peered up into the hills. "Just mind-ing our business heading home and someone blasted a hole in Morton." He hunkered down and shook his gun in Jace's face. "What's going on here, boy? We're still on your land. You got someone up there trying to get rid of your competition?"

Jace batted the gun away from his face. "None of my men are around here. They're all at the ranch waiting for me."

"You sure about that?"

Jace's fingers curled into fists. "They're at the ranch."

Grant peered up over the boulder. "Let's see if the shooter's still up there." He fired a round before Jace could say a word. No shot answered. "I say we go up and make sure."

Jace grabbed his arm. "You help Hank get Morton to the doctor. I'll go up and check things out."

"But —"

"I don't want your help." Hank stood and holstered his pistol. "You're nothing but a wagon load of trouble, and I want none of it." He bent down and helped Morton to his feet. "Do us all a favor, Kincaid. Move on before you get us all killed."

Jace waited for Hank and his men to ride off before heading into the hills. After several minutes of scouting around, they found nothing. Not even hoofprints to prove

20

anyone had been there. That fact fit right in with everything else happening on the ranch. Nothing made sense. Stolen cattle, and now a man getting shot, left him with more questions than answers. No doubt the sheriff would call on him. If not tonight then first thing in the morning. Shame of it was, Jace wouldn't have anything to tell him.

He looked up to find Bobbie staring at him, her expression one of doubt. Or maybe it was confusion. Didn't matter. If the day's events sent her packing, so be it.

"Let's get back."

What he wouldn't give to start this day over again. Maybe if he'd spent some time on his knees, things might have turned out better.

Bobbie likened her state of mind to a landslide. What was Roy thinking, sending her into the mess going by the name of the Double K Ranch? She'd deal with Roy later. Right now she had to figure out if she wanted to wade into this disaster or race down a trail in the opposite direction. Good thing Grant was leading the way. She couldn't think clearly enough to find the end of her nose.

She glanced back at Jace, who didn't bother hiding his stare. He never did give her a straight answer on whether or not she was hired. By his expression, he'd just as soon shoot her. Maybe it wasn't that bad, but no doubt he'd rather get bucked off his horse and land in a pit of rattlers than take her on as a wrangler.

Daddy often told her worrying would only get her an upset stomach. She'd succeeded in getting queasy. Now it was time to stop fretting. Either it would work out or it wouldn't. To relax, she only needed to immerse herself in the surroundings. She never got enough of gazing at the mountains, especially this time of year when new life was just a whisper after all the snow.

With a creak of saddle leather, she twisted around toward Jace. "From what I've seen, you have a beautiful ranch."

He looked at her long and hard before he said, "Yep."

So much for pleasantries.

By the time the ranch site came into view, her nerves were stretched tighter than her daddy's fiddle strings. Grant let out a whoop and galloped ahead, gaining the attention of every man working in the corrals. He'd already dismounted and was chatting with a couple men, pointing at her, when she and Jace caught up.

Jace led her between two of the three corrals, passing right in front of most of the men. Their stares burned hotter than a branding iron and spoke louder than the bawling calves in the furthest pen. Two of the men elbowed each other and burst into laughter. She sat in her saddle with all the pride she could muster and hoped she'd show them that their ribbing didn't bother her one bit, though the old ache in her heart returned.

The sight of a stallion so black he held hints of blue made her rein in her horse. Jace stopped next to her.

"He's beautiful."

"Isn't he?" Jace sat taller in his saddle. "He's the prize of the ranch."

"I can imagine." The stallion tossed his head and pawed the ground. "Is he broken?"

"Not yet. It's been slow going."

She scrutinized the horse and licked her lips. "I can break him for you."

Jace's snort matched that of the stallion.

She leveled her frown on him. "I can break him."

He rubbed at his day-old beard while eyeing her. "All right. Go ahead. Give it a try. I just hope you don't get yourself hurt." He nodded to his men. "Get him ready, boys."

Bobbie eyed the ebony beauty again. The thrill of working with such a splendid horse overrode her anxiety that she might fail to follow through on her claim.

She climbed into the corral and circled the stallion while the men busied themselves checking the bridle and tightening the cinches. The matted hair around the saddle and rope marks on the forelegs from being hobbled told her all she needed to know about the hours already spent gentling this horse. And the fact that the men were able to touch the steed without him fighting back meant he couldn't be far from being broken. Yet distrust shone from his eyes, and he held himself tense.

The stallion's shiny black coat gleamed over his rippling muscles. She caressed his cheeks and then ran her hands down to his nose. He snorted and bobbed his magnificent head. With quiet murmurs, she continued stroking his nose. She inhaled the scent of sweaty horseflesh and smiled.

After patting the horse's head and whispering to him one more time, she walked to his side, sliding her hand along his neck and shoulder. His flesh twitched beneath her palm. She pulled her hat down, fitting it snug around her ears. One of the men held his hands like a stirrup to help her mount, but she declined his offer with a shake of her head.

Moving slowly, Bobbie slipped her foot into the stirrup, carefully lifted her leg over the cantle, and slid onto the saddle. Once she'd settled in, the horse began to rear. He left no doubt about his strength, giving her a bone-jarring ride. She struggled to hold her neck stiff enough to keep her head from snapping around.

Bobbie watched the stallion's head for signs of his next move. He bucked in a rhythm — a short skip between each high kick. She settled into the pattern, certain she could break him. The burning muscles in her arms screamed for relief. The stallion dug in his front hooves and came to a jolting stop before bucking straight up, throwing her from the saddle.

Dust billowed around her as she lay in the dirt. Her lungs fought for air for the second time that day. Several faces appeared above her.

"You all right?" Jace reached to give her a hand up.

She jumped to her feet. "Let me try again. I know I can break him."

"I think that's enough for one day." Jace eyed her and smiled, so briefly she couldn't be sure he'd smiled at all. "You proved you could ride. You stayed on longer than I thought you would. Longer than I did. You sure you're all right?"

She nodded, still panting from the exertion. Her quivering arms made the simple task of climbing out of the corral an effort.

Jace followed her. "You'll eat supper with my sister's family and me tonight so we can discuss the terms of your employment. We eat at seven. That gives you about an hour to settle your horse in the barn and clean up." He motioned for one of the men to join them. "This is my foreman, Dew Wellman. He'll show you where to keep your horse." With a tip of his hat, he headed toward the big house.

Startled at the sudden acceptance, Bobbie barely managed a reply. "Mr. Kincaid?"

He stopped and spun around. "The men call me Jace."

She nodded. "All right, Jace. May I ask you something?"

"I suppose."

"The stolen cattle you mentioned. You still don't think I had anything to do with —"

"No." He exchanged a glance with Dew then cleared his throat. "Look, I apologize for that, but we're not taking any chances. We'll do the same to anyone else we find on the property without permission. At least until we catch the culprit."

"I understand."

"Is there anything else?"

Bobbie shook her head.

Her new boss strode away, and she bit back a smile. It couldn't have been more obvious he thought she had done well. She could hear it in his voice when he helped her from the ground. But even that thought didn't calm the fluttering in her stomach. She had a new job and was another step closer to attaining her dream. Still, Jace had made a concession hiring a woman. One big mistake, and she'd be out and floundering on her own.

Jace trudged toward the main house to tell his sister and her husband about their supper guest. Maybe Annie and Pete would take the news better than he did. The presence of his new female ranch hand made his steps slow to a complete stop.

The first message he'd received from Roy Simms arrived weeks ago telling him to expect a 19-year-old ranch hand. He should've known Roy wouldn't come right out and tell him the wrangler happened to be a woman . . . girl, really. Jace groaned and rubbed the back of his neck.

Roy had played on his sympathy in the first note, stating the wrangler had lost both parents. From experience, Jace understood how hard life could be when left on your own. Jace glanced back at the woman in question. She leaned against the corral talking to his foreman, one foot crossed over the other. She wasn't any bigger than a 12-year-old boy. Her clothes and neckerchief were dusty and her boots worn out. The dirty brown hat pulled low to protect her eyes couldn't hide their color, which reminded him of the new spring grass he'd seen reflected in the lake that morning.

Her hat covered a good deal of her dark blonde hair but couldn't disguise the thick braid hanging halfway down her back. His gaze paused at the sidearm belted at her slim hips.

A 19-year-old girl on the run from her past. What was Roy thinking? But then again, it should be no surprise. Roy was protective of those he loved. He'd been the same way when Jace and Annie's parents were killed. Roy wanted Bobbie where she would be safe. Purposefully mentioning God's mercy, Roy knew how to pour on the guilt.

Jace admired her grit. Moving all the way from the Boulder area had to be difficult, yet there she stood, ready to prove her abilities. He liked that she didn't seem afraid of a challenge. But something about her didn't sit well. The woman was a puzzle and that made him nervous, a feeling he never liked. Doubting the good judgment God gave him, he continued on toward the house.

"Stop him," a voice yelled. "Someone get hold of that horse!"

Jace spun around. Running at full speed and headed straight for the bridge was his prized stallion.

THREE

The black disappeared down the creek embankment and reappeared on the other side. Jace sprinted to the nearest horse. When he realized it was Bobbie's, he hesitated a split second, but then grabbed the reins and leapt onto the saddle. He tugged hard and spun around to give chase.

An instant later, he found himself flat on his back in the dirt. He rolled to his side, stunned and gasping for air as Bobbie ran past, her boots the only thing he could see. After catching his breath, he struggled to his feet while Bobbie mounted her horse and raced after the runaway.

The horse of one of his wranglers stood tied to the corral. Jace ran his hand over the mare's sweaty flesh. He frowned at its owner but mounted and spurred the animal into a gallop.

Bobbie descended the crest of the hill at the same time he reached the bridge, her rope around the runaway's neck. The relief of having his horse back diminished some of Jace's anger. He took the rope from Bobbie without a word and headed back to the corral.

After placing the lead rope into Dew's hand, he dismounted and flung the reins toward its owner. "I don't know what happened, and I doubt I want to know. Just don't let it happen again."

"Yes, sir," came the quick reply.

Once the gate swung closed, Jace strode over to Bobbie. "Who trained your horse? He bucked me off!" He spat the taste of dirt from his mouth.

"I did. He won't let anyone ride him but me. Mr. Simms gave him to me as a colt for my fifteenth birthday." Her voice dropped to a whisper. "We've spent a great deal of time together. We're very close."

Jace's irritation melted away. She looked and sounded like a 15-year-old girl with her arms folded protectively around her middle. Her gaze fell to the ground.

"I see. Well, you can be sure I won't try to ride him again." He smiled. "He threw me down harder than that black in there."

Activity at the corral suddenly sent her speeding past him. Jace turned in time to see Adam, his newest ranch hand and owner of the lathered horse he'd borrowed, raise a fist high into the air, a whip held tight in his grip. The end of the whip came down across the chest of Bobbie's horse with a *thwack.* The gelding reared and screamed, and his ears lay flat against his head.

Bobbie yanked out her sidearm and trained the barrel on Adam's face. "You whip my horse again and you'll draw your last breath. Do you understand?"

Jace walked between the two and grabbed the barrel of Bobbie's gun. "Let me have the gun, Bobbie."

She tore her gaze from Adam and looked at Jace. She released her hold, hand trembling, and strode to her horse.

"Give me the whip, Adam," Jace said.

The young man thumped his hat back with his knuckles. "That horse nipped at me, Jace. I only wanted to touch him, and he tried to take off my fingers."

Jace held out his hand. "I said give me that whip."

"You're not being fair."

"I told you when I hired you never to whip an animal on my place."

"But I was defending myself!"

Jace's temper ignited. Disobedience and disrespect were two things his father never tolerated. Adam was a kid. How many times had Dad taken on a roughneck kid and trained him to be an honorable man? Jace asked him once why he didn't fire the troublemakers. *"You may not consider ranchin' a ministry, son, but it's a way of life, and our lives are to be a ministry."*

Jace's anger died at the memory. "I'd like you to stay and work for me, young man, but if you don't turn over that whip, I'll have to ask you to leave."

Adam hesitated and his cheeks flushed red, but he slapped the whip into Jace's palm. He cast a resentful glance in Bobbie's direction. "Ain't no good can come of having a woman on this place. Any fool —" Adam clamped his mouth shut, but his hands curled into fists.

"You won't get this whip back until you're no longer in my employ. Understood?"

Adam jammed his hands into his pockets. "Yes, sir."

"Good." Jace turned to leave until he remembered the sweaty horse. He swung back around. "Where've you been, Adam?"

The boy's eyes widened. "What do you mean? I ain't been nowhere."

"Then why is your horse lathered?"

"It — he —" Adam tugged at his shirt front. "I took a ride into town."

"I told you to stay here." Jace studied him

with growing distrust. "Why'd you leave?"

Eyes to the ground, Adam shrugged. "I went to see a girl."

Jace clenched his jaw and waited for the good Lord to get hold of his tongue. "A girl?"

With another shrug, Adam raised his chin in a show of bravado. "Yes, sir."

Jace drew a long breath. "This girl must be something for you to risk losing your job."

Adam's head jerked up. "What? You're going to fire me?"

"Not this time. But disobey my orders again, and you'll be looking for work elsewhere. Got it?"

Nostrils flaring, Adam nodded. "Yes, sir."

"Good." Jace looked around at the other ranch hands. "All right, men, finish your work and call it a day."

"Yes, sir." They disbanded, but Adam turned back and speared him with his eyes before continuing on his way.

Just like Coop, Jace thought. Coop hadn't been happy when Jace decided to name his friend Dew as foreman after Jace's father died. Coop thought the position belonged to him since he'd been on the ranch the longest. Maybe the old hand did deserve that position, but Dew had been a faithful friend for years, and Jace trusted him like an older brother. With all the turmoil caused by his dad's death, Jace needed someone like that in a position of authority. In time, Coop calmed down. Jace figured it would be the same for Adam.

Jace walked to Bobbie's side. "Is he all right?"

Blood from the wound on her horse's chest tinged her kerchief. "He'll mend."

"Good. Come with me. I'll show you where to keep your horse. Then we'll put salve on that gash to keep it from getting infected."

She gave no indication that she'd heard him.

"Bobbie?"

She lifted her head. Tears filled her red-rimmed eyes.

Jace placed a hand on her shoulder. "Let's put him up for the night."

This time Bobbie followed.

Jace indicated the stall she should use for Mack, then handed her the salve. "Come to the house when you're finished here."

She nodded.

He walked out the barn doors but slowed his steps when her voice carried out into the still evening air.

"I'm sorry, Mack. I ain't sure what I got

us into, but if it doesn't get better, we'll leave."

Jace peeked through the doorway to find Bobbie with her arms around the horse's neck. As he walked away, the questions in his mind mounted. Had he made the right decision in taking her on? Would a woman working on a ranch with half a dozen men bring trouble? He shrugged. Only time would tell.

One day. Bobbie had worked at the Double K for only one day, and Jace left her to her own devices. Who knew he'd all but shut down his ranch on Sunday? Jace and his sister had invited her to attend church with the family, but she'd rather watch the men whittle and spit tobacco than pretend to be pious along with all the other fakers sitting in the pews. She'd met her share of hypocrites and had her fill of them. They'd be nice to her face, then laugh when she turned away. No, she'd avoid that kind of religion.

Instead, she spent a quiet morning grooming Mack. Most of the men had saddled up and gone off somewhere. She returned to the house and fried a couple eggs for her dinner, about the only meal she could make on a cookstove that didn't end up too black to identify.

36

She moved all the dirty dishes to the sink to get them cleaned up before Annie returned. Jace's sister made her feel right at home from the first night, as did her husband, Pete, by offering her the spare bedroom next to the kitchen. Their two children were adorable, especially little Ben. His long lashes could make a grown woman jealous. And baby Sara was a miniature of her mother, her dark hair just as curly. Without a doubt, Bobbie couldn't have found a better place to stay than with the Wallace family.

After a quick peek into the living room, she figured banking must be a mighty lucrative business. Pete provided quite well for his family. Fancy curtains danced in the light breeze flowing through the open windows. High-quality furniture filled the room along with several beautiful and expensive decorations. At least they looked costly to her, though her knowledge about such things might almost fill a thimble.

Restless with nothing to do and no one to talk to, she decided Mack could use some exercise. She entered his stall, laid the blanket over his back, and settled the saddle in place.

"Going somewhere?"

The deep voice raised the hair on her

scalp. Alarm skittered over her skin. She thought Grant had left with the others.

She didn't turn but reached for the cinch. "Just for a ride."

Footsteps shuffled closer. "Want some company?"

Her throat grew tight, and her heart hammered. She hurried to finish with the saddle. "Not really, but thanks for the offer."

He entered the stall and moved beside her. "Are you sure? I think the two of us could be good friends." He placed his hand over hers. "Know what I mean?"

His touch sent a hard shudder through her. She yanked her hand from under his. "I know what you mean, and the answer is no."

He moved still closer until his breath washed down her neck. "Now, that's not very friendly."

She turned away. He grabbed her arm and jerked her around to face him. She swung at him with her free arm. He seized it and shoved her backward until he pinned her against the wall.

"Stop it!"

His eyes gleamed so dark, they looked black. "If we're going to work together, we better learn how to get along."

He leaned down toward her mouth. She

twisted away. He chased her every move. She struggled only to have him grip her tighter. She opened her mouth to scream for help.

Then he was gone.

She leapt to the other side of Mack, then looked around. Jace had Grant by the shirtfront. Tears formed, and she panted from a mixture of exertion and relief. She swallowed hard to keep from sobbing.

Jace flung Grant out of the stall. Grant came at him and threw a punch. Jace ducked and rammed his fist into Grant's belly before shoving him to the ground. Grant stood and pulled his gun, but Jace already had his out and cocked.

"Pack your things."

Grant holstered his pistol. "Why? Because of her?" He jerked his thumb in Bobbie's direction. "She expected this to happen. Why else would she spend time with a bunch of men?"

"She deserves the same treatment and respect as anyone else on this ranch."

Grant crossed his arms. "You need me here."

"I don't need anyone on this ranch who would treat a lady that way." Jace waved his gun. "Get your things together. Then find Dew for the last of your pay. I want you off my place within the hour."

Grant didn't move for several seconds. "Fine. There's plenty of other ranchers who could use my help." He spat in the dirt. "I might even head to Texas. I've had my fill of this territory."

Jace stood as a silent guard while Grant saddled his horse. Once Grant left the barn, Jace finally replaced his pistol and turned to Bobbie.

"You all right?" He moved inside the stall and examined her face before lifting and looking at each of her hands. "He didn't hurt you, did he?"

A little embarrassed by his attention, she stepped back and shoved her hands into her coat pockets. "I'm fine." When he remained and didn't say a word, she tried to smile her reassurance. "I'm not hurt. But thank you for coming when you did."

He shook his head. "I'm sorry it happened."

"I hate that I caused you to lose a wrangler. Has he been here long?"

He shrugged. "About five months. A little longer, I guess."

"I'm sorry."

"No need. I don't abide men who . . . act like that." He patted the saddle on Mack. "Going for a ride?"

She grabbed the bridle from the nail. "I thought we both could use some exercise."

Once she had it on, she led Mack out of the stall. Jace followed on her heels.

"You feel up to some company? You'll need to know the boundaries of my property. I thought today would be a good day to get started. We'll be busy again tomorrow."

Bobbie sent him a sidelong glance, then shot him a smile. "Let's go."

"Great. Give me a chance to change clothes. I won't be long."

Bobbie had his horse saddled and ready when he returned. She spent a relaxing afternoon alongside Jace while he gave her a tour around a portion of his ranch. He showed her areas she hadn't yet seen, explaining why he ran the ranch as he did, and telling her how his father came to be the owner.

"My dad was foreman of this ranch years ago for Mr. Hillyer. The man had a daughter, but he hadn't seen her in years. They had some sort of disagreement and she left. From what I know, she never came back or kept in touch."

"How sad."

"I think that's the reason Mr. Hillyer and my father grew so close. Dad told me Mr.

Hillyer treated him like a son. When Mr. Hillyer became old and sickly, he told Dad that rather than have his land go to someone he didn't trust or like, he'd sell it to my father. The charge was one dollar."

Bobbie's mouth dropped open. "One dollar?"

Jace grinned. "That's really something, isn't it? Dad took care of Mr. Hillyer until he died, and then buried him under his favorite tree near the creek."

She shook her head. "That's an incredible story."

"Yes, it is. It's amazing how God provides."

Her back went ramrod straight. She turned and stared at him.

He returned her gaze. "You don't think God had a hand in that?"

She shrugged. "I think one man did something incredibly generous for another man."

"Well, I believe God has a hand in everything that happens, no matter how big or small." Jace stopped his horse and looked around. "If God can create the world and everything in it with so much detail and obvious love, why wouldn't He want to have a hand in what happens in our lives?"

His statement scraped across raw wounds.

42

"So, you're saying if He has a hand in everything, I'm right to blame Him for my parents' deaths and putting me in the position of fending for myself?"

Jace leaned on his saddle horn and looked into her eyes. "I've come to believe that most problems are self-inflicted."

A slap on the cheek would have been just as effective as his words. "How can you say that! You think I'm at fault for my parents' deaths?"

"No, but how you handle it is." His eyes turned sad. "Trust me. I know from experience."

The hairs on the back of her neck calmed. She remembered his loss. "Can I ask . . . how your parents died?"

Jace's jaw tightened. He refused to meet her eyes, and she thought he wouldn't answer.

"They were killed. Murdered." He sat up straighter and threw a glance at her. "Maybe I'll tell you about it someday."

They rode in silence until the sun started to dip toward the mountains in the west.

"We should probably head back," Jace said.

"Um, do you mind if I stay out and ride a bit longer?"

Jace stared at her, then cocked his head.

"You're not going to get turned around and make me come out looking for you, are you?"

She couldn't help but smile at his teasing voice. "I think I'll be fine."

He gazed at her a moment longer before touching a finger to the brim of his hat. He turned his horse toward home and prodded him into a gallop.

The number of years Jace sat in a saddle were evident with the ease and grace with which he rode. His strong back straight, one hand on his thigh, Jace flowed with the movement of his horse.

Bobbie turned Mack toward the mountains. The day had been a shower of new things, good and bad. She needed time alone to work through it all.

Jace wasn't like most believing men she'd met. Many were like Grant Wilcox, who acted like a gentleman when people were around, then would turn into a mongrel when alone. Jace's sister and brother-in-law were just like her new boss, kind and thoughtful. Maybe the church where they worshiped was different from others. She might have to consider taking them up on their invitation to join them some Sunday.

The beauty of the landscape surrounding her grabbed and held her attention. She loved this territory. She loved the mountains and all they contained. Their permanence gave her peace when life became unstable. The tall pines reached to the sky as though seeking to touch heaven. Bristlecone added texture to the open areas and flatlands. The mighty oaks demanded admiration for fighting the harsh winters in order to house a multitude of birds in the spring. She knew there was plenty of country yet to be seen, but why would anyone want to leave the Colorado Territory? Surely there wasn't a more glorious place on earth.

Movement in the distant sky caught her attention as she approached an area of scrub pines. Buzzards circled. She urged Mack into a canter.

When she broke through the cluster of trees, she jerked back on the reins. Mack's hooves skidded in the rocky soil. She jumped to the ground, a gasp stuck at the back of her throat.

FOUR

The pounding of a horse's hooves forced Jace to pause at the threshold of his house. He'd heard the urgent pace too many times lately. He strode around the corner. "Bobbie?"

She was headed toward him at a gallop and held what looked like a calf in front of her. She reached him and yanked back on the reins, dust billowing from the sudden stop. Bobbie dismounted just as fast, stumbling and losing her balance with the weight of a newborn calf in her arms. Jace braced her up, then took the animal from her.

"I think you have some cattle missing." Her chest heaved almost as hard as Mack's. "I can't tell how many. But there are plenty of hoofprints heading away from your ranch." She reached to scratch the head of the calf. "This one's mama is tied to a tree. She has a lot more brands on her than just yours. I left her there so I could get back here before dark."

Jace clenched his jaw and peered into the distance. "Find Dew. Tell him I need him." He ran to the barn, still holding the calf.

Jace, Dew, and Bobbie arrived at the copse of trees as the sun greeted the tips of the mountains. Shadows cast an eerie glow over the scene. Jace pulled his rifle from its scabbard, metal against leather the only sound beyond the chirping crickets and the crunching of rocky dirt under the horse's hooves. He searched the area before dismounting. Gun in hand, he headed toward the trees. Dew and Bobbie followed with their own rifles.

Without a word, they looked over the ground, their eyes trailing the hoofprints leading away. While Bobbie and Dew headed toward the cow tied to the tree, Jace dropped down beside one set of hoofprints — that of a horse. Maybe, just maybe, there was some outstanding mark on the shoe that his blacksmith friend, Cade Ramsey, would recognize. As usual, nothing.

"You need to see this, Jace," Dew called.

Jace headed toward them and stepped around the cow to stand next to Dew and Bobbie. With his finger, he traced the strange branding marks stamped on its side.

"What does it mean?" Bobbie asked.

"I have no idea. I've never seen brands like that before. Except for mine right in the middle of the rest."

Bobbie shivered and ran her free hand up and down her arm. Her gaze darted around the area. "I wonder how long ago this happened."

Jace grunted and traced the hairless markings the color of saddle leather. "Couldn't have been too long. Still looks fresh." He saw her shiver again. "We need to get back, but we can't leave this cow out here. Dew —" but his foreman had already moved to get his horse. Jace removed the rope.

Dew maneuvered his horse behind the cow and gave a shrill whistle to get the beast moving.

Bobbie all but ran toward Mack. Jace would have smiled at the look of relief on her face, but he couldn't find anything funny in the situation. With a flick of his tail followed by a cloud of dust, Mack raced off.

Why would someone steal only my cattle? Jace wondered. Not that he wished any trouble on his neighbors, but why only him? And what were the brand marks saying? The answers eluded him on the ride home.

Those same questions continued to haunt

him the next morning. He didn't get much sleep during the night, adding to his already foul mood. He poked his head inside the door of Annie's house. "I'm not staying for breakfast, Annie."

His sister hurried to the door. "Do you know something about the cows?"

"No, not yet. I'm on my way into town to see Morgan. Maybe he can wire some other sheriffs in the area and find out if they've seen anything like this. Or at least they can keep an eye out for my brand." He didn't wait for a reply and strode toward the barn.

Standing in front of the sheriff's desk a short time later, Jace couldn't believe his ears.

"Calm down, Jace."

"What do you mean, calm down? Someone is stealing my cattle, and all you can tell me is to calm down!"

Morgan Thomas leaned forward over his desk and peered up at Jace above the rim of his spectacles. "Getting all riled up won't help us catch the men who did this. Besides," he smoothed the ends of his mustache, "I'm not the one you're angry with, so stop shouting at me."

Jace took a deep breath, ready to tell Morgan exactly what he thought about his methods of keeping the law, but the sheriff was right. The breath left him in a hiss. He had been fighting his temper since the day he found out about his parents' death, and his frame of mind seemed no better today. They still needed to find his parents' killer, and now he had another mystery to solve. He dropped down on the chair near the desk. He'd never been so weary.

"I'm sorry, Morgan."

Morgan pulled off his spectacles and rubbed the bridge of his nose. "I know. Now, let's take a minute to pray. Then we'll look at these brands you drew from the cow and see what we can figure out. After that, I'll send out some wires."

An hour later, atop his horse and taking in the beauty of the mountains, peace settled over Jace. The time in prayer with Morgan worked wonders on his attitude. He couldn't stop his mind from wandering to his father as he rode home. Had his dad ever run into a similar problem? He couldn't remember, but it didn't matter. The ranch was *his* problem now, and he needed to figure out what to do about the latest challenge.

FIVE

Bobbie and Mack zeroed in on their next target. Since she'd been hired almost a week ago, their main task was cutting and roping calves while Jace and Coop tossed and branded them. She learned in a hurry not to question Jace's decisions. The first day he'd told her they'd be branding calves. She'd looked up at him. "Branding? Don't you think it's a bit —"

"Early? Yes, but I'm not about to let the rustlers get away with any more of my calves without at least getting my mark on them."

And in that moment, Jace had her convinced of his ranching abilities. She didn't mind roping and branding. The work was hard but honest, and the help capable.

Jarvis Cooper. She smiled at the sight of him. When they had first been introduced, he was in the middle of stuffing his jaw with tobacco. He'd scooped his finger along the inside of his cheek when he saw her and discarded the brown wad into the dirt with a flick of his wrist. After wiping his finger on his pant leg, he extended his hand. Once they exchanged greetings, he restuffed his cheek.

A shudder went through her at the memory. She guessed he was only trying to be polite by removing the wad, but she would have preferred he left it alone. Since then, Coop became comfortable with her and apparently no longer felt the need to do away with his tobacco. She'd found him kind and thoughtful, as were all the men. Even her opinion of Adam changed once she got to know him better, though she could tell he still burned because of their encounter that first day. She didn't miss Grant Wilcox in the least, though the ranch could have used his help.

With a quick jerk of her arm, Bobbie sent her lasso flying around the head of the next calf. She whistled a quiet tune, more confident than she'd been the first few days. Her decision to ignore the stares, work hard, and prove she could do her job helped set the tone. Everyone soon relaxed and began treating her as one of the men.

Bobbie drew the calf in and pondered the fine job Jace had done in selecting his hired hands. Her stomach grumbled, and Beans came to mind. The cook reminded her of her father, and that gave them a special bond. He did more grunting than talking, but he treated her with kindness.

Dew Wellman, Jace's foreman, deserved the position. He worked harder than all the other men and knew a great deal about cattle. The rest of the wranglers, Sonny Marshall, David Lundy, and Adam Taylor, had followed Dew out early that morning to round up more cattle. That left Bobbie at the ranch to do all the calf roping while Jace and Coop did the branding.

Determined to make a good impression, she made certain she had a calf ready for Jace and Coop at all times. She looped her rope three times around her saddle horn and sat back to wait until they were ready.

The sight of Annie hanging clothes out on the line made her smile. The lady was easy to like though she was as completely opposite from Bobbie as two women could get. Bobbie towered over Annie by a good five inches, and Annie was an open, kind, and giving person, while Bobbie kept to herself. Still, given time, they might become great friends.

Coop approached and sent a disgruntled glance in her direction. He flipped her lasso from the calf's head. "Hey, Bobbie, you try-

53

ing ta kill us?" Coop tossed the calf on its side and then sat on its head, struggling with the legs while he waited on Jace with the branding iron.

She dismounted in stunned silence and grabbed the calf's hind legs, pulling them back and holding them tight while casting a questioning glance at Jace. He met her gaze for an instant before turning his attention to the calf. He pressed the hot iron against the calf's hip. It let out a loud *baw-w-w.* Moments later the scent of burned hair and seared flesh drifted across Bobbie's nostrils.

Jace looked at her and squinted against the bright sunlight. "What he means by that is, you can stop working yourself into a sweat. You're doing fine, and your job is secure. But as I'm sure you've noticed, I'm a bit shorthanded. You're keeping us so busy, we don't have a chance to breathe."

"And we ain't getting no younger," Coop said with a wink before spitting a stream of tobacco juice into the dirt.

She stared in silence while Jace notched the calf's ear. Then a smile crept across her lips. "Sorry."

The men nodded and went back to work. She returned to the saddle, meandered toward the calves, and returned Annie's wave. Because of the distance she couldn't see if Annie was smiling, but she had no doubt it was there. Besides, how could Annie not be happy? She had a thoughtful, loving husband and two cuddly children. It didn't hurt that she lived amidst such beauty.

Tall trees lined the creek bank that ran along the ranch. In order to enter, a person had to cross a bridge that spanned the creek. Huge oaks also grew along a small ravine that separated Jace's house from Annie's. Mountains rising up in the background gave the scene a finished look. This place was even prettier than the Simms ranch.

Mack tugged at the reins. She smiled and heeled him forward. Her horse loved the job of ranching almost as much as she did.

As the day passed, some of the larger calves struggled with the men. If one fought itself free, she'd jump from the saddle to help. She'd been kicked more than once and bore the bruises for proof.

Another calf managed to break loose from Coop's grasp, and Bobbie lunged from her saddle to drop onto its head. The calf dragged her several feet before knocking her loose and scampering away.

Her battered ego now matched her injured behind. She stood and brushed the dirt from her clothes. Jace and Coop rocked with laughter. She grinned, shook her head at them, and remounted Mack to find that calf before the setting sun made any more work impossible.

She returned before long with the calf in tow, and after dismounting, she headed across the pasture toward the two men. The long day had left her with an ache in every bone and muscle in her body. She caught Jace watching her, his mouth twitching.

She shook her finger at them. "Stop laughing." She had to hide her own smile. "I'm tired of calves, and I'm tired of saddles. If I have to spend another day in that saddle, I'll have to start wearing dresses just to hide my bowed legs. And I'm so hungry that if I have to rope one more calf, I just might cook it and eat it."

"Stop, Bobbie," Coop said holding his side. "I can't breathe."

The smile she'd been hiding claimed her face. She desperately wanted to rub her backside, but instead, she rocked side-to-side in an attempt to get the circulation going again.

The thud of hoofbeats drew their attention to the top of the ridge. Calves herded by the wranglers appeared at the crest and plunged down the slope into the creek. Her groan escaped before she could rein it in.

Coop sent her a teasing grin. "Stoke the fire. Here comes supper." He headed toward the empty corral. "I'll get the gate."

"Thanks, Coop." Jace turned to her. "Why don't you take care of Mack and then head to the house? I want to talk to Dew a bit and I'll be in as well."

"You won't get an argument from me." She was already walking away.

"I didn't think I would."

She took plenty of time caring for Mack while telling him he had worked harder than any of the others. His head dipped lower and lower while she ran the brush over his back.

Her one-sided conversation with Mack continued until Jace entered the barn. He leaned against the stall opposite Mack's, his gaze soft and his hat pushed back on his head. She kept on brushing. *It's his barn after all,* she reasoned. Why shouldn't he stand there if he wanted, his arms crossed and looking for all the world like he felt at ease.

"Do you always talk to your horse?"

She glanced at him before returning her attention to the task at hand. "Yes."

"You've done a good job training him. He really knows his business."

She shrugged. "He's a good horse."

An awkward silence fell between them. Jace cleared his throat. "Annie has supper about ready."

She set down the brush, fished for a lump of sugar in her coat pocket, and said a quiet good night. After patting Mack's neck, she followed Jace to the house.

The washroom sat just off the kitchen, and she stepped inside to clean up. The tub in the corner looked inviting. A hot bath would do wonders for her sore muscles and the smudges of dirt and sweat the mirror revealed.

Jace leaned against the door frame waiting for her to finish. "If you'd like, I could help bring in water for a bath tonight."

Her mouth dropped open. "I'd like that. Thank you."

Jace inclined his head, his gaze questioning.

Questioning what? The fact that his offer surprised me? Surely he realized she didn't know many gentlemen. She smiled and walked past him into the kitchen to offer Annie some help, but Annie had the food on the table and everyone sat waiting on them.

"I'm sorry." Her glance encompassed the sea of faces that met her.

Annie nodded. "You look like you've had a long day."

"Long enough." Bobbie sat down beside Sara. "I think I'll see and hear bawling calves in my sleep tonight."

Ben giggled and imitated a frightened calf while everyone laughed.

"Did I hear Jace offer to help draw bath water?" Annie arranged her napkin in her lap and then looked up.

Bobbie remained silent, letting Jace answer for himself. She didn't expect any favors. He reconfirmed his offer.

"Would you like me to help you wash your hair?"

"That would be wonderful."

An hour later, she leaned back and relaxed in the hot water, relishing the feel of her muscles unwinding. Her eyelids drifted closed as the steam rolled off the surface. She blinked, trying to keep from succumbing to the urge to sleep.

She had stayed up late the night before, her mind going over the thoughts and plans her father had shared for a ranch. For many years she had watched Roy Simms and now observed the way Jace ran his place. She took notes on all she had learned, writing down each item she could recall, not stopping until the words blurred before her eyes.

The sound of the door opening startled her into wakefulness. Annie entered with a pail of warm water. "Are you ready?"

Annie washed Bobbie's hair, then rinsed away the soap with the water in her pail.

"Bobbie, you have the most beautiful head of hair I've ever seen."

She laughed at Annie's remark. "Thank you."

After dressing, Bobbie joined Annie at the kitchen table, where she waited with a steaming cup of black coffee. Annie pushed it toward her as Bobbie ran a brush through her tangled locks.

Annie set aside the newspaper she was reading and watched. Minutes later, she groaned. "I can't stand it." She took the brush from Bobbie and continued the job. "I can't wait until Sara's hair is longer. I've dreamed of doing this with her like my mother did with me."

An ache tore through Bobbie's heart. No one had brushed her hair since her mother died. The memory was wonderful and excruciating at the same time.

"So, tell me about your trip from Boulder. How long did it take, and where all did you stay?"

Bobbie took a deep breath. "It took about

ten days. I didn't rush to get here. I've never been too far from home, so I wanted to take in the sights, do a little exploring."

"It's beautiful, isn't it? Our parents took us on a trip to see more of the territory. I can't imagine there's a prettier place than right around here."

She nodded. "I have to agree."

"So what towns did you stay in?"

Too many questions. "I didn't stay in any towns."

The brush stopped halfway down the length of her hair. "Why not?"

She sighed. "People who live in town have very little tolerance for women like me."

"Women like you?" Annie turned Bobbie's shoulders and peered into her face.

"Unfeminine women in trousers. Men can be rude, and women's tongues often sting. The country held much more peace." She traced a crack in the table with her thumbnail. "I only went into a town if I ran low on supplies. I own a couple old dresses just for trips into town, but I didn't take the time to change into one."

Annie remained quiet for several moments. "I'm sorry, Bobbie. I hate that that happened to you." She hesitated a moment longer before moving the brush again.

Bobbie shrugged but stayed silent. The

61

large clock ticking off the seconds clicked louder as each moment passed.

"What possessed you to leave the safety of the Simms Ranch anyway? I can't think of a single woman brave enough to venture out on her own like you did."

"I don't know if it was bravery or stupidity. Actually, I'm chasing a dream."

When Bobbie didn't say more, the brushing stopped again. "Now, Bobbie. You can't just leave me hanging like that. Don't make me wring this out of you."

The humor in Annie's voice made her laugh. "During the last couple years, my dad and I started talking about buying a ranch of our own. It began as a joke with the two of us stating what we'd do with our own place. We didn't do much about the idea at first, but then the dream took hold of my dad. The more he talked, the more I wanted the same thing. He was to be the boss with me as his foreman.

"We'd always been careful with our money, but once we had something to save for, we watched every penny. We knew it would take less money to buy a small, established ranch than having to build from nothing, so Daddy started watching the papers for just the right place to come along."

Watery eyes set within tough leathery skin flashed before her. Her father's eyes would glaze over as he described the type of place he wanted. By his faraway expression, Bobbie knew he could see it right in front of him — and could picture himself riding across his own property. Tears burned behind her eyes.

"Then . . . he died." Saying the words burned her throat.

Annie's arms encircled her. When Bobbie sniffled, Annie removed her tattered apron. "Here, use this for your nose. It's only a little dirty. Okay . . . it used to be white."

Bobbie reached for the apron and wiped away the moisture, and then placed it in her lap.

Annie crossed her arms. "I still don't understand why you couldn't stay on the Simms Ranch. Not that I'm not glad you're here."

She shrugged. "There were several reasons, really. But I guess the main thing was my fear that if I stayed with Roy and Maggie, I'd get too comfortable and talk myself out of following the dream. I figured if I could venture away from the only home I could remember, I'd take that last step and find the place Daddy and I dreamed about."

"Do you have a location in mind?"

A yawn escaped before she could answer. "No, but wherever it is, I hope it's a lot like here. You and Jace have a beautiful ranch."

"Thank you. So, how long before you think you can fulfill that dream?"

She bit her bottom lip. "I'm not sure yet. I still have a lot of things to work out."

"Like what?"

"Well, I guess the biggest problem is the fact that no man would want to take orders from a woman. I'll have to find a foreman I can trust who knows all about ranching. I also have to gain a little confidence. I was all for the idea of owning a ranch when I thought Daddy would run it." Her voice dropped. "I'd hate to try this alone and end up failing."

Annie stepped behind her to finish brushing her hair. "Now you sound like Jace. Those were almost his very words when the responsibility of running the ranch fell to him. He tried to convince me to sell the place. Claimed he was too young. But I knew the man he was and would yet become." She tapped her finger on the back of Bobbie's head. "I can see a lot of those same qualities in you. You're a hard worker, and I have a feeling that once you start something, you'll be determined enough to see it through."

Bobbie reached back and patted her hand. Annie handed out encouragement like a nutritious meal. Another yawn pushed through.

Annie set the brush on the table. "There, your hair is finished and so am I. I'm going to bed. Help yourself to the paper, if you'd like. Good night."

Bobbie returned the wish, picked up the newspaper, and started reading, a luxury she rarely had time to enjoy.

Jace sat in his office with the newspaper in his hands. Details of a bank robbery filled the headlines, reminding him of some bank notes he'd left with Pete. Jace intended to work on them tonight. He set the paper aside and headed toward the main house, thankful to see a light still burning in the kitchen.

A whistle just started to form on his lips when he crossed the threshold. He stopped short. Bobbie sat at the table with her head resting atop a newspaper. Her long hair fanned across her back and down her side. He cleared his throat, but she didn't move. He leaned against the door frame. This was the first time he'd ever seen her still.

The day replayed through his mind. The sight of woman and beast working together as a unit amazed him. Bobbie and Mack knew each other well. If he didn't know better, he'd think they could read each other's minds. He had exchanged many glances with Coop throughout the day and admitted the admiration and appreciation evident on Coop's face matched what he felt.

The way she'd dismounted at the end of the day brought a grin to his face now. Stiffness had her walking different than usual, though she tried her best to hide it. Her great sense of humor surprised him. She seemed too quiet and reserved to have such an amusing side.

No grumble or complaint about the hard work crossed her lips until they were finished, and that had been in jest. He made a mental note to mail Roy a letter thanking him for sending such great help. In no time she'd earned the men's respect, never flinching from any task nor asking for help.

He pushed away from the door and entered the living room to search for Annie. Someone would have to help Bobbie to bed. The room as well as the rest of the house was dark.

"Now what?" His thoughts went back many years to a night his mother fell asleep while sitting in a chair mending clothes. When his dad picked her up to carry her to their room, Jace asked him why he didn't just let her sleep there.

His dad's voice echoed through his mind. "Because she won't be able to sleep soundly and will probably wake up feeling sore. I wouldn't want that."

Jace stared at Bobbie several more seconds, then leaned down and, with slow and careful movements, lifted her into his arms. Her head slid down to rest on his shoulder as he stood, and her breath feathered across his neck. He all but ran toward her room. Good intentions aside, the last thing he needed or wanted was the memory of her hair brushing against him or the feel of her slender body cradled in his arms.

The moment he laid her on the mattress, Bobbie curled onto her side. Prepared to beat a hasty retreat, the sight of an extra blanket lying at the foot of the bed made him stop. He unfolded the blanket and threw it across her sleeping form. The sound of her soft sigh drove him from the room. He closed the door and leaned against it for a minute to clear his thoughts.

He shook his head in self-derision at his foolish reaction. He wasn't about to let a female wrangler get under his skin. After turning down the lamp, he strode out of the house.

Jace was halfway home before he realized the papers he'd gone after still lay on Annie's kitchen counter. He stopped and turned to go back but couldn't make his feet move. Better not to risk it. He headed home.

Sleep eluded him. Even pounding his pillow with his fist to make it more comfortable didn't work. His eyes fluttered open and he forced himself to consider what it was about Bobbie that made him nervous. Maybe it was just that they didn't know her well enough yet. It wouldn't be the first time one of his ranch hands turned out other than how they presented themselves.

He soon found himself asking God to show him how to help lead Bobbie to Him, and that He would help make his walk with Christ a shining example to her.

He ended his prayer and flipped onto his other side. One last thought crossed his mind as his body shut down. Tomorrow was Saturday. Somehow he needed to find a way to ask Bobbie to join them for church on Sunday. For some reason, he had a feeling it wouldn't be easy.

SIX

What a foul mood.

Bobbie glanced at Jace one last time before heeling Mack into a gallop to catch up to Dew. Today was the first time Jace sent her on the roundup rather than have her stay at the ranch to help with branding, and she couldn't be happier. If she had to put up with his grouchiness much longer, she might have to rope and truss him same as the calves.

Maybe he didn't sleep well last night. She hadn't had that problem. She was too exhausted to remember going to bed. Though well-rested, every muscle in her body moaned and creaked as she dragged herself out of bed at sunrise. She hoped Jace got some rest tonight. He was way too prickly to bear for long. Poor Coop and David would have to deal with him all day.

They rode close to an hour before Dew reined to a stop. He sent Sonny and Adam one direction around a bluff while he and Bobbie would ride the other side. The way he had it figured, they should have close to 50 head when they met up somewhere in the middle. With the memory of Jace's stolen cattle still fresh on her mind, she feared they might venture across far fewer than that during their search.

She and Dew managed to find eight cattle, seven with calves, on their first sweep. They turned south into a gully hoping to locate more. With the face of the bluff to her right and a rock wall to her left, Bobbie had the uneasy sense of being trapped. She urged the cows on faster by increasing Mack's pace. The sooner they were out of the gully, the better.

A low rumble overhead grew louder. She exchanged a glance with Dew before they both looked up. Dust clouded the sky. Tiny pebbles rained down on their heads, followed by larger rocks.

"Landslide!" Dew whistled and hollered to get the cattle running.

Bobbie did the same. The panicked cows tried to scatter and turn back, slowing their progress. Dread rolled through her faster than the stones falling from above.

Bobbie peeked up. Something large hid the sun. Then another. And another. The bawling of terrified cattle echoed off the walls and filled her ears.

"Boulders, Dew! Get out. We'll be crushed!"

The bellowing around her drowned her words. Dew's horse reared, almost unseating him. He looked at her, eyes wide. His mouth moved, but she couldn't hear him. No matter. They raced for the opening.

A loud thud followed by a scream made Bobbie look back. One of the rocks had scuffed the haunches of Dew's horse. Dew leapt off to one side and scrambled to get away from flailing hooves. Bobbie stopped and turned back only to have Dew wave her on.

"Get out! I'm fine."

Bobbie forced Mack forward while keeping an eye upward. A large rock crashed mere feet to her left, but there was no turning back. Mack danced and whinnied but obeyed. She waved to Dew. He ran and jumped up behind her. Without any urging, Mack spun and sped out of the gully.

Once in the open, Dew dropped to the ground, his chest heaving. Bobbie dismounted and knelt beside him.

"Are you all right? You're not hurt, are you?" Though she didn't see any blood, his shirt had tiny tears where it'd been scraped.

"A little sore, but I'm fine. The rock only brushed down my back before hitting my horse."

Dew looked up at the top of the bluff. Bobbie did the same. A brief glimpse of an unknown horse and rider stood in silhouette against the sun before they vanished from sight. Bobbie jumped to her feet and ran for Mack.

Dew stood and reached for her arm. "Stay here, Bobbie."

She hesitated. "But I might be able to catch him."

"No. I won't let you go alone."

Bobbie pulled her arm from his grasp. "Then come on. Hurry!"

Dew grabbed the reins. "Listen to me, Bobbie. Do you really think your horse is strong enough not only to get us both to the top of the bluff but also to overtake someone who's probably riding off as fast as he can? Mack may be strong, but trust me, he can't do it."

Frustrated and angry, Bobbie slapped her palm on the saddle.

Dew retraced their steps into the gully. "Let's go back in and see how many cows those rocks killed. Then we'll find Sonny and Adam before heading to the ranch to report more bad news." He slowed and waited for her to catch up. "Jace is strong, but I don't know how much more he can take."

Who would do such a horrific thing? And why? Careful of her steps and mindful to keep checking above, Bobbie counted the cattle. A cow and her calf were wounded. Miraculously, the rest had survived.

Dew stood eyeing his horse. Bobbie moved to his side. "She doesn't look too bad."

Dew pulled the kerchief from around his neck and wiped at some of the blood. "Nope. With proper care, she ought to be fine in a week."

Dew's voice sounded upbeat, but by his expression, Bobbie figured the misery Jace and his wranglers faced had just begun.

Jace sat low in one of Annie's plump armchairs situated next to the living room window. His head rested against its back while he jiggled his bootless feet on the matching footstool. Any attempt to focus on the bank papers Pete handed him earlier met with failure.

Failure. The word defined his life since his parents' deaths. If he didn't find the person stealing his cattle and attempting to kill his wranglers, his efforts to run the ranch would be described the same way.

After ordering Dew to stay at the ranch, Jace and Sonny returned to the bluff to do some exploring. The two sets of tracks they found proved his suspicion that he fought more than one man.

He could have lost Dew and Bobbie today. Every time he thought about it, his mind went into chaos. Anger and fear mixed with helplessness and resentment. In the end, dropping to his knees and praying for help was the only thing that calmed him. The pleas were frequent since he couldn't stop thinking about how close he came to losing friends. Dew had scrapes and bruises down his back to prove how near he came to death. Since they didn't work on Sunday, at least he'd have time to recover.

Then there was Bobbie. The memory of her in his arms haunted his dreams . . . when he managed to get a bit of sleep. With very little rest, he woke up moody and with a headache gnawing at his temples. When he got to Annie's for breakfast and found Bobbie looking good and bright-eyed, he took out his irritation on her by sending her away and putting her in danger, not to mention removing any chance to invite her to church. After the way he'd treated her this morning, her refusal would serve him right. He could tell by her eyes that she didn't understand why he had barked orders at her, and he wasn't about to explain. Besides, if she planned to work with men, she needed a thicker skin. His other hands wouldn't think a thing of a bad mood.

But she's a woman.

The soft feel of her in his arms served as a vivid reminder. He set the financial papers aside giving up on any pretense of getting some work done. Bobbie entered the room, pricking his self-conviction even further. She sent him a glance, then looked away. She walked over to Annie's porcelain doll collection and fingered the frilly dress on one. He figured her fascination with the dolls was an act to avoid him, but when Annie entered the room, she asked about them.

"My mother started the collection when my father gave her one the day they married," Annie said as she moved to Bobbie's side. "I fell in love with them and continued the collection."

"Which one did your father give her?"

"This one right here." Annie picked up a doll from the highest shelf. It stood about eight inches tall and sported a dainty white face with black curls molded into the head.

"It's beautiful. So this was her wedding gift?"

"Yes. They'd been looking in a catalog for

75

things to put in their new house, and Dad noticed how Mom stopped and stared at this doll. He went back to the store the next day and ordered it."

Bobbie fingered the dress. "That's sweet."

Jace had heard that story so many times, he usually quit listening whenever it was retold. He watched Bobbie's face and thought it odd she would be interested in something so feminine, doubting she even played with dolls as a child.

Annie replaced the doll and moved to sit beside Pete. Bobbie plopped herself on the floor and leaned against one of the chairs, which didn't surprise Jace. He'd seen her do it once before. The action drew the attention of the two children. Ben walked right over and dropped himself onto her lap with a book.

"Read this, please." Ben craned his neck to look up into Bobbie's face.

Ben's long dark lashes made him irresistible to everyone, Bobbie included. She wrapped her arms around the boy before she took the book from his grasp.

Bobbie read with animation, waving her arm in the air. Her voice changed pitch and depth to match the characters. Everyone listened as her storytelling brought the book to life. Little Sara was drawn to her side and looked over her shoulder at the pictures. Sara fiddled with Bobbie's braid with one hand while she found her mouth with the thumb of her other hand.

Bobbie finished the story with a flourish and snapped the book closed — breaking the spell with a move that startled them all. Ben laughed and clapped his hands in approval, and Sara followed suit.

Pete pushed himself out of the chair. "That's the perfect note to put them to bed on, Bobbie. Thank you."

"You're welcome." She moved aside to allow Pete to scoop Sara up in his arms. Annie stood and called Ben to her. The boy obeyed, but turned and hugged Bobbie's neck and planted a kiss on her cheek. She returned the hug. "Good night, Ben."

"Night." He ran to take his mother's hand.

In the next few moments while they were alone, Bobbie managed to look everywhere but at Jace.

"You've captured the hearts of my niece and nephew." He held his breath when she smiled and rose from the floor, but instead of retiring for the night, Bobbie sat in the chair she'd been leaning against. He watched her pull her long legs under her and snuggle down into the softness of the chair.

"I ain't —" She pursed her lips before starting again. "I haven't stolen their hearts. I've just placed myself inside of them."

"You've definitely done that. You've got a kind heart, Bobbie." She didn't respond, but a pink tinge spread over her face. "And you blush rather easily."

Pete and Annie chose that moment to return. "What did you say to cause that blush, Jace Kincaid?" Annie grinned as she sat down.

"I just told her that she has a kind heart and that she blushes easily."

Annie shook her finger at him, then looked at Bobbie. "Don't mind him. He's a terrible tease. Always has been." Annie cast a look at Jace but then turned back to Bobbie. "We're all going to church in the morning. Would you like to join us?"

"Oh, I don't know. I haven't been to church in years."

Pete wrapped his arm around his wife and pulled her close. "Why did you stop?"

"My mother died." Bobbie shrugged and gazed at each of them. "Mama used to attend church, and she always brought me along. My father never joined us because he was always busy working. So when Mama died, I just stayed home with my father."

Pete picked up his newspaper and set it in

his lap. "Did you ever miss it?"

"No, not really. I still went to school and saw my friends, so I didn't feel the need for church."

"We'd love for you to join us tomorrow," Annie said.

Bobbie rubbed her hand back and forth on the leg of her trousers. "I think I'll just laze around tomorrow."

Jace swallowed his disappointment. "That's fine. But if you don't mind, we'll continue to invite you."

She smiled, but it didn't seem to reach her eyes. "That'll be fine. Thank you." She stood and stretched. "I think the pillow is calling my name. Good night, everyone."

The men stood. "Good night."

Annie sat for a moment, then followed Bobbie out of the room.

Bobbie shut the door and dropped onto her bed, glad to escape their inquisition. At the light tapping on the door, she took a deep breath. When would the questions end? "Come in."

Annie poked her head inside with a smile and entered. She closed the door and moved to sit on the side of the bed. "You told me you had two old dresses. If you had a nice one, would you be more willing to attend church?"

Bobbie rubbed her thumb along the seam of her denims. Being rough and tumble never bothered her until the last few years when the comments from other women about her lack of decorum left scars.

"Something nicer would probably go a long way in making me feel more comfortable around other people."

Annie reached over and covered her hand. "Were people really that rude to you?"

She gave a small nod. "If they didn't say something rude, they either snubbed me or treated me badly."

Annie looked into her eyes. The compassionate smile warmed Bobbie's heart.

"Would you be willing to wear one of my mom's dresses? I'd have to make a few adjustments to the bodice, but you're about the same height. I'd love to let you have one."

She didn't answer but stared at the hand covering her own.

"Bobbie?"

When she looked up again, tears pooled in Annie's eyes. Try as she might, she couldn't stop moisture from blurring her own vision. Annie moved closer and pulled her into a tight embrace. Bobbie hesitated and then lifted her arms to return the hug.

"I'm sorry if my questions hurt you, Bobbie."

"Oh no!" She pulled back enough to see Annie's face. "That ain't it at all. It's just . . ."

"Just what?"

Annie sat waiting for an answer.

"It's a mixture of many things," she said finally. "I've felt a bit alone since Daddy died, but I guess it's mostly the fact that you've been so kind. It's nice to have someone around who tries to understand me. Female companionship has been scarce." She wished she'd bit her tongue long before she'd finished.

"Bobbie, do you know that you're an answer to my prayers? I've been praying every day for more female friends in my life, and in you rode, near my age and sweet to boot." Annie squeezed her hand. "God may have sent you just to shut me up, but I'm thankful all the same. Not only have you found a place in my children's hearts, but you've wrangled your way into mine as well."

Tears trailed down Annie's smooth skin, marred only by a freckle here and there.

"Thank you, Annie." They both mopped up the tears and laughed.

"Now back to my original question. Would

you accept one of the dresses?"

"I don't know, Annie. That sounds like an awful lot of work. I'd hate to be a bother."

"It's not a bother. It'll only take me a few hours to have one ready for you."

"Are you sure?"

"Definitely. Come on, Bobbie. Just one dress."

She sighed. "All right."

"Great!" Annie embraced her again, then jumped up and spun around, her hands clasped in front of her. "I'm thrilled."

Bobbie laughed. "I can tell."

Annie smiled and shook her finger. "You're as bad as Jace with your teasing." With a shake of her head she strode to the door. "Good night, Bobbie."

"Annie?"

Annie turned, her hand resting on the doorknob.

Bobbie fought the lump in her throat. "Thank you."

"You're welcome. Good night."

"Good night, Annie."

Annie's kindness reminded Bobbie of Ginny Bennett, whose husband worked for Mr. Simms. Ginny hadn't always been kind. Not by a long shot. Only months ago, she was known for her brash behavior and coarse way of talking. Her husband matched her in actions and speech. She could be found sitting in a rocker wasting away the day, not caring about a thing in the world, least of all her appearance or the manner in which she spoke to others.

Mrs. Simms must have seen something special in Ginny. She spent time with her, teaching her to cook and clean and sometimes invited her over for a cup of coffee so they could chat. Soon, Ginny began joining Mr. and Mrs. Simms Sunday mornings on their way to church. A slow change took place in Ginny. She started combing her hair and washed more than once in a month's time. Her speaking became quiet and refined. Her face glowed with happiness, and her actions were kindness itself. If anyone asked her about the changes, she wasted no time giving the credit to her newfound faith in Jesus Christ.

The transformation caught Bobbie's attention and led to curiosity about God. Roy and Maggie Simms tried on many occasions to get her to attend their church. She always balked at the idea, and they finally quit asking. At the time, she didn't feel a need to include God in her life. Truth be told, she blamed Him for taking her mother away. She couldn't think of one good thing He had done for her, but the change in Ginny couldn't be ignored. The peace that seemed to fill her appealed to Bobbie, and thoughts of attending church with Ginny and the Simmses came with frequency . . . until her father died.

Bobbie undressed down to her long underwear and hung her denims and cotton shirt over the bedrail. She moved to the small mirror on the bureau and unwound her braid. What she'd give for a nice cotton nightgown. She hadn't owned one since she was 10. If she wanted to continue saving money and fulfill her dream of owning a ranch, she wouldn't have one for quite some time.

She picked up her brush and ran it down her long hair. Now, once again, she lived in the midst of believers. Annie, Jace, and Pete reminded her of Roy and Maggie. Annie seemed sincere in her friendship, and Jace . . . she made a face at herself in the mirror, aware of how foolish she acted in front of him. How was it she would try to show him up in the corral, yet without Mack and her hat, he could make her blush so easily? At least he was kind about his teasing and not crude like so many others.

Finished with her hair, she set down the brush, blew out the lamp, and climbed into bed. The idea of attending church terrified her. When it came to her choice of clothing, church-going folks often acted the worst. Their stares burned with a conviction she couldn't ignore. Only when presented with a dress would she even consider following through with Annie's plan.

SEVEN

Bobbie woke early the next morning, dressed, and stepped outside. Serenity filled her as the bright orange sunrise blazed on the horizon, and she wanted to chuckle at the insecurity she experienced the night before. She leaned against the house, drinking in the colors as they advanced across the sky.

"Is something wrong?"

The deep voice made her jump. She turned to find Jace standing at her shoulder.

"I'm sorry." Jace wore a teasing smirk. "I didn't mean to startle you."

"That's fine. I was just watching the sun come up." Her gaze moved down to his feet then back up to his face. "You're all dressed up. You look nice." She closed her eyes as heat burned her cheeks. "I'm sorry."

He smiled and gave a gallant bow. "Thank you."

How humiliating! She turned back to the

sunrise, though her heart still thumped at the fright he gave her . . . or was it his presence?

"There's nothing like the colors of dawn. I think it's my favorite time of the day." She inhaled deeply as if the hues held a scent. "It's as if each morning is a brand new start, a new beginning. Just look at it." She refused to look at him and continued staring at the sunrise.

Stained with pink and purple, the sky appeared as though someone had spilled their paints. The sun added a tinge of orange and gold as it reflected itself on the array of clouds that an unseen wind had whipped into a wispy froth.

"The heavens declare the glory of God; and the firmament showeth His handiwork."

Bobbie switched her gaze to Jace. "What?"

Jace repeated the verse. "That's found in the Psalms. I can only marvel at how anyone can see such beauty and not believe in God, the Creator of all things."

Bobbie wanted to question him about his beliefs, but he had turned and walked toward the door.

"Shall we go in for breakfast?" he asked.

She followed, only to be caught staring at him again. If only he didn't look so good. How would she make it through the meal when she knew it would be impossible to swallow? Thankfully, Jace acted as though nothing had happened outside.

After breakfast, Annie asked Bobbie to join her, and she found herself in Pete and Annie's bedroom. Annie pulled from the closet a dark navy dress with white lace around the collar and sleeves. Bobbie walked over and touched the material. It shimmered in the sunlight.

"This is very pretty, Annie. Is this what you're wearing to church?"

"No, Bobbie. This is your dress."

She gasped and touched the dress again. "Really? Is it really, Annie?"

"Yes. It'll look great with your light hair color. Are you ready to put it on?"

"What? Oh. You mean to try it on."

"No, I mean are you ready to wear it today?"

"But I thought . . . you said . . ." Her mouth went dry.

"I did, but it didn't take much altering. I liked it so much, I planned to see if I could alter it to my size. But now with this third child on the way . . . Well, needless to say, I doubt I'll ever get into this dress, altered or not."

"You're going to have a baby?" Bobbie glanced at Annie's stomach before giving her an awkward hug. "I had no idea."

"Oh, Bobbie, you make me feel good. I already feel like I've swollen to twice my size."

"Well, you sure don't look it. Congratulations."

"Thank you. Now back to the dress . . . all I did was take it in a little. I stayed up for a while last night to work on it so you could come to church with us today."

Bobbie lifted her gaze from the worn wooden floor. "I ain't got — I mean, I don't have any nice shoes. I've always just worn my boots with the other dresses."

"I've already thought of that. I still have some of Mom's shoes. See?" Annie pointed at several pair she had placed near a chair. "You're about the same size Mom was. I'm sure some of these will work." Annie paused. "Do you want to do this today, or would you rather wait?"

Bobbie's hands slicked with moisture. She looked from Annie to the dress that would turn her into another person. The excitement in Annie's eyes outweighed her fears, and knowing she'd stayed up late to do this for her made her feel guilty.

"All right. I'll do it," Bobbie blurted before she could change her mind.

A squeal escaped from Annie as she

89

embraced her. "I'm so happy. But we'll have to hurry so we won't be late."

After they threw on their clothes, Annie pushed Bobbie onto a chair to fix her hair. When she finished, Annie held up a mirror. "What do you think?"

Bobbie stared in disbelief. Annie had coiled her braid into a bun and pulled some tendrils free to hang in wisps around her face. Bobbie nodded her approval with a forced smile. She stood and slipped into the shoes beside her.

Annie touched her arm. "Are you ready?"

Bobbie peered into Annie's eyes and saw nothing but warm friendship and assurance. "I think so."

Annie put her arm around her shoulders and squeezed. "You look great."

Bobbie could give only a weak smile of thanks as Annie led the way down the stairs. "Are you men ready?"

Pete's snort echoed up the stairs. "What do you mean are *we* ready? We've been waiting on *you!* You know, it doesn't matter, Jace. A woman could be on her way to clean out the barn, and she'd still take forever to . . ." The smile froze on his face and disappeared as he stared up at Bobbie.

"Pete?" Jace frowned at his brother-in-law and followed his shocked gaze up the stairs.

Bobbie didn't know what she expected, but Jace's reaction wasn't it.

His jaw dropped open and both hands fell to his sides. She paused at the head of the stairs. It wasn't too late to turn around and forget about church, except Annie had worked so hard, and she'd hate to hurt her feelings. She reached out to take hold of the banister with a shaking hand and forced herself to take the first step.

Unsure of her footing in the fancy heeled shoes, she descended the stairs slowly. She knew she looked feminine, had even stared at herself in the mirror as Annie fastened up her hair, but it felt like a shell, not like her at all. Still, as Jace continued to watch her progress down the stairs, she couldn't help but be pleased. The look on his face made the whole ordeal worthwhile.

Annie walked past Jace, placed her fingertips under his chin, and pushed up. Bobbie caught the movement and couldn't help but chuckle under her breath. Jace smiled.

Without another word, Pete scooped up his children in his arms and followed his wife through the front door and out to the waiting wagon. Bobbie moved to follow.

"You're all dressed up," Jace whispered as she passed. "You look nice."

She attempted a curtsey, doing her best to

mimic the response he had given her earlier. "Thank you."

Jace grinned and motioned for her to exit in front of him. She tried hard to disguise her anxiety but felt her lips tremble.

"Relax, Bobbie. No time like the present to get used to dressing up and facing groups of people."

If only that would make it easier, but she was completely out of her element. She stopped at the side of the wagon and stared in dismay. When she wore denims, she just hopped into it. Now, wearing a dress, she wasn't sure what to do. She'd have to start paying more attention to those things.

She started forward, determined to climb on and do her best not to trip and break her neck. Before her hand touched the wagon, Jace was at her side. He took her by the waist and lifted her up to the seat. She gasped, then slapped a hand over her mouth. The only man who'd ever done that had been her father when she was young.

Bobbie sat behind Ben, Sara, and their parents, and worked to arrange her skirts as Jace slid up next to her and leaned close. "I hope I didn't offend you just now, Bobbie, but I couldn't see any other way to get you aboard."

"It's all right." But she refused to meet his

gaze as her face flamed hotter.

Because they were late, Pete dropped them off at the front of the church. Jace helped her down in the same way he'd placed her in the wagon, his strong hands clamped around her waist. Could she ever get used to being treated in such a style?

They entered the small clapboard building and filed into a back pew. Bobbie sat between Jace and Annie. The congregation sang a few hymns before the pastor stood up at the front and began the sermon. Several minutes later, she still could not get engrossed in the message. She sat on the edge of the wooden pew as straight as a fence pole, her gaze glued to the older woman in front of her, though she couldn't help but notice the frequent glances of several people sitting ahead of and around her.

Besieged by a strong desire to run, she tossed a sideways glance at Jace just in time to catch the frown he shot at Annie, who gazed at her curiously. Bobbie stared at her hands clasped in her lap. She didn't want to disappoint Jace and Annie. They wanted her to like church, but she didn't feel comfortable here. With a small sigh, she at least managed a prayer . . . that the sermon wouldn't last much longer.

After the service, Bobbie forced a smile as Annie introduced her to members of the congregation. She shook hands with everyone, their names and faces a blur, feeling very much like that black stallion she'd been helping Jace break. She wanted out. Somewhere outside these church walls lay familiar territory — a place where she could run, hide, and be herself. She could see the bright light of freedom beckoning to her from the door.

She looked at Jace, willing him to notice her discomfort and help her make an escape, but what she found was the same annoyance he'd had for the black. Is that what she had become — a challenge to break into submitting to his faith?

Jace led her to the door and introduced her to Pastor Robbins and his wife, Garnett. Garnett gave her a warm hug, and Bobbie relaxed for the first time since they arrived at the church.

She remained subdued on the ride home and couldn't seem to bring herself to join in their chatter, nor did they press her with questions. As soon as they were in the house, Annie stopped Bobbie's escape into the kitchen by clasping her arm and holding her until Pete took the kids upstairs.

"Bobbie, would you like to tell me what's bothering you?"

Lips tight, she shook her head. "Nothing."

"You and I both know that's not true. If you tell me about it, I may be able to help."

Though her words were to the point, Annie's voice sounded kind and concerned. Bobbie dropped her gaze to the floor. Jace paused at the door. Instead of going through, he closed it and leaned against it with his arms crossed. She had the distinct feeling he had cut off her escape on purpose.

Annie called her name. She looked up. "Talk to me, Bobbie."

She heaved a sigh. "I guess I just thought the people in your church would be different."

"What do you mean, 'different'?"

"They were the same as everyone else I've come across since I left the Simms Ranch. I've been stared at and talked about everywhere I go, and the same thing happened at the church today. And I wasn't even wearing my trousers." The sentence came out in a sob.

Her last comment caused Annie to smile. Jace looked away but not before she saw his grin. "It's not funny!"

"Well, actually it is," Annie said, still smiling. "You see, it's not what you're wearing that causes people to stare . . . although that dress does look wonderful on you."

Annie laid her Bible on the couch before she took Bobbie by the shoulders, spun her around, and directed her to a mirror hanging on the wall.

"What do you see?"

Bobbie shrugged without really looking at herself. She tried to pull away, but Annie held her in front of the glass with firm hands.

"Come on. Humor me. What do you see?"

Uncomfortable with Jace in the room, she wished she could be anywhere else. "I just see a girl, a cowhand."

Annie nodded. "That's what I thought. Now, let me tell you what everyone else sees when they look at you." Their eyes met in the glass. "They see a very beautiful young woman they would like to know better."

Bobbie looked away, shaking her head in disbelief, but Annie wouldn't let her go. Jace chose that moment to step in.

"Do you remember watching the sun come up this morning? You could hardly look away because it was so pretty. That's the way it is when people, especially men, look at you. They see something beautiful and want to see more. So they either continue to try to catch glimpses of you or they just flat out stare."

Bobbie frowned and backed away. He was making sport of her.

Jace crossed his arms. "I can see that you've spent way too much time working and not enough time socializing. You still don't believe me, do you?"

"It's true, Bobbie," Annie said. "Just look at the way even my little four-year-old Ben can't keep his eyes off you."

She shook her head. "That's just because I'm a stranger."

"No it's not. And if you don't believe me, just ask him. A child will almost always tell you what he's thinking. He already said you were pretty."

Bobbie stared at Annie. The woman seemed determined to win this argument even if she had to stand there all afternoon.

"People know it's rude to stare, but sometimes they just can't help themselves. Once they get used to seeing you, the staring will end, just like at the Simms place. Trust us, Bobbie." Annie gave her a hug. "We wouldn't lie to you." Annie stepped back and looked deep into her eyes. "All right?"

She felt her anger melt away and tears rise.

Annie stepped away. "Oh, now don't start that or you'll get me going."

Bobbie laughed as Annie walked to the

kitchen, her hands shaking in the air. "I cry way too easy when I'm with child."

With the smile still on her face, Bobbie turned back to Jace.

He motioned for her to enter the kitchen. "So what did you think of the message?"

"I honestly can't say. Maybe next time."

His brows rose. "So there will be a next time?"

She shrugged and headed to her room to change. "We'll see."

EIGHT

Bobbie pushed away from the table, filled with enough of the noon meal to prove Annie was a good cook. The fact that she'd spent the last two days branding calves didn't hurt her appetite either. Jace refused to let her help with the roundup. She wanted to argue, but something in his eyes, almost a haunted look, kept her silent.

Jace wiped his mouth and leaned back. "So Bobbie, would you mind taking a trip to town for me?"

Annie returned to her chair, apparently waiting for the answer.

"Sure. You need me to pick something up?"

"Just go into the mercantile and tell them you're there for me. I gave them a list of items when I stopped by on Monday. They'll load my order into the wagon for you."

Bobbie nodded her agreement and stood.

Annie rose with her. "Would you like some

company?"

"Sure. In fact, you'll come in handy as I'll need to stop by the bank on some business. I may need you to soften up the manager for me."

Annie smiled. "I can do that. And how about a little shopping?"

Jace groaned and headed for the door.

Bobbie grinned and shook her head at him before turning to Annie. "That's fine. Apparently, I have all afternoon."

"Great! The kids and I will be ready in no time, once I finish with these dishes that is."

Bobbie started clearing the table. "I'll help."

"And I accept."

With the kitchen tasks finished, Bobbie changed into one of her old dresses, and they were on their way. Bobbie drove the horse and wagon so Annie could hold her children. By their excitement, a trip to town must be a real treat. They wriggled and chattered until Annie looked worn before they'd reached their destination.

Their afternoon began at the bank. When Bobbie entered with Annie and her kids, the nearest teller offered a friendly smile, then tapped on a door and announced to his boss that his wife had just arrived.

Bobbie cast a quick look around the building as they waited. The light-colored wood counter gleamed with polish. White paint reflected the sun off the walls, making the room bright. The place smelled clean and looked new, but she knew Pete had been working here for several years. The orderliness told her a lot about the man who ran the bank.

At the far window, a man stood with his back to them, leaning against the counter talking to the other employee. The bank sported three teller windows, and Bobbie suppressed a smile. Whoever built the bank must have been a visionary with great dreams for this small town's growth.

The man chatting with the teller turned. Bobbie was surprised to see that it was Coop. She nodded a greeting, and he tipped his hat with his index finger, sending his familiar tobacco-stained smile in her direction. He looked like he was about to speak, but the teller's strident voice reclaimed his attention with a description of a string of recent bank robberies. Bobbie turned away and tried to close out the sound of the teller's voice.

Pete must have heard the conversation as he entered the room. He scowled in the teller's direction before approaching, gave Annie and the kids a kiss, then turned to Bobbie.

"Hello, Bobbie. Are you all here on business or is this visit strictly for my pleasure?" He bent to ruffle Ben's hair and then sidestepped the boy's disgruntled jab.

"I'd like to open an account, Pete. Is my money acceptable?"

"Sure! Follow me and I'll get you set up." Pete led the way to the first teller window. He located the necessary paperwork, and then waited while she filled it out. "So how much will you be depositing today?"

She reached down and hefted her saddlebag onto the counter. The puff of dust flying into the air along with the dirt now marring the once clean wood made her cheeks burn with embarrassment. She lifted the bag and prepared to wipe the counter with her sleeve, but Pete held up a hand.

"Don't fret, Bobbie. Men carrying much more soil than that have been through here. It all cleans up." He smiled and patted the wood. "Let's see what you have."

She pulled out stacks of bills, quoting the amount she had double-checked that morning as she handed them to Pete. When his eyebrows raised, she grinned at his obvious surprise.

"You left this much lying around?" Disbelief as well as disapproval coated his tone.

She looked about the room and found Coop's gaze glued to her stack of money. She pushed it further toward Pete.

"I didn't just leave it lying around, Pete. Besides, are you saying I can't trust you and your family?"

Pete's expression changed from chagrin to amusement. "No, I'm not saying that at all. You'll have to excuse that comment. I guess there's more banker in me than I thought."

"There's nothing wrong with that. It tells me you'll take good care of my money."

"Without question." He applied his signature to the paperwork and slid the sheet toward her. While she signed, he pulled out a new bankbook and stamped it before handing it to her to keep for her records. "Just bring this with you every time you need to make a transaction. But I guess you probably already know that."

She nodded. "Thank you."

"I'm glad to be able to help you, Bobbie."

Pete motioned for one of the tellers to take care of the money before stepping around the counter. He followed them to the door and bid them farewell.

Outside, Annie stopped Ben from heading to the mercantile with a touch to his shoulder. She switched Sara to her other hip.

"Goodness, Bobbie." Annie grabbed hold of Bobbie's elbow. "You said you and your dad had been saving, but I had no idea. I can't believe you've been running all over the territory with that kind of money."

Coop exited the bank, interrupting her response.

"I didn't know ranch hands could make such a wad of cash. Could be I need to think on moving north." He spit a stream of brown juice into the street before tipping his hat. "Good day, ladies."

She exchanged an amused smile with Annie. Coop's crude behavior no longer took her aback, but it surprised her to see him act that way in front of Jace's sister. Across the street, a lady Bobbie recognized from church beckoned and then hurried toward them. She offered a flustered greeting before asking to speak with Annie.

"I'll meet you in the store," Bobbie said.

She followed Coop's footsteps down the boardwalk with mild fascination. He grabbed the reins of his horse and led it between two buildings — in the opposite direction of the ranch. Unsure what prompted her curiosity, she trailed Coop to that same alley. She peeked around the corner of the building. Seeing nothing, she stepped off the boardwalk and headed for the back.

When she reached the opening, she caught sight of Coop again. Two men she didn't recognize accompanied him. At least one was a man. The other rider was hidden by bushes with only the horse's head showing. She moved into the shadow of the structure, never taking her eyes off them. The one man had his back to her, his long, light-brown hair blowing in the breeze. The hidden rider appeared to do most of the talking, though she heard no word of the exchange. Coop handed over a piece of paper, turned his horse, and headed in the direction of the ranch while the other two turned up the hill behind the bushes away from town.

She leaned against the building and re-played the strange scene in her mind. When she first saw Coop at the bank, she assumed he was there to do some business for Jace. But why would he send two ranch hands? And Coop's furtive actions weren't those of someone conducting honest business.

"Why you back here, Bobbie?"

Her heart leapt to her throat. She swallowed hard when she saw Coop staring down at her from atop his horse.

She forced a weak chuckle that sounded tremulous even to her own ears. "Coop, you scared me."

The man didn't say a word as his eyes narrowed.

She slowly stood up straight as she scrambled for an explanation. "Wha — ah." Her mouth went dry. She licked her parched lips. "I was just doing a little exploring of the town. Other than going to church, it's my first trip here since Jace hired me."

"Strange way to explore. Most women stick near the boardwalk and peer in the windows. But you ain't like most women, are ya, Bobbie?"

Anger replaced her fear. "No, I ain't. But I do have feelings, Coop."

Coop's shoulders drooped. "Right. Sorry, Bobbie. That weren't how I meant it."

She gave a quick nod and tugged the brim of her hat down lower over her eyes. "Apology accepted. I need to get going now. Annie's expecting me at the mercantile. See you back at the ranch, Coop."

She felt his eyes boring into her back as she headed for the boardwalk. Not until she slipped around the corner was she able to take another breath. With trembling legs, she made her way to the store, not looking over her shoulder until she stepped inside. Though she was safe amidst the other patrons, she couldn't resist the quick peek out the window to make sure Coop hadn't followed.

Inside the store, merchandise packed the walls from floor to ceiling. Everything and anything anyone could need lined the shelves in neatly labeled barrels and jars.

She approached the clerk to let him know she would be picking up Jace's order and that the wagon sat out front. She tried to ignore his gawking as she turned and began a slow walk up and down the aisles. Her fingers skimmed over the bright linens and flowered napkins that painted one of the tables. She eventually found herself at the back of the store where Annie spotted her and held up a piece of green cloth. "What do you think of this?"

Bobbie touched the material and loved its softness. "This is very pretty, Annie. Is this going to be your new dress?"

"Actually, I thought this could be *your* new dress."

Her jaw dropped open, and she snapped it closed. "Oh, Annie. I don't know how to make a dress."

"No. But I do."

"But I couldn't ask you to do that for me."

"You didn't ask me to. I'm offering."

"But Annie —"

Annie cut her off with a wave. "Look, Bobbie, I want to do this for you. Besides, it will give me something to do with my hands. I already have all the baby clothes I need from the first two." Annie ended her plea with a shrug. "So you see, you'll be helping me out."

She shook her head at Annie and took Sara from her arms. "You're hopeless."

Annie grinned, then ran around collecting the thread and buttons she would need to complete the dress. Bobbie went up to the front to see if all of Jace's supplies had been loaded into the wagon, waited for Annie to rejoin her, then paid the bill.

Once home, she let Annie and the kids off at the house and then changed back into work clothes before pulling the wagon around to the barn to unload Jace's supplies. She jumped from the seat and lifted a bag of grain.

"Stop right there," a voice growled behind her.

She dropped the bag and raised her hands in the air. She straightened her shoulders, fighting the urge to turn toward the voice, and wishing she had worn her sidearm.

NINE

"What are you doing, Bobbie?"

"I beg your pardon?" She peeked over her shoulder. The second she saw Jace, her hands dropped to her sides, and her face flamed bright red.

"Why'd you put your hands up?" Jace walked toward her and the wagon.

"Y–you're command. I reacted instinctively."

"I just wanted you to drop that bag."

"Well, it worked. I dropped it." With a half-hearted laugh, she glanced over her shoulder at the bag. "It ain't too heavy if that's what you're worried about."

"That's not what I'm worried about, but you don't need to be carrying stuff like this." He lifted the bag onto his shoulder. "I gave you the afternoon off. Relax."

She stood rooted near the barn door as if she didn't know what to do with herself.

"Go on, Bobbie. I'll take care of this."

"All right. If you insist."

"I do." She was nearly inside the barn when he dropped the bag, caught up with her, and touched her elbow. "Did everything go all right today?"

"Yes." Her smile looked forced. "Annie and I had a great time."

He searched her face, sure that something had happened in town that she didn't want to tell him about. He veered toward the wagon and paused with his hand on the side rail. "Bobbie, most women scream when they're frightened, but not you. Your hands went up."

She took a step toward him. "That incident with your cows and the falling rocks left me a bit shaken, Jace. It seems someone is after you, and if that's the case, who's to say they wouldn't also come after your ranch hands? I didn't want to take any chances."

He liked that she looked him in the eye the entire time she spoke. He nodded. "Completely understandable. I'm sorry I spooked you."

"It's all right." She retraced her steps.

"Did Annie mention anything to you about Bible study tonight?"

"No." She turned but held her ground halfway to the barn. "Why?"

110

"Just wondering if you might like to go?" Seeing her in that dress with her hair fixed up nice and no dust to mar her features was a sight he couldn't shake from his head.

Bobbie's smile spoke to him before her words. "Yes, I think I'd like that."

"Great. We'll need to leave shortly after six thirty."

"All right. I'll be ready."

He smiled and hoisted the bag on his shoulder, maybe too pleased she'd be joining them.

She'd disappeared into the barn but reappeared moments later. "Jace, I know you've set up a night watch to keep an eye out for whoever stole your cattle. You never told me when it's my turn."

"You don't get a turn."

He dropped a roll of wire inside the barn door and went back for more. With the answer he'd just given her, he expected a battle. The way she stood with her hands on her hips proved he would get it.

"Why not?"

"Because you're a woman."

Bobbie's mouth dropped open about the time he saw flames leap into her eyes. "I'm a ranch hand, Jace. *Your* ranch hand."

"You're a *female* ranch hand, Bobbie. Protection for you will force one of the men to pull double duty, and I won't do that to them."

She crossed her arms in front of her. "I can take care of myself. I think I've proven that."

"The answer is no." He grabbed another roll of wire.

"But Jace, you know whoever's stealing the cattle will need a fire if they do anymore branding. If I see a fire, I promise I'll come back for help."

He gave an inward groan. *Women!* His men would have accepted his answer and moved on. He shook his head. "I'm not going to discuss this any further with you, Bobbie. You're not getting a turn."

He started past her, and her mouth fell open again to continue arguing. He stopped next to her and leaned his face toward hers. "No."

Without another word, she headed toward her horse. He hid a grin, certain Mack would either get a vigorous brushing or the ride of his life.

Evening settled in as Bobbie made her way toward town following the wagon at a comfortable distance. In her current mood, she didn't feel like wearing a dress. Donning clean trousers, she decided to ride

Mack and wouldn't take no for an answer. She didn't feel much like meeting with the townsfolk either. Convincing them she was glad to be there would take some good acting on her part.

Little Ben turned in the wagon and waved. She forced a smile and waved back, seeing Jace out of the corner of her eye do the same. He had insisted on riding horseback with her, which proved he didn't trust her to ride into town alone. If only he could be as sweet as his nephew. Right now, he irritated her like a biting mosquito. She'd rather have the mosquito. At least then she could swat it.

An owl screeched off to the east where darkness touched the scrub pines. Mack snorted and shook his head and she patted his neck.

"Easy boy. There's nothing out here we can't outrun or outsmart." Tonight, holding her tongue would be her greatest challenge. She'd love nothing more than to give Jace an earful of what she thought of his chivalry.

Her musings came to an end when Mack stopped.

"Here we are." Jace reined in his horse in front of a large, two-story house. He jumped down and tied his horse to Pete's wagon.

Matt and Rebecca Cromwell's home

rested at the edge of town, far from the bustle of the Half Moon Saloon she'd heard so much about from the other wranglers. Bobbie twisted the reins in her hands as a wave of homesickness washed over her. Rose bushes just starting to say hello to the new season grew along the picket fence that circled the house.

"You coming?" Jace offered his hand to help her down. Her eyes met his. His expression looked as pleasant as the tiny purple flowers peeking out beneath the rose bushes. He didn't seem a bit remorseful that he'd made her feel incompetent. She ignored his hand and jumped down beside him.

The front door of the house opened and an older couple stepped onto the porch as another wagon rumbled up to the house. Jace grasped Bobbie's elbow and directed her up the path toward the waiting couple.

"Bobbie, do you remember meeting the Cromwells Sunday?" Jace made the introductions again, reminding her that Matt owned the livery.

Rebecca smiled and put an arm around Bobbie's shoulders. "Not to worry, Bobbie. It's hard to remember everyone at first." Rebecca waved at the young couple that had arrived behind them. "That's my oldest daughter, Amy, and her husband Mike Cowling."

Bobbie nodded her greeting. Annie must have noticed Bobbie's tension because she looped her arm through Bobbie's while giving her a sympathetic smile. A girl Bobbie guessed to be in her teens entered and led Ben and Sara away.

"That was my other daughter, Mandy," Rebecca informed her. "She watches the kids during our study time."

A burst of sweet, warm air tickled Bobbie's senses as Rebecca opened the door and waved everyone inside. Brownies, or better yet, chocolate cake, she thought with a smile. She hadn't eaten much for supper. Jace's attitude had made her lose her appetite.

They all moved into the living room, and Pastor Robbins and his wife, Garnett, stood to envelope her in a hug.

"It's good to see you again, Bobbie," the pastor said.

Bobbie gave a self-conscious nod. "Thank you."

Pastor Robbins continued the introductions. "Here we have our town sheriff, Morgan Thomas, and his wife, Beth. And next to them is Ella Ramsey, the Cromwells' neighbor." The pastor turned. "Last but not

115

least is Cade Ramsey, Ella's son. He works at the livery with Matt."

Cade rose and Bobbie looked up, her mouth opening in surprise. He stood a good two inches taller than Jace and looked as though he could lift the horses he worked with in the livery. She took his extended hand, and for the first time ever, she felt delicate.

He flashed an even, white smile. "I knew I was saving this seat for a reason." He motioned toward the piano bench where his Bible rested. "I just didn't know that reason would be so pretty." Cade picked up his Bible and sat on the floor beside it.

She wanted to laugh. He hadn't saved any seat. Jace moved around her to take a chair across the room. With a defiant attitude, she lifted her chin. Sitting next to Cade would be a wonderful idea.

The pastor opened with prayer and then read from the book of Romans. Upon finishing, he asked for thoughts about the verses. Bobbie listened to the comments about never speaking badly of her enemies and the need to spend time with them, trying to befriend them.

In her 19 years, she never had enemies of any real sort. Once, a band of rustlers tried to steal some of the Simmses' cattle, but that hadn't been personal to her, and Roy Simms told her it was important to love everyone, even those rustlers who might not believe a God existed.

She gazed at the faces of the people around her, stopping at Jace. Apparently, he had enemies, yet he hadn't said a word about revenge. Did he take the cattle thefts personally? How would he handle it when he found out who was causing the trouble? His eyes met hers. Maybe he was mulling over those very same thoughts. He gave her a tight-lipped smile. She looked away as Cade made a comment.

"I think the important thing to remember is that Christians are to be an example of peace and love, not revenge and hatred."

The hour sped by, and she was stunned to hear the pastor conclude by reminding everyone that it took commitment to the Lord not to let evil reduce them to evil. He closed the meeting the same way he'd started, with prayer.

Good-byes were said in haste because of the lateness of the hour. Jace and Bobbie reined their horses into a slow walk behind the wagon. Her mind scrambled to find a way to fill the silence and landed on Cade.

"Why isn't Cade married?" she asked Jace. "He seems like a gentleman."

117

"Oh, he's a gentleman all right. He has the softest heart of any man I know."

"Sounds like you two are good friends."

"Been best friends for as long as I can remember." Jace heaved a sigh. "He thought about marriage once. To a girl from school. But when she moved away with her parents without a backward glance, he doubted she felt the same way. We assumed she'd be back every so often because her aunt and uncle run the mercantile, but we haven't seen her. He hasn't been serious about another woman since."

"I imagine there have been plenty of women interested in him though."

"Mmm. So, Bobbie, what did you think of the study?"

"I really enjoyed it. Was Sunday's service as good as that?"

He laughed. "The Sunday services are always good, but I like the Bible study better. It's informal, and we get a chance to compare thoughts and ideas. We also get to dig a little deeper into the Scriptures."

They moved on in silence, the drone of locusts surrounding them with an endless chorus. Jace cleared his throat. "Do you have any questions?"

She had been waiting all evening to tell him how she felt. "Who do you consider your enemy, Jace? I mean, do you think unbelievers are your enemies?"

"Anyone who is ruled by Satan could be considered an enemy to a child of God."

"So, since I ain't what you call saved, I'm considered one of your enemies?"

He remained silent for a time. Maybe she had offended him. Worse, what if he did think of her as an enemy?

"If you try to lead me away from God or do something that goes against what's written in His Word, then yes, I would have to consider you an enemy. But we're talking about a spiritual enemy, Bobbie, not a physical one. Do you understand the difference?"

She sat quiet and held the reins loosely in her hand, glad for the shadows that guarded her expression.

"I can't see you very well in the dark, Bobbie, so I'm going to have to ask. You gave every appearance of being tense earlier. Are you upset?"

She snapped her head in his direction. "The way you order me not to help with this job makes me feel like your enemy, Jace. I don't need you to look out for me. I can take care of myself. I think I've proven that in the last few weeks."

"Yes."

Was that all he could say? "If you won't let me do my job —"

He reached out and grabbed her reins, interrupting her outburst and bringing them both to a stop.

"I don't know how many men are involved in this, Bobbie. It could be one, or it could be a group. If they have men keeping watch, one of them could see you coming long before you knew they were there. I firmly believe these men would be much worse on a woman than they would on a man." He cleared his throat. "They may do things to you, Bobbie, that they wouldn't do to one of my men. I couldn't bear for that to happen."

His last few words came out just above a whisper, and her resolve weakened. Even in the dark she could tell his eyes were trained on hers, not more than two feet away. Horrible images raced through her mind. She thought she could take care of herself, but hearing Jace's speech made doubts rise to the surface. She also had to admit he wasn't acting any differently than her father or Roy would have in this situation.

"You'll have to forgive me for trying to be a gentleman, Bobbie. My mother worked hard to instill that in me, and believe me, it was no easy task." She heard him sigh. "I'd like to think my mother would be proud of the way I've handled the situation."

She understood his stance, maybe even sympathized with him over the loss of his parents. His voice sounded so solemn. Her heart ached for him.

"I think I can safely say she would be, Jace." She exhaled, and her fury drifted off on the wind. "Thanks for your concern." She hoped her voice didn't reveal the reluctance she felt saying those last words.

He grasped her arm. "I have no doubts about your abilities, Bobbie. I want you to know that up front. You also need to know that my employees are my responsibility, and I'll do all I can to protect them. That includes you."

He released her and walked his horse on ahead. She stared at the dark shadow of his back and lagged behind on purpose. He cared about his ranch and the people helping him run it. She could respect that, but she could also shoot better than half of his men, and she was smart enough not to get caught alone on the range. Unless she wanted to drive herself crazy, she'd have to accept his position and believe his sincerity. Still, that presented a new problem. No man had ever treated her like a woman.

Mack snorted, making Bobbie look up

and realize Jace stopped to wait for her.

He moved his horse next to her. "Can I ask you a question?"

"Sure."

"Do you at least believe there is a God?"

"Yes," she said without hesitation. "I believe there's a God out there somewhere. My mother used to talk about Him. But I don't know that I would put my entire trust in Him like you and Annie do."

"Why not? Is it because your mother died?"

She paused. First her mama, then her daddy. "That may have something to do with it, I guess." Bitterness rose up in her chest, and she swallowed hard before she could force the next words from her dry throat. "I can't think of one good thing God has done for me, which makes me wonder if He really cares. Besides, I've done fine on my own without Him." She shrugged. "I don't know for sure, Jace, but for some reason, I'm holding back when it comes to trusting Him, and until I know what that reason is, I don't plan to change."

Silence reigned for a time as she wrestled with her anger and disappointment. How could she come to any definite conclusion until she knew more about this God that Jace and Annie held in such high regard?

She knew of only one way to find out more.

"Is there a spare Bible lying around the house, Jace? I think I'd like to do a little reading."

"I'm sure either Annie or I could dig one up for you."

She heard the smile in his voice and grinned in the darkness. The remainder of the ride home was silent as his question returned her thoughts to the Bible study. She had heard a lot of interesting ideas from the others, and she had every intention of looking into each one of them.

Once they reached the ranch, they saw Dew's taut figure outlined in the lamplight flowing from the open barn door.

"Jace," Dew called out.

Something in his voice sent a shiver down her spine.

TEN

Jace reined in his horse, certain he didn't want to hear what his foreman had to say.

"You've been sent another message." Dew strode toward them, the lantern in his hand shaking along with the fury in his voice. "Someone left a cow tied to the bridge. Its hide's been branded." Dew's voice lowered once he reached Jace's side. "I'm thinking you were meant to find it on your way home, but I found it first and moved it out of the way."

Jace clenched his jaw. "Any more missing?"

"That's all I saw at first. I rode around a bit hoping to run into whoever did it." Dew shrugged. "I never saw or heard a thing, but I did find more hoofprints. Too dark to tell if they've been rustled."

Dew's eyes flashed toward Bobbie, and Jace bit back his response. He'd forgotten about her. "Take Bobbie to the house, Dew.

Then meet me in my office."

Bobbie dismounted. "I need to put Mack up for the night."

"I'll do it. You go with Dew."

For once, she didn't argue. He knew his clipped commands had done nothing to ease Bobbie's frustration, but he didn't have time nor was he in the frame of mind to ease her irritation. Tension curled his hand into a fist.

If you're fighting, you're not thinking.

His father's words came back to him like a flash of light. *Maybe if you'd have fought, Dad, you'd still be alive.* His fingers uncurled, and he took a deep breath.

"All right, Dad." He led the horses into the barn. "So now what do I do?" Unable to face his foreman yet, Jace dropped onto a bench and cradled his face in his hands.

Dew sat in a chair waiting for him when Jace walked into the office. "Pretty gutsy fella, don't ya think, Jace? I mean, he was almost in your front yard. So now what?"

Jace had spent some time in prayer while stabling the horses and felt much more calm. "At first light, we'll take another look around. Then I'll go talk to the sheriff again. Whoever is doing this is getting bolder. It just may lead to their first mistake." He reached for a pearl-handled letter opener and tapped the desk. "Who's on watch tonight?"

"Coop. He headed for the hills before nightfall — said he wanted to get close to the cattle before it got too dark."

Jace nodded. "Tell him I want to talk to him before we head out in the morning."

After Dew left, Jace sat in silence and thought about the watches he'd set up. Did they do any good? One man couldn't cover all of his territory. He needed more men. Bobbie's face popped into his mind unbidden.

He ran through the conversation they had on the way home, especially the fact that she didn't trust God. Trusting God didn't come easily. He could attest to that. He'd struggled with it since his parents were killed. But his parents left behind a wonderful model, and he was determined to follow their example. Not only that, but now he needed to be an example to Bobbie. He blew out his breath in a gust. Too many problems. His mind went back to the stolen cows.

The cattle thief seemed to know his every move. His thoughts ran over each of his neighbors. Could one of them be capable of this crime? He and his father had been friends with most of them for years. There was only one he didn't know well, Lyle Phipps, and he kept mostly to himself. Jace's chair squeaked as he sat back and rested his chin on his fist. He'd have to ask Morgan about Lyle in the morning. Then he'd have to start making plans for an early cattle drive. If he wanted any cattle left or the money he could get for them, he'd have to get them to Pueblo in a hurry or face the possibility of losing everything.

ELEVEN

Bobbie sat on the porch, her feet propped on the wooden barrel Annie used to catch water for her flowers. Two weeks had passed since she and Jace returned from the Bible study to find more of his cows gone. They spent most of their time riding around the ranch checking on the cattle. Because of the long hours and the tension of the situation, Jace started giving each of his ranch hands a few hours off once in a while. Sitting in a chair and taking a break from the workload was a wonderful change.

She shook out the newspaper she'd bought in town earlier. Most of the stories centered on the bank robberies plaguing the area from Dale City to Rockford. So far the bank in town remained untouched. If she didn't like Pete so much, she'd be tempted to remove her money.

Her gaze drifted to the date at the top of the paper. May thirtieth. Hard to believe

128

she'd been on the Kincaid ranch for over a month.

"What are you thinking about to make you shake your head like that?" Annie dropped onto the chair next to hers, then scattered some toys across the porch to keep the kids occupied.

Bobbie tickled Ben as he walked by then turned toward Annie. "How quickly my first month here went by."

"Has it been a month already? It's strange, but at times it doesn't feel that long. Other times, it feels like I've known you a lot longer."

Annie's expression made her laugh, though she felt the same. She'd become friends with the people in the Bible study, but she didn't feel as close to them as she did to Annie, who now reached over and bumped her arm.

"I finished your new dress. Once I've gotten a chance to sit here and rest a bit, we'll go in and try it on. Make sure it fits right." She rubbed her tummy. "If it weren't for this little rascal, I'd make another for myself out of the same fabric. The material is beautiful."

Bobbie nodded. This was the second dress Annie had made for her. If she weren't careful, Annie would have her acting downright

129

feminine.

Jace rode by and tipped his hat, his familiar smile in place. He seemed much more relaxed than he had a couple weeks ago. Though they'd found no evidence as to who rustled the cattle, he didn't appear upset with the lack of facts, which surprised her. Then again, his faith managed to surprise her several times.

Since the latest stolen cattle, Jace and Sheriff Thomas had spent a great deal of time looking for evidence. Jace allowed her to join them on a scouting trip but no further. That left her with little to do beyond mundane chores. She decided to continue the task of breaking the stallion to fill her time.

As Jace rode by, the length of hair showed below his hat. His locks were long when she hired on and remained uncut a month later. "How often does he get his hair cut?"

"It is getting pretty long, isn't it?" Annie said. "He considers it a great inconvenience to go into town just to get it cut."

"My father was like that. I finally got tired of seeing him looking so shaggy, so I made him let me cut his hair before he could eat."

Annie stopped rocking. "You knew how to cut his hair?"

"Not at first, I didn't. It took a few times

to figure out how to do it right." She laughed at the memory. "My father wouldn't take his hat off for days after the first few times I cut it."

Annie leaned forward to look into Bobbie's eyes.

She returned the gaze. "What?"

"Let's do that to Jace."

"Do what to Jace?"

"Let's make him sit and get a haircut before we feed him tonight." Annie twisted one of her dark curls around the end of her finger, her head cocked to the side. "Would you mind cutting his hair, Bobbie? You don't have to if you don't want."

"Actually, it might be nice to tell *him* what to do for once instead of the other way around."

Annie stood and paced in front of her as she laid out the plans. Bobbie nodded as she watched Annie's animated movements. After she heard all of Annie's ideas, her laughter rang out, and the children looked up, their giggles mingling with hers.

Jace stepped out of the barn and headed toward the house, thankful for the end of the day. A light breeze blew across his face. He tipped back his head, closed his eyes, and took a deep breath. Water trickling over the rocks in the creek provided the perfect background for the song of the crickets, frogs, and birds that blended their tunes into a calming chorus.

Dad always enjoyed nights like this. He'd sit on the porch listening to nature's music, and Jace would sit with him until bedtime talking about ranching. He learned a lot working alongside his father, but the chats meant the most. They revealed his father's thoughts. Those special times ended all too soon.

With a sigh, Jace looked up to find Bobbie standing next to the house. The last time she needed him, cattle ended up missing. This time, she held what appeared to be a bed sheet in her hands with a chair sitting next to her. *Now what?*

"Good evening, Jace." Her smile appeared more like a smirk, and he didn't like the feeling it gave him.

"Good evening."

"Did you have a good afternoon?"

"Yes, I did." He lifted his hat to give his head a scratch. Before he could replace it, Bobbie reached for it. He pulled it away.

"Don't bother putting that hat back on, Jace."

"What? Why?" He frowned, his hat held above his head in uncertainty.

132

Bobbie leaned on the chair with one hand and propped the other on her hip. "Because I'm going to cut your hair."

Jace finally smiled and placed his hat on his head. "I don't think so."

Annie came out and stood next to Bobbie. "Jace Kincaid, you will sit down in that chair and let Bobbie cut your hair or I won't feed you tonight." She crossed her arms as if to punctuate what she said.

He narrowed his eyes. "If this is what you girls came up with this afternoon, you've got way too much time on your hands." He moved to walk around them only to have Bobbie block his path. He looked down and studied her face. "You're serious, aren't you?"

"Yes, we're serious, Jace." Annie swatted at his arm. "You're beginning to look like your shaggy dog. In fact I think your hair is even longer than his."

"Well at least he's more loyal than my sister."

Still, neither woman budged. He surrendered with a sigh. A trim might not be so bad. Maybe. He moved to the chair and dropped down onto the seat.

"Oh, Jace, for mercy sake. Stop pouting." Annie's posture changed to match Bobbie's. "Bobbie sure can't make it look any worse than it already does."

Jace looked back at Bobbie. "Do you even know how to cut hair?"

Stone-faced, she shrugged. "I'll do the best I can. Besides, you have a hat to cover any mistakes I might make."

Bobbie removed his hat and tossed it toward a bench next to the house before draping the sheet around his shoulders. She walked around him and ran her fingers through his hair. The breeze he appreciated earlier became a curse as it swirled around his head the smell of the rose-scented soap she used.

He swallowed hard, not sure he liked having her so close. The little imp he tried to protect from trouble was preferable to this — this feminine side. In an instant, he realized making her mad had been one way of holding her at arm's length. Shivers raced through him and moved down his back and arms.

About to stand and put an end to the torment, he stilled when Bobbie stepped behind him and snipped at his hair. He watched some of the clippings fall in front of him. "Are you sure you're not taking off too much?"

"It'll grow back." Bobbie continued cutting.

The scissors fell to the ground, and his heart fell with them. Did this girl know what she was doing? For someone so graceful in the saddle, she seemed all thumbs at the moment.

She picked up the scissors. "Sorry."

Several minutes later, he heard "Oops." He started to stand. "What do you mean, 'oops'?"

Bobbie placed her hands on his shoulders and pushed him back down onto the chair. "You probably won't even notice it, Jace."

"No, *I* won't since it's at the back of my head. But the question is, will everyone *else?*"

"I can't speak for when you're not wearing your hat, but I'm sure the men around here won't notice a thing."

His jaw ached from clenching his teeth. Each snip of the scissors grated on his nerves like an annoying fly buzzing around his ears. He held his silence several more minutes and had decided to put this whole game to an end when Bobbie announced she was finished.

She walked around him, running her fingers through his hair, ending her examination by putting her fingers under his chin to make him look at her. He watched her gaze flash from one side of his head to the other several times, never once looking him in the eye. He wanted to grab her chin so she had to look at him. Instead, he rubbed his palms on his legs to get rid of the moisture.

Finally, with a nod of approval, Bobbie removed the sheet and stepped back. He wasted no time striding into the house, not only to put some distance between them but also to check her work. Annie met him in the hall with a grin on her face. His scowl sent her ducking out of the way. He glanced into the kitchen and saw Pete seated at the table, a corner of his paper flipped down.

"You should try to control your wife, Pete."

"That'll be the day." He chuckled. "The sooner you learn to succumb to their wiles, the better off you'll be."

Jace grunted in response, then stood in front of the mirror in the washroom. Moving his head from side to side, he slowly started to smile. Panicked at what he'd find, it was a relief to see that Bobbie had done a better job than Mooney, and she smelled better too. He ran his hand under his chin where the tingle of her fingers still lingered, never planning to use the town's barber again.

He returned to the door, opened it, and

leaned against the frame. Bobbie lifted the chair and carried it toward him, then stopped right in front of him with a knowing grin. His breath caught in his throat as an incredible urge to kiss her raged through him. He frowned.

"Is it okay?"

He took the chair from her. She stepped past him, and he followed her to the kitchen. "It is. In fact, I'm impressed."

"*Are* you now?" She moved to stand next to Annie.

The entire family had taken their seats around the table and sat staring at him. Even Sara stopped sucking her thumb long enough to point her pudgy finger at him.

Jace returned the stares as he shifted from one foot to the other. "What?" He quit smiling. "What?" Comprehension dawned as he took in everyone's expression. His gaze jumped back to Bobbie. "You knew how to cut hair all along, didn't you?" His audience burst into laughter. "Why you little . . ."

He lunged for Bobbie. She gasped and ran to the opposite side of the table, still laughing.

She stopped long enough to point at Annie. "It was all her idea."

"Really?" He picked up a glass from the

137

table and swirled the water around. "So it was my *sister's* idea to scare me half out of my mind."

Annie stood and backed away from the table, her hands out toward Jace. "Now Jace, you know you needed a haircut."

"Yes, I did." He took another step toward Annie. "But you didn't have to put a terrifying weapon into the hands of someone so good at acting that she had me thoroughly convinced she didn't know what she was doing."

He turned and prepared to empty the glass of water on Bobbie.

"Jace looks pretty." Ben proceeded to clap his hands.

Jace dipped his fingers in the glass and flicked the moisture toward Bobbie before doing the same to Annie.

"You two enjoy your trickery now, but beware . . . I'll get even." He sat and reached over to ruffle the hair on top of Ben's head. "Thank you for the compliment, Ben."

He couldn't stop his gaze from sliding back to Bobbie and found her grinning at him as she took a seat at the table. His focus remained on her lips until her head dipped. He gripped the napkin. Best to keep his thoughts and feelings under control.

The next day, Bobbie rode up to the chow hall for the noon meal. The other ranch hands surrounded her as she dismounted. She stared at them in uncertainty. "What's up, boys?"

Coop removed his hat and ran a hand through his hair. "Well Bobbie, we all seen what a good job ya done on Jace's hair, and we was hoping you'd do us the same favor."

Several yards away, Jace leaned against the barn with a satisfied smile. He wiggled his eyebrows and hooked his thumbs through the loops of his trousers.

"Come on, Bobbie," David Lundy said. "It'd sure save us the hassle of going inta town ta get it done."

Sonny Marshall stepped up and pulled off his hat. "Not to mention the money we'd save."

"Who said I'd do it for free?" She feigned exasperation.

Sonny's eyes grew wide. "Jace said you didn't charge him."

She looked over at Jace again and noticed his shoulders shaking in quiet laughter. "Yeah, well, he's the boss."

The men crowded a bit closer. "Come on,

Bobbie," Coop said again. "Will ya do it?"

She took a step back to gain some room but found Mack blocking her escape. Finally, she put her hands up. "All right. I'll do it tonight after we're through working."

The men cheered and patted her on the back before entering the hall to eat. She walked over to Jace, who still leaned against the barn with a smirk on his face. She couldn't help but smile in return.

"I warned you I'd retaliate."

"Now, Jace," she said in her sweetest voice, shaking her finger at him, "you know very well that revenge is not your responsibility. We just heard about that in church last Sunday."

He grabbed the finger she shook at him. "You know, you're right. I guess I'll have to go home and confess that sin tonight while you're cutting all those heads of hair."

She stuck out her tongue, and he grinned.

"Come on." He pushed away from the barn. "We'd better get in there and get some food before the men eat it all."

"Really. I need to eat so I'll have plenty of energy for tonight."

He put his arm around her shoulders and gave her a quick squeeze. She gave his arm a playful push. "Don't go trying to make it up to me now. It's too late."

Her heart did a funny little dance at the sound of his laughter. He tipped the rim of his hat and gave a mocking bow as he held the door open for her.

TWELVE

Jace spotted the man he sought. Coop lounged with his feet up on a barrel surrounded by men engrossed in his latest tale.

"Coop, can I talk to you a minute?"

"Sure. Whatcha need?"

He led Coop away from the rest of the men. "You know we're leaving on Monday to drive the cattle to the stockyard in Pueblo."

"Yep."

"I'd like for you to stay behind and watch the place for me." Coop's face darkened with that angry look Jace had come to know well, and he raised his hand to staunch an outburst. "I know Adam and Bobbie were the last to arrive here. They should be the ones staying behind, but I really don't like the idea of leaving Bobbie here. That just leaves women and children to take care of things. And I don't know or trust Adam enough to leave him behind to watch everything.

"I hope you're not angry about my choice, Coop, but I've got to get these cattle to the stockyard before I lose any more. With so many of them to move, I need every available hand. Will you take over for me while we're gone?"

The compliment rubbed the redness from Coop's face. "Sure. I'd be happy to. Ya got nothing to worry about while yer gone. I'll take care of everything."

Jace stuck his hand out for Coop to shake. "I've already talked to Annie. You'll be taking all your meals with her while we're gone. We should be back in a week if all goes well. Thanks again, Coop."

He patted Coop's hunched shoulder, appreciating that his men respected his decisions. If only Bobbie agreed to do the same. She'd not said more about their argument or their conversation after the Bible study, but even after the fun she'd had cutting his hair, he couldn't help but feel as if he'd lost something — respect or trust, he wasn't sure.

"You bet. Don't worry 'bout nothing."

Jace swung toward the stable.

"Ah, Jace? I could sure use a trip inta town 'fore ya'll head out. If I go now, I shouldn't

143

need to go again till ya git back."

Jace paused, his hand on the carved wooden latch. "Sure, Coop. That's not a problem."

Coop tugged his hat over his eyes before heading for his horse. Jace went back to work with a clear head.

Two days later, the cattle drive was finally under way, much to Jace's satisfaction. The anticipation always seemed harder than the drive itself. After countless trips, it still surprised him how tense he became.

He reined in his horse and glanced back, keeping a careful eye on the new men he'd hired for the drive. *Men.* The corner of his mouth twitched at the thought. Two of them were fresh out of the schoolyard. With a lot of talking and all the charm he could muster, he finally convinced their mothers to let them go.

He glanced at the sun, now halfway up in the sky. They'd left before daylight and were making good time. Looking ahead, he spied Dew leading the way with Beans nearby on the chuck wagon, flaps fluttering like two great white sails in the breeze. Bobbie had told him she'd been on cattle drives with Roy. His face flaming, Jace asked what she did about changing clothes and such. She laughed and said as long as the chuck wagon had flaps, she did all of her changing inside. He decided they would do the same on this trip.

Dust billowed in the air, blocking his view of the woman in his thoughts, but he didn't doubt she would be nearby performing the job she did so well. He pulled his kerchief up to cover his nose and mouth. The alternative was a snout full of grime at the end of the day, and a headache bad enough to cripple a man.

A heifer darted out of the group at a full run with its tail up and ears back. Jace reined his horse to give chase but stopped when he saw Bobbie atop Mack appear from the dirt cloud. Bobbie's long braid bounced against her back with each of Mack's strides. Jace caught himself grinning as he watched her cut off the heifer's escape, turning it back toward the herd. Mack pranced as if he were in his element. No doubt Bobbie felt the same way.

The day passed uneventfully, and as night fell, everyone hankered to get out of the saddle. Earlier, he'd caught many of them standing with feet still in the stirrups trying to remove some of their knots and get their blood circulating again. He dismounted and did some stretching of his own before removing his hat and beating it against his legs, arms, and back. Around the campsite, others did the same.

Beans found a good place next to a stream to set up for the night, and the tantalizing scent of his wonderful stew and biscuits filled the air. Jace posted watches for the night. Dew and David would stand watch the first night, and he and Bobbie would take the next night. Sonny and Adam would be responsible for the third. Upon hearing that, Dew quickly downed some food and left with instructions for David to relieve him around midnight.

The rest of the group dug into the stew. They finished in a short time and relaxed around the fire while sipping on coffee. Bobbie excused herself, and Jace set down his coffee cup, prepared to follow if she took too long. Needing her to stand watch galled him, but he couldn't use the boys he hired, and he needed Sonny and Adam for the third night. He wouldn't ask any of his men to pull double duty. Besides, if he wanted to earn her respect, he needed to trust that she could pull her own. At least they'd be far from the trouble at the ranch, and she knew how to use her weapons.

He remained watchful until Bobbie's return. Annie hadn't liked the idea of

146

Bobbie going on the drive, and had given him stern instructions. He planned on following them to the letter.

When David finished his coffee, he pulled his guitar out of the chuck wagon and began playing a lively tune, much to the enjoyment of the group. Jace took that opportunity before bedding down for the night to check on his horse and talk to Beans about where they might stop tomorrow. The day had gone well. He prayed the rest of the drive did too. He'd had his belly full of trouble.

Bobbie prepared her bedroll next to Jace's, looking around to make sure she wasn't being watched. After making some adjustments on Jace's bedding, she returned to the fire to listen to David sing and play his guitar.

David's slow ballad wafted on the night air, his soft tenor voice ebbing and swelling like she'd pictured the ocean at full tide. Bobbie closed her eyes, soaking in the words she'd known since childhood. Unable to help herself, she joined him in singing the last verse and chorus, her clear, strong alto providing the perfect harmony.

When the song ended, the men clapped their enthusiastic appreciation. Her face heating, Bobbie was grateful for the darkness. Jace came up and sat next to her.

"That was beautiful."

"I agree," Sonny said. "Do you know another one?"

"I don't know." Bobbie looked at David.

"How about this one." He began another ballad. This time the entire group joined in the laughter and singing. Groans of disappointment filled the air when the song ended and David reached for the canvas bag to store his guitar.

"Sorry, fellas. It's late, and I'm next on watch."

He ignored the pleas for more and finished stashing his guitar before plopping onto his bedroll. To his good fortune, David ducked his head under his pillow in time to avoid the barrage of boots that pelted him from every direction.

Bobbie crawled under her covers facing Jace and waited for the fun to begin. Through lowered lids, she watched him drop onto his pallet. Moments later, he flung off his covers and jumped up.

"What in the world? Is that a snake?" He rushed to the fire, picked up a lighted stick, and returned to his bedding.

She pulled her blanket up over her face and fought the laughter that shook her as she heard the other men question Jace. She peeked over the top of her covering and saw Jace grab his blanket and throw it off the rest of his bedding.

"What's this?" Jace reached down. "A coiled piece of rope. And it's wet." He looked around at the men, a smile curling his lips. "All right. Who's the prankster?"

He held the fire stick higher. When his gaze rested on her, she shut her eyes tight and curled the blanket around her face.

The wet piece of rope landed across her. She burst into laughter, and the men joined her.

"Jace Kincaid." Bobbie sat up. "I can't believe you're afraid of a little piece of rope. You're supposed to be our fearless leader."

He knelt down in front of her, a slow smile curving his lips. "I guess you forgot that I like to retaliate." His voice was quiet. "You'd better watch your back, Bobbie."

The night was long as she spent it tossing. She just made out Jace's face in the firelight and couldn't help but watch him sleep. His handsome face looked peaceful in repose. And his lips. What might they feel like . . .

She wasted no time clearing camp the next morning. She tied up her bedroll, gulped down some breakfast, and climbed onto her

149

saddle, anxious to get as far from Jace as possible.

The best part of the day was spent looking over her shoulder as she kept a wary eye on Jace's whereabouts, trying to anticipate his every move. She rubbed at the aching muscles in her neck and back.

A nearby cow moved with slow steps, its head hanging low. Absorbed with trying to decide if it was hurt or sick, Bobbie almost shrieked at the voice only inches from her ear.

"You look just like that cow, Bobbie."

She leaned away as she turned toward Jace, her mouth dropping open. "Why, thank you. I've always wanted to be likened to a cow."

His head went back with spirited laughter as he spurred his mount forward.

After the long, hot day, she rode toward the chuck wagon yearning for a bath. None would be forthcoming this far from home with nothing but dirt and hills for miles in every direction. Beans stood at the fire with a plate full of food and pushed it into her hands the moment she slid from the saddle. The first night watch was her responsibility, and she needed to eat fast so she could start her assignment.

She finished her meal and stood, ready to

get back to work. Jace stood at the same time. After checking the cinches on her saddle, she climbed astride, ready to find the best place to keep an eye on the herd.

"Bobbie . . . hold up." Jace walked toward her and mounted his horse. "I'll show you where to sit for the night."

She spurred Mack on.

He caught up. "Is there something wrong, Bobbie? You look awfully tense."

She couldn't help but hear the humor in his voice. "As if you don't know."

"Let me remind you that you started it."

"I know, but you've got to admit it was pretty funny." She cut her eyes at him, annoyed by the smug set of his chin.

"After the fact, yes, but when I laid on what felt like a snake, my heart about jumped out of my chest."

She burst into laughter all over again.

"You laugh, my dear, but let me warn you yet again. I *will* get even."

Bobbie shook her head, though she felt a small thrill at his endearment.

Jace stopped his horse at the mouth of a small valley. The gorge was surrounded on three sides by large rocks that made up the foothills of the mountains. They had driven the cattle inside for the night. Jace led the way to a large, wide ledge just above the herd. She followed close behind carrying her canteen and rifle.

He motioned along the ridge. "Will this be all right for you tonight?"

"It's perfect. With the clear night and being above the herd, this will be an easy watch."

"That's what I thought. I'm going to head back and try to get some sleep. I'll relieve you around midnight."

"All right. See you then."

When he'd left, she proceeded to get as comfortable as possible on the rocks. After fighting the hard dirt floor for almost an hour, she retraced her steps to get the blanket from her saddle. She grabbed her jacket and slipped into it, knowing the night air would get cold. Bobbie returned to her vantage point, placed the folded blanket on the ground, and settled in for the rest of her watch. With her back against a large boulder and the rifle sitting across her lap, she hummed tunes to stay awake.

Several hours later, guessing it close to midnight, a twig snapped above her head. She tightened the grip on her rifle. The sound of pebbles crunching carried through the still air.

"Jace?" Bobbie held her breath, searching the darkness. "Jace, if that's you, you'd bet-

ter let me know so you don't get yo
shot." There was no answer.

She got up on her knees. Below, Mack an
some of the cattle acted skittish. When
pebbles rained down on her head, she
cocked her rifle. The noise must have
alarmed whoever stood above her. She saw
some movement in the moonlight. With a
grunt, the person sprang from a hiding
place above her head. At the last moment,
she swung her gun around, getting two shots
off in quick succession before the impact
knocked the rifle from her hands.

THIRTEEN

Jace yawned as he tightened the leather strap beneath his horse's belly. Staying awake until daylight would be a struggle. Worry over Bobbie and the two greenhorns he'd been forced to hire had kept him awake, and here it was, almost midnight. He'd never had a woman on a drive before, and the strange responsibility made him uncomfortable . . . and protective. He moved to the edge of the stream, knelt, and splashed water on his face. In the distance, a coyote howled its mournful tune.

The sharp crack of two gunshots echoed across the range. Jace stood and ran for his horse. Fully awake, he mounted and took off at a full gallop.

He slowed at the opening of the valley. There was no sign of cattle on the run, no dust choking him or cattle bellowing in panic. He reined in his horse and sat listening. The silence was eerie. He whirled his horse and raced the short distance to the ridge, pulling his rifle from its sheath and jumping from the saddle before the horse came to a stop.

"Bobbie?" He ran up the ledge. No response. "Bobbie?"

"Jace?"

Relief rushed through him. "Where are you?"

"Over here, Jace. Help! I can't hold on much longer."

He ran toward the sound of her voice. "Where are you?"

"I'm hanging off the ledge. Hurry! My fingers are slipping!"

In three steps, he stood over her. He heard her panting. Her boots scraped against the rocky wall. He dropped to his belly and ran a hand along the edge. His fingers brushed hers. He scooted forward so half of his shoulders hung over the edge in open air. If he wasn't careful, he'd send them both careening down on the herd below. With his foot anchored behind a boulder and one hand on a tree root, he reached down and grabbed Bobbie's wrist. She let loose of the ledge and screamed.

"I got you. It's all right, Bobbie. I've got you." He grabbed her other hand. Muscles straining, he pulled until Bobbie's upper body rose over the edge of the cliff. He struggled to his knees, still holding tight to her, and helped her climb up the rest of the way.

She flung herself against him, almost knocking him off balance. He led her away from the edge and helped her sit. They leaned against the bluff, breathing hard. Her quiet sobs reached his ears.

"Are you all right?" She didn't answer. He reached up and pushed a tangled strand of hair from her face.

She sniffled. "I'm fine."

"Are you hurt?"

"Not really. Just a bump on the back of my head."

His fingers barely touched the forming knot when she winced and pulled away. He dropped his hand. "What happened? I heard gunshots." Galloping horses sounded in the distance. He knew it would be his men. "Bobbie?"

"A man jumped me."

"What? A man? What man?" He glanced around in the darkness. He reached for the rifle he'd dropped. "How'd you end up hanging over the ledge?"

She sniffed again. "I didn't know I was that close. When I rolled away from him, I fell over."

"Jace? Bobbie?"

"Over here, Dew." He was thankful his foreman thought to bring along a torch. Behind Dew, Sonny scrambled up the ledge, eyes wide and hat askew. Bobbie struggled to get up, holding her head. Jace slipped a hand under her arm and helped her to her feet.

She searched the ground around her. "Do you see my rifle? It's around here somewhere. He knocked it from my hands."

"He?" Dew shoved the fire toward them. "What happened?"

"Some man attacked her." Concerned by the way she held the back of her head, Jace moved close enough to grasp her shoulder. "Are you sure you're not hurt?"

"I'm fine. I bumped my head on the rocks when he knocked me down, but it's not bad." Dew bent to pick up her rifle and hat. "I'm sure it's nothing a bit of rest won't take care of."

Bobbie pulled away and walked toward her horse. Sonny trailed after her and helped her descend the ledge.

"Dew?" Jace waited for Bobbie to move some distance away. "When you get back to camp, have Beans check her head."

"Sure thing, Jace." He paused. "You sure you don't want me to take your watch?"

"No, but thanks. It's my watch. I'll take care of it. Besides, I couldn't sleep now if I wanted to."

Jace hunkered down with his back against the rock wall, his rifle across his knees. Not sure what he expected to see, he peered into the dark over the cattle. Thoughts and questions careened through his mind. Who attacked Bobbie and why? Was he after Bobbie alone or whoever happened to be standing watch? Did this have something to do with his rustled cattle? Were they looking to take the herd?

He thought again of Bobbie, and an ache began in his heart. He couldn't imagine the ranch without her.

He stared up at the star-studded sky. What was he thinking? He was running a business. How could he have let a ranch hand become so special? He shook his head and sighed. She could have died tonight, and she would have spent her eternity separated from God. *And from me.* He almost laughed at his inability to convince himself that Bobbie wasn't important to him. The ache in his heart grew. He started praying for her and the feelings inside him that he hadn't acknowledged until now, but he kept both eyes wide open.

Bobbie took her time waking up. She had to force her eyes open. Her head pounded with pain, and she rubbed at her temple. Her blurred vision started to clear, and the first thing she saw was Jace perched on a log sipping from a blackened coffee cup. The men spoke in whispers, and guilty surprise was written across their faces when she tried to sit up.

She gasped at the pain that cut through her shoulder.

Jace dropped to one knee next to her. "Are you hurt, Bobbie?"

She shook her head. "Just a little sore. The man that threw me down was huge. He hit me pretty hard."

Jace looked past her. "Beans, check her."

She tried to turn away, but a beefy hand clamped onto her chin as Beans turned her head in his direction.

"You can fight me or be agreeable, but I aim to take a look-see at your head."

Bobbie couldn't help but smile. Beans tried to sound gruff, but his eyes showed his concern. Most cooks worth anything on a drive doubled as doctor, always carrying medical supplies. Beans seemed to take the role seriously.

"Now, that's a nice sight — your smile. Just turn back that a way and let's see the other side o' your head."

Beans gave her chin a push, and Bobbie complied. Her gaze met Jace's. The look on his face sent warmth flooding through her. She didn't have time to ponder the feeling. Beans's fingers pressed on the tender spot, and she winced.

"She's still got a lump but nowhere near as big as last night."

Jace moved back to sit on the log. "I want you to ride in the wagon with Beans today."

She shook her head and flinched at the ensuing ache.

"Bobbie —"

"No, Jace. All riding in that wagon's gonna get me is a worse headache. I'd be better off in the saddle."

"I'm gonna have to side with the little lady here, Jace." Beans still knelt by her side. "If we was on a road, I'd be agreeing with you, but crossing the prairie is jarring enough to rattle your bones."

Jace emptied his coffee cup with a flick of his wrist. He opened his mouth as if to speak, but Dew galloped into the camp and reined in his horse. He dismounted in one smooth motion, his eyes on Bobbie the entire time. His gaze dropped to the coat lying at Bobbie's feet. He grabbed it and began an examination.

"When it got light enough to see, I looked around for tracks." Dew spoke as he scrutinized her coat. "I found drops of blood on the ledge." He stopped, then poked a finger through a hole in the jacket. His gaze went to her. "Left shoulder, Bobbie. You hurt?"

"Check your shoulder, Bobbie," Jace said.

She pulled the blanket down. "I told you I'm not hurt, Jace. I think I'd know if . . ." The tear in her shirt stopped her words. Shock rolled through her as her eyes sought Jace's.

"Beans." Jace jumped to his feet, his gaze never leaving hers.

The cook moved around to her other side. "I'm just gonna check real quick." Beans poked a finger through the rip. After her hiss of pain, he tore the material a little more to get a better look. "Just a scratch. Not much blood to speak of. I'll get the kit."

She tried to peek at her shoulder to see if she could apply a bandage to it herself and made a face when she realized it would be too awkward.

"The blood on the ledge must've come from the man." Dew's voice cut into her thoughts. She looked up and met his gaze.

161

"I guess you hit him."

Her heart thudded. She'd never shot anyone before.

"I want you to stick close to one of us at all times today, Bobbie." Jace's voice sounded stern, but the look on his face was more so. "I won't give in on this, Bobbie. Either you agree or I'll tie you to the wagon myself."

"All right. But you know, Jace, I'm sure that man wasn't after me. He probably wanted to hurt whoever happened to be on watch last night."

"I realize that, but I'm not taking any chances." He jammed his hat on his head. "Just stick close."

Dew tossed Bobbie's coat back where he found it. "You want me to have Sonny follow the tracks, Jace?"

"No, I need every wrangler here. I'll talk to the sheriff when we get to town."

Dew nodded and grabbed the reins of his horse. "All right, men. Let's mount up."

"James." Jace waved to one of the boys he'd hired. He came running. "Stay with Bobbie until she's ready to go. Then ride with her to catch up. *Stay with her.*"

"Yes, sir."

Bobbie looked at him. "But Jace —"

"I don't want to hear it. Catch up when

you can."

He mounted up and rode off. She urged Beans to hurry with his ministrations and tried to move away after he applied the bandage, but he sat her back down.

"Let's do some stitching on the hole in your shirt."

Sitting still wasn't easy. When Beans finished, she jumped up and ran to Mack. Riding hard to reach the herd, she felt sorry for James as he struggled to keep up. She moved into position at left flank, and James hung back over her shoulder.

Bobbie rubbed at her temple in an attempt to ease the throbbing. She moved back and took up a conversation with the boy named her guardian for the day. The thought made her smile. If anything were to go wrong, she'd be the one doing the guarding.

The day and night passed uneventfully except for the drizzle that slowed them down, raising the level of Jace's frustration. They didn't arrive on the outskirts of Pueblo until early afternoon on their fourth day out. Jace rode ahead to prepare the stockyard for their arrival. He stood with the manager at an open gate of a large corral and counted each head as his cattle were herded inside. The cattle bellowed and bumped into one another as their hooves made sloppy sucking noises in the mud. Jace was glad to see the end of them.

He stuffed the money for his cattle into his saddlebag, then mounted and led his men to the livery. He paid the owner to leave the horses overnight and led the men back out to the street.

"I'll reserve a couple rooms for the night. Take the rest of the day off, but make sure you're able to ride tomorrow. We're leaving early. I'm ready to get home."

Bobbie turned to walk away with the others.

"Bobbie, we still have some business to attend to." She paused, confusion knotting her forehead. Jace nodded toward the sheriff's office. "We need to report what happened." She scowled and shook her head but followed him without argument.

A short time later, Jace stopped pacing in front of the sheriff and leaned over the desk toward the man. "What do you mean, there's nothing you can do? She coulda been killed." He slapped his palm on the desktop. "You're the sheriff. Go out there and look for the man. Follow his tracks. Do *something!* It's your job."

The sheriff rubbed at his chin, eyebrows

raised. "Look, mister . . ."

"Kincaid."

"Look, Mr. Kincaid. From what the little, uh, lady has said, she didn't get a good look at the attacker." The sheriff leaned back in his chair and propped his booted feet up on the desk. "And it's been raining. There ain't gonna be any tracks left to follow. They're bound to be washed away by now. And from what you've described, that's quite a distance from here. I can't leave my town unattended for that long."

Jace gripped the edge of the desk before pushing away. "Well, at least let a marshal know about it. Maybe he'll be more inclined to do his job."

He took Bobbie by the elbow and led her out of the office toward the hotel. Several steps later, he realized she was almost running to keep up. He slowed his stride and then stopped.

"I'm sorry. I guess he got me a little riled." He looked at her face. Amidst the streaks of dirt, he could see her weariness. "I think it's time we get some rest. I'll arrange for baths, then have a warm meal sent to your room. Is that all right?"

"That sounds wonderful."

He placed his hand at the small of her back as they continued down the boardwalk.

165

"You won't be disturbed and can go to sleep whenever you want. I'll come for you in the morning."

After making arrangements for Bobbie to have the tub first, Jace then gave the maid some money to take a plate of food to her. Once he delivered her safely to her room, Jace sat in his own tub of steamy water and allowed the heat to melt away his tension. He thought back on the last couple days. He'd been quiet. The looks he received from the men told him they'd noticed.

Bobbie hadn't said much about the attack. He'd overreacted, treating her different from how he would have one of his men. Annoyance rode him hard. He knew better than to bring along a woman, and yet he'd done it anyway. Not only had he gone against what he believed, he also discovered his feelings were more than a boss should have for his hired hand. Much more. At least she'd found a way to avoid him, keeping herself occupied teaching the boys rope tricks. And it made her feel useful, not even suspecting he'd already asked the boys to keep an eye on her.

He ran his wet hand over his face and stared at the ceiling. What would he say to her the next time they were alone? Somehow he had to convince her that she had no place

166

working the range even if she was one of his best hands.

The next morning, Jace led Bobbie and the men down the boardwalk toward the livery. A man cut through the group, hurrying in the opposite direction. He gave Bobbie a rough shove with his elbow.

She stumbled. "Hey!"

Dew reached out to help Bobbie catch her balance. The man stopped and turned back. Jace moved to her other side to make sure she wasn't hurt, but the look on her face caught his attention. His gaze moved between the stranger and Bobbie as she stared at the man who'd hit her.

"That's no way to treat a lady," Sonny said.

The man turned to him. "If she dressed like a lady, she'd be treated like one."

Sonny stuck his finger in the man's chest. "She's more a lady than you'll ever be a man."

The man shoved Sonny's finger from his chest. The rest of Jace's men surrounded the two of them. After the space of several heartbeats, the man held up his hands.

"Sonny," Bobbie said as she laid her hand on his arm, her gaze still glued to the man's face. "It's all right."

"No, it's not." Sonny continued to look

the man in the eyes.

"Let's go, men." Jace took Bobbie by the arm and pulled her toward the livery, expecting the rest to follow. "Do you know him, Bobbie?"

"I don't think so. He seemed familiar at first, but I don't think I know him." She made him stop when she pulled her arm away from him. "If I'm going to work for you, Jace, you're going to have to recognize that people don't accept me."

"That's nonsense." He couldn't imagine anyone treating Bobbie so rudely, but then not everyone felt about her the way he did. Did she remember the way he reacted to her when she first arrived on his ranch? He wanted to apologize. Then he shook the thought away. The way he was feeling about her right now, he might say something he shouldn't.

The first day's ride home started out with very little chatter. They plodded along only as fast as the chuck wagon allowed, following behind it in a tight cluster. Bobbie appeared anxious as she gazed at each man's face. Jace knew the men were protective of her, but she hadn't expected their defense. He'd wanted to flatten the man himself but obeyed the strong desire to be a good example.

"There was one night when I was about 14," Bobbie said all of a sudden, "that I became envious of all the other hands going off into town for a night of fun."

Jace stared at her. Rarely did Bobbie talk about herself, let alone her childhood. He perked up, not wanting to miss a word.

"They always came back laughing and talking about how much fun they had. I was never allowed to have that night off and got more and more upset about it as each weekend rolled around. I decided that if I couldn't join them, I'd at least get into town to watch them."

Jace glanced around. She had their undivided attention, and the smile on her face told him she knew it.

"I came up with a plan I was sure would work. I already had men's clothing. All I needed was the whiskers, or so I thought. The only thing I could come up with that would look like whiskers was the charred end of a burned stick. So I waited until my father was asleep and rubbed the soot of that burned stick all over my cheeks and under my nose and chin. I wound all my hair up under my hat and went off to have a good time."

She paused in her story, and Sonny said, "Come on, Bobbie, you can't stop there. We wanna hear what happened."

Bobbie grinned. "In all my excitement, it never dawned on me that everyone would recognize my horse, clothes, and hat. I rode into town hoping to come across as a stranger they wouldn't give a second look. I spotted the horses of the other hands and tied mine near them. I walked into the saloon and found a table in the corner. I sat down in a chair, pulled my hat a little lower" — she tugged at the rim of her hat much like she must have that night — "and proceeded to find out how the men had so much fun every weekend. I didn't know they recognized me instantly and came up with an idea to teach me a lesson.

"They filled in one of the saloon girls on their plan, offering to pay her to be a part of it. She accepted and sashayed her way over to my table. She leaned over, smiled and batted her long lashes, and said, 'Need some company, cowboy?' "

Bobbie had altered her voice to sound like the saloon girl, all soft and sultry. The men roared with laughter.

"I shook my head at her and pulled my hat even lower. She wasn't dissuaded. I wanted to run, but she had pushed the table out of the way with her hip, cutting off my escape. Then she said, 'Aw, come on. Every cowboy needs a little fun,' and she plopped herself down on my lap and lifted the hat off my head. I jumped up, which made her fall to the floor, but she was laughing along with everyone else in the place as I ran from the saloon. I had never been so embarrassed in my life. It took a long time to live that down."

The men's laughter rolled across the plains. Jace reined his horse next to hers. "What did your father do to you?"

"He scolded me for several minutes but that was all. He knew I was miserable and humiliated and that the men were going to give me a pretty bad time about it. I guess he thought that was punishment enough."

Bobbie smiled at him. Jace shook his head. This woman was full of surprises, and he didn't doubt they'd seen only the surface.

The men spent the rest of the day telling their embarrassing moments, making the time speed by. Before Jace knew it, they stopped to camp for the night. He climbed into his bedroll and pulled the blanket up to his chin. If they rode hard, maybe they'd make it home the next day.

He'd just drifted off to sleep when he heard a commotion around him.

"Stampede!"

The word echoed in his mind, bouncing

him from deep sleep to sudden awareness. He jumped from the ground and felt for his boots, his heart racing.

"Where are my boots?" It was the question every person asked — all but one. Bobbie still lay in her bedding. Then it came to him. He had no cattle.

"Here they are," Beans called out.

Jace looked toward the chuck wagon. Beans straddled a pile of dusty boots, his hands planted on his hips, before tossing them back to their owners.

Jace's gaze went back to the only person still lying down. "Bobbie?"

"Hmm?" She rolled over. "What?"

She stifled a yawn he suspected was meant to cover a grin. She sat up and rubbed her eyes. "Oh, sorry. Bad dream."

The men groaned and threw their boots at her as she pulled the blanket over her head.

The pelting finally ended, and Jace nudged Bobbie's blanket with his toe. "How do you come up with this stuff?"

She moved the blanket and peeked up at him. "Why, I don't know what you're talking about, Jace Kincaid."

Jace shook his head. "How did your father ever control you?"

"He rarely tried."

Jace watched her a moment longer before climbing back into his bedding. He had never paid her back for that first prank. With all that had happened to her on her watch, he lost any desire to get even. After this latest prank, he might have to come up with something just to keep pace before she moved on. That thought made him roll to his side to look at her. What would he do if Bobbie ever decided to leave the ranch? The notion hit him like a punch to the gut.

Jace rose early the next morning and rousted everyone but Bobbie out of bed, motioning to the men to be quiet. They joined him several yards away, and he filled them in on his idea to get even.

Several minutes later, plan and men in place, Beans clanked his spoon on the pot. Jace kept his eye on Bobbie from under the rim of his hat as she sat up, stretched, and yawned. Tossing off her blanket, she reached for her boots and slid one on. In seconds, the boot went flying from her foot. A small snake slithered out and away.

Bobbie peered up at him, accusation in her eyes. Jace grinned before nodding his cue at the men. They turned to face Bobbie and chorused, "Good morning!" She burst into laughter when she saw their faces, all blackened with soot as she had described in

173

her childhood story.

She rose to her feet shaking her finger at each of them. "As much as I hate snakes, it was worth putting my foot next to one just to see you all like this."

Sonny stood and stretched before dumping the rest of his coffee. "Jace, can we make it home today? I don't know if I can handle another night with this woman."

"Sounds like a good idea to me."

"I pity the poor man who marries you, Bobbie," Sonny said. "He'll have to be wary at all times."

Bobbie finished rolling her blanket. "What gave you the idea I ever plan to marry?"

Bobbie's voice was tinged with humor, but an uncomfortable silence followed. Beans gave Jace a questioning look, and the other men remained mute. Were his feelings for Bobbie that obvious?

Sonny handed his plate to Beans, then reached down and touched Bobbie's shoulder. "I'm sorry. I didn't mean nothing by that."

"It's all right, Sonny. I took no offense. I've just always accepted it as fact."

They cleared camp as fast as they could. They rode hard and arrived home after dark, dusty and exhausted. Annie met them at the kitchen door, her smile aimed at

Bobbie. "It's so good to see you. You have no idea how much I missed you." Annie reached to give her a hug, but Bobbie stopped her by raising a hand.

"You may not want to do that. I'm filthy, and I'm sure I smell bad."

"I don't care." Annie wrapped her arms around Bobbie. "I'm just glad you're back."

Bobbie returned the hug. "You're a sight for sore eyes yourself. A week with a bunch of men is more than any woman should have to bear."

"I heard that." Jace waited on the steps. Bobbie tossed a smile over her shoulder as she threw her belongings into her room.

Annie pulled him into a hug. "Jace, have you talked to Coop?"

He took in the look on his sister's face, and his heart sank. "No."

"More of your cattle are missing."

FOURTEEN

Bobbie sat on Mack's back as Jace swung his arm to keep the horses from scattering and escaping. "Get that gate open, Adam!"

They'd spent the morning rounding up every horse Jace owned. He wanted them near the ranch, hoping to keep them from getting stolen like his cattle. Eighty head had been rustled. A blow for any rancher, but Jace had just sold off over twice that amount, leaving him with a small herd.

An ache formed in her chest for Jace. How would he be able to survive the loss?

He'd gotten upset, angry even, hollering Coop's name all the way out to the barn the night they returned from the drive. Bobbie followed him at what she hoped was a safe distance. Sheriff Morgan Thomas stood between the two men as if he expected trouble. Coop blubbered that he couldn't be everywhere at once — that there was no way for him to stop the thief.

Jace amazed her. After the initial shock, he'd calmed down and spoke of ways to preserve what he had left.

The next morning, she had walked into the barn looking for Jace. She'd wanted to encourage him but stopped when she heard his voice. At first she thought he was talking to one of the wranglers, but what she heard let her know he was praying, thanking God it wasn't worse.

Bobbie shook her head at the memory. Time and again he'd proven his faith was strong. Something like that would have sent her running even further from God, but Jace seemed to draw closer to Him, as if God was all he had left. Maybe that's exactly how Jace felt.

Bobbie eyed the beautiful black stallion in the first corral as she reined Mack in and wiped the sweat from her brow. Summer hadn't arrived yet, but the temperature gave a foretaste of what was to come. The stallion tossed his head at the arrival of possible mates. She hadn't had as much time to work with him lately, but she'd been able to ride him around the corral the last time. He was nearly broken.

She heard someone yelling behind her and looked toward the house. Annie came running, skirts flying.

"Ben!"

Bobbie turned Mack in that direction and urged him into a gallop. "What's wrong, Annie?"

"I can't find Ben." Annie's dark hair clung to her face and tears coursed down her cheeks. "I left him alone long enough to put Sara down for a nap, and now he's gone. He's just disappeared." Annie took off at a run again calling Ben's name.

"Annie, wait!" Either the call went unheard or Annie didn't want to stop.

Fear gripped Bobbie's heart. With all that'd been going on around the ranch, she didn't even want to think about what could have happened to the boy. Tears filled her eyes as she went for Jace.

"Ben's missing."

Jace rushed toward the house. She followed and continued to scan the area while Jace went after Annie.

Where could he be? Did someone take him or did he run off? In between the wranglers' shouts and Annie's frightened calls, Bobbie heard the water running over the rocks in the creek. She spurred Mack toward the sound.

Ben was squatting at the edge of the creek, playing in the water. He'd waded in too far, getting his shoes wet. His hand darted into

178

the water, then pulled back. He opened his hand and his shoulders slumped.

Bobbie dismounted quietly so as not to scare him and walked near him before she crouched down. "What are you doing down here, Ben?"

"I like the water." He dipped his hand into the creek again. "Turtles are in here. Baby fish too." He pointed one out to her, the end of his finger dripping creek-bottom slime.

"Did you ask your mama if you could come down here?"

Ben looked up as the first inkling that he might be in trouble occurred to him. Moisture pooled in his big blue eyes as he shook his head. She scooped him up in her arms and gave him a hug.

"Let's go find your mama, shall we?"

Ben rubbed his grimy sleeve under his nose, still not looking too happy.

Setting Ben up on the saddle, she climbed up behind him and held him tight against her, then pointed Mack up the incline toward the house. They had just ridden over the crest of the hill when she heard Annie screaming. Jace followed right behind Annie and appeared to be trying to get her to calm down.

When Bobbie stopped next to Annie, Jace

reached up and removed Ben from the saddle and handed him to his mother. Annie dropped to the ground with Ben on her lap and sobbed as she held him to her chest. Bobbie dismounted and sat next to Annie, trying to comfort and calm her. Several minutes later, Annie's sobs finally slowed to hiccups, then to quiet sniffles.

Annie held Ben away from her. "Why did you run off, Ben? You know you're not supposed to do that. You scared me to death!"

Ben's bottom lip began to tremble. "I'm sorry, Mama." He started crying.

Annie held him tight again and whispered in his ear. Whatever she said worked because he quieted. She held his face in her hands. "I don't ever want you to do that again, all right?" Ben nodded. "If you want to go someplace, you *must* come and talk to me first. Do you understand?" Ben nodded again.

Annie's attention turned to Bobbie and with her free arm, gave her a hug. "Thank you so much, Bobbie. I don't know how I could ever thank you enough."

"You just did. I'm thrilled I was able to find him." She rose to her feet, and Jace helped Annie to stand. They all walked toward the house.

"How did you know where to look, Bobbie?" Annie said.

"I heard the water running in the creek. I did the same thing when I was little."

"You ran off from your mother?"

"I was playing in the water just as Ben was doing, and when Mama found me she blistered my backside. Then she began to cry, and that hurt me much more than the spanking. I never did that again."

Jace smiled. "How old were you?"

"Around six, I guess."

They followed Annie into the house and, seeing her settle on the sofa with her son, they retreated to the kitchen.

"Jace, if it's all right, I'd like to stay with Annie for a while."

"I was going to suggest that. Just plan on staying the rest of the day. I'll put Mack up for you."

"Thanks, Jace."

"Nope. I thank you. I don't know what we would've done if anything had happened to that boy."

Jace held her gaze, and something in his intense brown eyes rendered her mute.

Bobbie glanced away. "He was fine really. The turtles fascinated him. I'm sure he was planning on coming back soon."

"Nonetheless, thank you again."

She smiled and gave a casual wave of her

hand. Still, something was making her heart pound hard. "You're welcome."

"Do you think I should get word to Cade that maybe he should come out a different night?" Jace referred to the supper invitation extended to his friend.

"I don't think that's necessary. You've all been friends for so long, I doubt that Annie would be uncomfortable with him here tonight."

"You're probably right."

After Jace left, Bobbie wandered into Annie's kitchen. She forced her thoughts to what she could do to help Annie. An idea came to mind. She checked on mother and son one more time before returning to the kitchen to cook supper. Nervousness assailed her. She was more comfortable on a saddle than in the kitchen. Determined to help her friend, she pushed the nerves away and got to work. Besides, she'd tackled calves and broken wild horses. How hard could it be to cook a meal?

An hour later, Bobbie felt she had everything under control — except maybe her heart. Jace was her boss, and she was only a ranch hand. She best not read anything into his lingering look. Or the way his lips turned up in a half smile.

Supper bubbled on the stove, and a loaf

of bread sat waiting to be popped into the oven. She heard Sara awaken and call for her mother, so she went to get her. Walking through the living room, she saw Annie and Ben asleep on the sofa, their heads touching.

Sara saw her and grinned. She held her arms out to be picked up. Bobbie scooped her up and planted a kiss on her cheek. She took Sara back to the kitchen, distracting her while walking through the living room so the little girl wouldn't see her mother.

Bobbie scattered some toys around in a corner of the kitchen to keep Sara occupied, then set the little girl down. She checked the pots on the stove and peeked in at the roast. Pete came through the kitchen door just as she popped the bread loaf next to the roast and put vegetables on to cook. "Hi, Pete."

"Papa!" Sara clapped her hands at the sight of her father. Pete bent to pick her up and, after giving her a hug and kiss, turned back to Bobbie.

"What's wrong, Bobbie? You wouldn't be in here doing the cooking if everything was fine."

She filled him in on the events that had taken place that afternoon. He thanked her and left to find his wife. She watched as Pete gently woke Annie and then embraced her when she started to cry. Bobbie returned to the kitchen to allow them some privacy.

Sometime later, Annie entered the kitchen and gave her a hug. "Thank you, Bobbie."

"I'm just glad I can help."

"You've definitely done that. Now what can I do to help in here?"

"Well, I found some beef and have that cooking. The potatoes and beans are done, as well as the bread. The only thing I'm not quite sure how to do is make the gravy. If you tell me, I'll get to work on it and you can go relax with your family." She was proud of her accomplishment and heard it in her own voice.

"Oh, let me do that for you. I haven't done anything all afternoon. I can at least make the gravy."

"Absolutely not. Just tell me how to make it and then leave."

Annie grinned and explained the procedure. Then she left as ordered.

Jace and Cade walked in as Bobbie put the finishing touches on the table. Jace stopped in the doorway. "How's Annie doing?"

"Better, I think. I gave her the afternoon off so she's resting in the living room with her family. Hi, Cade." She received a smile and nod in return.

Jace hadn't moved from the doorway. "You cooked?"

She feigned disdain at the surprise in his voice. "Yes, I cooked. And if you're nice, I just might let you eat some of it."

He held up his hands. "All right. Just let us wash up and we'll be ready." He sniffed the air. "It smells . . ." He sniffed again. "Interesting."

Bobbie couldn't wait to see that doubtful look change to one of appreciation once he tasted the meal. She moved to the living room to announce that supper was ready. Jace blessed the food and thanked the Lord for the safe return of his nephew.

The food was passed and everyone started eating. A look of shock passed over their faces when they bit into the beef. She had been sitting back to see if they liked her meal, but at the look on their faces, she stuffed a bite of the beef into her mouth.

She chewed just a moment. "Oh my!" *I'd have an easier time chewing on the toe of my boot.*

Jace bowed his head again. "And Lord, give us the strength to chew this meat." He smiled. "I'm sorry, Bobbie. I shouldn't tease you like that."

She raised her brow at their mirth, her

lips twitching. "Oh, well, don't hold back. Just go ahead and let it out."

"Well, at least we have the rest of the meal to fill us up," Annie said.

"That's right." Pete reached for the loaf of bread. He sliced at it, but the knife hardly made a mark. He stood then to get some leverage and sawed at the loaf as he would a log. "I'm sorry, Bobbie." He looked over at her and immediately started laughing.

Jace held out his plate. "How about a slice of that gravy to go with my meat?"

Bobbie stuck out her tongue then looked over the food. "Is there anything edible on this table?" She stuck her fork into the potatoes and took a bite. Her eyebrows shot up. "These are pretty good. What do you think of the potatoes, Ben?" He only eyed them with suspicion. She gave him a playful push. "Well, you're a big help."

Bobbie looked at Annie. "I'm so sorry. I ruined all this food."

"Oh, Bobbie, it's not ruined. I can make a stew or hash out of it tomorrow. I'm just so thankful you're here and that you wanted to help." Annie stood and leaned over to give her a squeeze. "Besides, I really needed the laugh."

"Well, I'm glad I could help with *something*."

Jace stood and smiled. "I'll go see if Beans has any food left over."

Bobbie made a face at him before he turned to go. He soon returned with a loaf of bread and a pot of stew. Ben clapped his chubby hands as he smiled at his uncle.

"Traitor," Bobbie mumbled loud enough for everyone to hear. She eyed Ben a bit closer and noticed a lump in his cheek. "What's this?" She tapped his cheek. He shrugged, looking uncomfortable.

Annie held her hand under his mouth. "Spit it out, Ben."

The boy opened his mouth and got rid of the offending item. Annie held it up for closer inspection. "It's chewed up meat. I guess he couldn't get it down."

The room echoed with laughter. Even Bobbie couldn't contain her mirth. Yes, she was born a ranch hand. She pulled Ben into her arms and kissed his cheek.

Pete patted her arm. "You took all this teasing well, Bobbie."

"It ain't like I didn't deserve it. If you're up to it, Annie, I want you to teach me to cook the next time I have a few hours off. Give me a rabbit and a campfire and I'll do okay, but I can't seem to do a thing in a kitchen."

"It'll probably take more than a few

187

hours," Jace whispered loud enough for her to hear.

She made another face at him. He smiled at her and winked.

Jace watched the pink color Bobbie's face and knew his wink caused it. He tried to fight back the thrill it gave him but with little success. He had an effect on her. Good or bad he didn't know, but right now, he just wanted to enjoy the knowledge.

FIFTEEN

Bobbie rode along the north range at Jace's request, a surprise considering how protective he'd been lately. Maybe his trust of her had finally grown. But the cattle had to be checked, and someone needed to see how the calving was going. Leading Mack around the outskirts of the range before moving inward, she thought Jace would be pleased with her report. Many of the cows had already birthed, and their young looked healthy. Spring could be a tough time for calving. The good news would be most welcome. And soon, another round of branding would begin.

As Bobbie circled Mack around a cluster of pine trees, the sun dipped toward the western ridge. Tall scrubs dotting the rocky ground loomed overhead casting long shadows across her path. She slowed so Mack wouldn't step in a hole. As she dodged between the pines and wove in and through the trees, she noticed something large and dark nearby. A familiar chill moved through her.

Bobbie pulled out her rifle and dismounted. She took a slow turn all around, keeping Mack between her and where she looked. Seeing no movement, she headed toward the cow. This one bore the same strange brand markings as the first cow they had found tied to a tree a couple months earlier.

A quick scout around the area revealed the remains of a campfire, one that looked recent, but nothing more of any consequence. She returned to Mack and the branded cow, all the while feeling as if a pair of eyes bored into her.

She untied the rope from the tree and led the cow to Mack before heading for home. Halfway there, she came upon another cow, this one having trouble calving. The cow lifted her head and then let it fall back down.

With another quick glance around, Bobbie dismounted and walked around the cow, groaning at the job she knew needed to be done. After retying the branded cow to a tree and retrieving a rope, she placed her lasso around the cow's horns before looping her end around the saddle horn. Then she pushed Mack back to tighten the rope. No sense taking a chance on the mother getting a burst of energy and trying to get up, although she looked too weak to attempt such a move. Bobbie stepped behind the cow and saw the calf's head near the opening.

She'd assisted a calving once before and wasn't thrilled at the prospect of doing it again. She squatted down, took a deep breath, and plunged her arm in next to the calf. She felt around for anything that might be blocking its progress and found the cord wrapped around the calf's front legs. After a bit of struggle, she finally managed to pull one leg free, allowing the other to move more easily. She grabbed the calf behind the ears, braced herself by placing her boots against the mother, and pulled.

At first, she didn't seem to be making any progress. Frustration mounted when her slick hands kept slipping from the calf. She rose to get another rope, looped it around the calf's legs, and tugged. The calf came sliding out, throwing her backward with the calf almost on top of her. She wiped as much of the slime from the calf's nose as she could before she wiped it from herself. She took off her neckerchief and rubbed on his chest while she tickled his nose with her other hand. After a moment the calf gave a sneeze as it struggled to lift its head.

"Well, hello, little one. Welcome to the world." She couldn't help but smile. A glance at the mother told her it was gone. She hated this part of the job.

She retrieved the branded cow and tied it to the saddle, then pulled the blanket from behind the cantle. After wrapping the cover around the calf, she laid it over her saddle before mounting. A tiny shudder rippled through her body at the thought of the slime still clinging to her clothes. A bath — as soon as she got home.

Stares and then smiles from the other hands greeted her as she rode onto the ranch site. Coop opened his mouth to say something. She put up her hand.

"No comments, Coop." She handed the calf to him and the rope tied to the branded cow to Sonny. "I'm going for a bath!"

"What do you want me to do with this calf?" Coop said.

Jace came out of the barn. "My goodness, Bobbie, what happened to you?"

She glanced at the calf in Coop's arms. "You lost a cow but gained a calf."

"You had to pull that calf?" He sounded shocked, but a smile spread across his face.

"Don't you start laughing too. If I didn't know better, I'd almost think you knew about that cow and sent me out to help her. I thought you'd be able to feed it from your milking cows."

Jace's eyebrows rose. "And who do you think will want to do that?"

"Beans."

"If you want him to do it, you ask him yourself. I'm not going to. I value my head."

She made a low growling sound in her throat and took the calf from Coop. She shook her head at the two of them, walked to the chow hall, and entered the kitchen. The men followed her to the doorway but no farther.

Beans turned and saw her. "Get that thing out of my kitchen!"

She rushed out and put the calf in Coop's arms. "I'll be right back." Several minutes later, she came out feeling as if she'd just faced down a bull and won. Beans followed on her heels carrying a bottle. She grabbed the calf again and headed toward the barn, this time with everyone trailing behind and Beans at her side. She laid the calf on some bedding in a stall.

"Whenever you need help, Beans, you just ask me. I'll help raise this little orphan."

He stroked the calf's head, his calloused

hands surprisingly gentle.

"But right now, I'm going for a bath."

Jace walked with her to the house. "How'd you get Beans to agree to feed that calf?"

"That's between Beans and me."

"Come on, Bobbie. I may need to use your technique one day."

She stopped at the threshold, this time a full smile on her face. "I'll never tell because I may need it for *you* one day." She laughed at the look on his face as she headed in to prepare a bath. She hadn't taken many steps before she turned and said, "While I'm cleaning up, Jace, you need to take a look at that other cow I brought to the barn. Someone left you another message."

Jace stayed up late trying to decipher the markings on the cow. He'd never seen the like before — except for his Double K brand intermingled amongst the others. Frustration rode him hard, but he tried to push it away.

The next morning, he sent his men out to scout the ranch for any other cattle while he headed out to question his neighbors. It'd been two weeks since he'd talked with any of them. The idea that he was the only one facing the problem troubled him. Even Lyle Phipps, the neighbor he didn't know well, thought it odd and had promised to help in any way he could. The sheriff had wired the town Lyle came from and received nothing but praise about the man. Jace no longer suspected him.

He rode up to Hank Willet's house first since he lived the closest. The smug look on the man's face as he descended the porch steps made Jace wish he'd waited to visit with Hank.

"I thought I'd be seeing you soon, boy, what with all the stealing going on. Come on inside and we'll discuss how much your ranch is worth." Hank turned on his heel and headed back up the steps.

"I'm not here to sell the ranch."

Hank spun back around. "Then what do you want?"

"I'm checking with all the ranchers to see if they've started having any problem with their cattle."

"There's not a rancher around these parts that hasn't heard about your troubles. We've always thought you were too young. This is a man's job."

"I'm not here to discuss my age or capabilities. I just wanted to know if you've had any problems."

"No. I have things well in hand. We all do. Not a single rancher has complained about troubles, except you. But then, you're no rancher, are ya, boy?"

Jace gritted his teeth, turned his horse, and headed to the next ranch.

"I'll see you around, *boy.*"

Hank's laughter followed him like a dark cloud. The man wanted his ranch, of that there was no doubt. He made it clear each time they met. How far would Hank go to get it? The thought hounded him the remainder of the day and clung to him during the evening meal, dampening his appetite. He was thankful his family didn't question him about his silence.

A knock on the front door interrupted the end of their meal. Pete rose to answer and returned with Sheriff Thomas.

Jace stood and shook his hand. "Good evening, Morgan. What brings you out here tonight? Did you find out anything about my cattle? Anyone seen them or the brand show up?"

Morgan looked uncomfortable as he stood in the kitchen, his eyes zeroing in on Bobbie. "I have some business to discuss with Bobbie here."

All eyes shifted to Bobbie, and Jace saw a look of surprise cross her face.

The sheriff shuffled his feet. "You may want to do this in private, Bobbie."

She looked around at all the faces in the room. "These are my friends, Morgan. Whatever you have to say to me can be said in front of them."

Morgan appeared to give that some thought and then nodded. "Fine."

Annie rounded up the two children and hustled them into the living room. Morgan found a place at the table, and Annie returned to her seat.

Morgan leaned forward and rested his arms on the table. "I waited until tonight to do this because I really didn't want to come out here about it. But my deputy wouldn't leave me alone, telling me that it was my duty to come and check it out. I finally had to agree."

"Check what out, Morgan?" Pete said. "You're not making much sense."

The sheriff took a deep breath. "You're a suspect in all the bank robberies, Bobbie."

SIXTEEN

The blood drained from Bobbie's face. Her chest ached. She couldn't take a breath. Much as she wanted to see the expressions on the faces around her, she couldn't pull her gaze from Morgan's.

"I received a letter from the sheriff in Silverton. It informed me about some bank robbers that I needed to be on the lookout for." Sheriff Thomas didn't look away. "There's a witness who describes you almost perfectly. The letter also went on to say that this female robber, who dresses like a man, had at least one male accomplice, possibly two."

Jace snorted. Her gaze moved to him. His face was flushed. "You can't be serious, Morgan. You know Bobbie. She's no bank robber."

Morgan sighed. "I understand you wanting to protect your ranch hands, Jace, but I have to check out the possibility. It's my job."

Jace leaned forward. "You said the witness described Bobbie *almost* perfectly. So what are the discrepancies?"

Morgan sat back in his chair. "The woman in question wears a black hat. I know Bobbie's is brown but" — he looked at Bobbie again — "do you have a black hat?"

She shook her head.

"I can answer that with a definite no," Jace said. "What else?"

"The letter also said this female is about six feet tall and that the length of her hair is just past her shoulders. Obviously, Bobbie isn't that tall and her hair is far longer."

Jace leaned back and crossed his arms. "Anything else?"

"No, that's about it."

"That sounds like a lot of discrepancies, Morgan. What are the similarities?"

"Hair color, the fact that she dresses like a man, and she rides a bay horse." Morgan eyed her. "You've been awfully quiet, Bobbie. Do you have anything to say about all this?"

Bobbie swallowed past the dryness in her throat. "I don't know what to say, Morgan, except that it ain't me you're looking for."

"Where were you the night of April thirteenth?"

"Oh, for mercy sake, Morgan!" Jace jumped to his feet.

"Jace!" Annie looked flustered.

Jace glanced at Annie and raked his fingers through his hair as he sat back down.

The sheriff swung back to Bobbie. "Well?"

She shrugged. "I was on my way here, but where exactly I stopped on that night, I don't remember."

"Did you go through Silverton on your way here?"

She thought for a moment, picturing the trip in her mind. "I didn't go *through* it if I remember right, but I did go around it. I think I camped at a creek near there."

"Why didn't you spend the night in town?"

She looked down, flicking at a piece of meat that had fallen off her plate. "Because I didn't need supplies at the time."

Annie touched her hand. "Tell him, Bobbie."

"Tell me what?" Morgan's gaze flashed from one to the other.

Bobbie looked at Annie and received a nod of encouragement. "People don't accept a woman in man's clothes. I get tired of the rude comments."

The sheriff nodded. "How 'bout you,

Pete? Do you have anything to say?"

Pete shook his head.

"All right then." Morgan stood. "I guess that'll be all for now. I'm sorry about all of this, Bobbie. I'm just doing my job."

"That's all right, Morgan. I understand."

"I'm not going to take you in because there's not enough proof. But I'm going to have to ask you not to leave the ranch. I have to know where you are at all times."

"I'll be here." Her voice came out in a whisper.

"Thank you." Morgan turned to all of them. "I'm sorry to disturb your evening."

Pete stood. "I'll see you out."

Annie went to Bobbie, putting her arm around her shoulders. Bobbie fought to keep the tears from falling.

Jace's chair scraped the floor in his haste to stand. "I can't believe this."

"Jace, you're not helping matters any," Annie said.

He took a deep breath and ran his hands over his face. "You're right. I'm sorry." He paused for a moment. "Is there anything I can do for you, Bobbie?"

She shook her head. "I'm all right." She wiped the tears from her eyes. "Really. I'm fine."

Annie patted her arm. "Go relax, Bobbie.

We'll take care of the dishes. Won't we?" The look on Annie's face dared the others to argue.

Bobbie wanted to smile, but her lips trembled instead. "I can help."

"No, you can't. You just go on into the living room and relax. Go on now." Annie pushed Bobbie out of the kitchen.

In the living room, Ben and Sara sat playing with their toys. Bobbie dropped onto the sofa and watched them only a few minutes before she needed some fresh air. She moved out the front door and sat in one of the chairs on the porch. The stars were out in force, but she couldn't enjoy them. She couldn't focus, so she stared at nothing.

Her mind couldn't grasp what had happened. She'd always tried to be honest, to do the right thing. Daddy expected no less. Bank robbery was the last thing she would ever consider.

Daddy. A lonely ache grew within her. He wouldn't doubt or question her innocence. He'd stand and go to battle for her, dragging her with him, teaching her to fight for herself.

Stand tall in your saddle, Bobbie, he told her on more than one occasion. *Don't give no one reason to look down on ya. If they do, it's a battle within themselves they're fightin'.* She didn't need to hear the words to know her father felt proud of her. She never dreamed standing alone would be this scary.

She remembered the day she decided to set out on her own. Finding that perfect piece of land to start a ranch both excited and frightened her more than anything ever had before. Maybe she should have given up on the dream and stayed with the Simmses where it was safe. No one there questioned her motives or suspected her of anything but working too hard.

Jace's angry voice came back to her. He must have believed in her innocence to become that upset. That thought edged out some of the chill she felt inside. Though Annie never said a word, her hug conveyed her support. Bobbie's anguish receded. She had friends here too — people who cared about her. There was no need to be scared.

She had no idea how long she'd been sitting out on the porch with only her tears to keep her company, tears she pushed away with an impatient hand. She wiped them away again when she heard the door open.

Pete stepped out. "There you are. May I join you?"

Bobbie nodded, and Pete placed a lantern on the small table between them. For a while, only the soft creak of his rocking chair filled the silence before he turned toward her. "I hate to ask you this with all you've been through tonight, Bobbie, but I feel I must."

She straightened to give him her full attention.

The rocking stopped. "Where'd you get all of that money in your account?"

An ache rose in her chest. She leaned her head back, hoping to keep the drops from rolling down her cheeks. She took a deep breath and blinked back the tears.

She heard Pete draw a deep breath. "I'm sorry, Bobbie. You don't have to answer that if you don't want to."

"Yes, I do. This is your house, and you wouldn't have asked if you didn't want to know the truth." Bobbie sighed and leaned toward him over the arm of her chair. "My father and I hardly ever left the ranch, and Mr. Simms provided all our meals. Even our housing was free. About the only thing we spent our money on was clothing and occasional gifts. With both of us earning a salary, over a period of several years, our bank account grew rather fast. We hoped that if we were careful with our money, eventually we would be able to buy our own ranch."

"Oh, I remember Annie mentioning something about that. If I would've given it any thought at all, I could have figured that out. I'm sorry, Bobbie."

"It's all right."

"No, it's not. But I felt I needed to know all the facts before I could help you fight this." He paused, running his hands over his face as he leaned forward. "Bobbie, you've got to know how special you've become to us. You're like a member of the family. If anything happened to you —" His voice cracked.

She heard his heavy breathing, and the light from the lantern revealed the moisture in his eyes. Tears burned in her own. She reached out and grasped his hand.

"Thank you, Pete. You have no idea how good that makes me feel."

They both stood and embraced, unable to say any more.

After the kids had been put to bed, Jace followed Annie into the living room and flopped down onto a chair. No surprise that Bobbie was gone. He could only imagine her pain and need for solitude.

Annie sat in the chair nearest him. "You never used to have such a temper, Jace. Not until Dad and Mom died. Now, even the smallest thing seems to set you off."

"What happened tonight wasn't a small thing, Annie."

"No, it wasn't. But the only person who had reason to be angry was Bobbie, and she chose to remain calm." Annie paused and leaned toward him. "You're in love with her, aren't you, Jace?"

"No." His gaze fell to the floor. When he looked up again, he found Annie's gaze on him, a smile on her lips. "She's my ranch hand, Annie. All my wranglers are important to me. You know that."

"Yes, I know that." The smile never left her face.

"What's that grin for?"

She shrugged, and he pushed to his feet. "I'm going to bed."

"Good night, Jace. Pleasant dreams." Humor colored her voice.

He strode through the kitchen and out the door, pausing to take a deep breath of fresh air and listen to — voices? He stepped toward the edge of the house. Pete and Bobbie's voices drifted toward him. He chanced a peek around the corner and saw them embrace.

"I thought I'd lost all my family." Bobbie choked on the words. "But you claim me as one of your own. I'd been doubting my decision to come here, but now I know it was a blessing. I've never had such good friends."

Annie joined Pete during the last of Bobbie's words. She took Bobbie in her arms, and the three shared an embrace. Jace ached. He should be the one consoling Bobbie. He gave in to the knowledge that Bobbie had taken up a special place in his heart. A big place that he never knew needed filling before he'd met her.

Jace woke the next morning, weary from the restless night he'd just been through. Between trying to decide what to do about his newfound feelings and wanting to help Bobbie, he caught only bits and pieces of sleep. He sat down across from Bobbie at the breakfast table. Her puffy, red-rimmed eyes told him she'd had the same kind of night. He tried to catch her gaze to give her a reassuring smile, but she spent most of the meal staring at her plate.

When they finished breakfast, he gave Bobbie a few different jobs to do around the ranch site. Her shoulders slumped, and he felt he'd just added to her burdens. He touched her arm to stop her from walking away.

"We're going to get through this, Bobbie.

Don't you fret about anything."

Her mouth twitched as if she attempted a smile. It never formed. Without a word, she turned and went to work.

Jace and Pete rode directly to the sheriff's office. Morgan looked up when he heard the door open, and his expression let them know they were expected.

"I was pretty sure you two would be paying me a visit today."

"We'd like to see that letter, Morgan," Jace said.

Morgan already had it sitting on his desk and tossed it in his direction. Jace scooped it up and started scanning.

Pete leaned against the desk. "You know she's not guilty, Morgan."

"I'm almost certain of that, Pete, but I'll need some proof to be absolutely sure of it, both for my sake and for the judge. Not to mention all the other lawmen in the area." Morgan leaned back in his chair.

"Have you already informed the judge that you may have a suspect?"

"No, I don't want to do that unless I find out she's guilty or have more proof against her."

Jace finished reading. "This letter says that more than one bank has been robbed. When and where did the others take place?"

Morgan raised his hands and let them drop. "You just read the letter, Jace. It doesn't say, so I don't know. The only date stated in there is from the first bank robbery, the one in Silverton. But it sounds like most of them have been around this area. The sheriff even warned me to be careful about the bank in this town. I told you that last night, Pete."

Pete and Jace looked at each other and then back to Morgan. Pete grinned. "Well there's your proof."

"Where? What proof?"

Jace tossed the letter onto the desk. "Morgan, since Bobbie showed up at the ranch, she's always been with us. It sounds like the majority of these robberies have taken place since she arrived."

Morgan still looked skeptical. "You mean to tell me she's been with someone at all times since her arrival? You're telling me that someone can account for her whereabouts every day and every night since she started working for you? You can swear to me that she's never left the house after you've gone to bed?"

Jace exchanged an uncertain look with Pete.

"That's what I thought." Morgan leaned

forward and rested his arms on his desk. "Gentlemen, unless you can verify that Bobbie has been with you or any of your other hands every day and night since she came to this town, she will remain under suspicion, not so much by me, mind you, but by the Colorado Territory. I'm sorry."

Jace stared at Morgan for a moment. "What about the discrepancies? You can't discount the difference in the height or the hair . . . or the hat for that matter. I've never seen her with anything but her brown hat."

Morgan shrugged. "Her cohorts could bring a different hat with them, and she could somehow tuck some of her hair up under that hat. As for the difference in height, they could just be guessing wrong."

"For pity's sake, Morgan," Jace said. "You sound like you're beginning to think she's guilty."

"Not at all. I'm just showing you what most of the other lawmen might think."

Jace eyed the sheriff for a few moments before he turned to leave.

"Jace, I'm serious about keeping Bobbie at the ranch," Morgan said. "It's for her own good. If another robbery takes place and she can be accounted for, that would go a long way in helping to prove her innocence."

"I know. She's there now."

Morgan nodded.

"If I'm with her or send her out with one of the hands, would that be all right?"

Morgan shrugged. "I don't see a problem with that. As long as her whereabouts can be accounted for."

Jace headed home. At least he had some good news for Bobbie.

SEVENTEEN

Bobbie sighed as she stepped out of the barn. Seeing her horse had done nothing to boost her spirits. Mack hung his head and pawed at the ground. He wanted out. So did she.

A week had passed since the confrontation with Sheriff Morgan Thomas. She hadn't left the ranch site since, except to take Annie into town, or to go to church and Bible study. She didn't want to go, but Pete, Annie, and Jace convinced her it would be in her best interest to continue doing things and going places like she normally would. Not even wearing the new dresses Annie made managed to boost her sagging spirits. She'd been so preoccupied she couldn't recall a single word spoken during those outings.

If she couldn't leave the ranch, how could she go about proving her innocence? But then, she didn't have any idea how to do that anyway. How did a person produce evidence for something they didn't do?

She spent her days pacing the ranch like a trapped animal. She had taken her freedom for granted. Freedom to come and go as she pleased. Freedom from worry and fear. Now, the restraints sucked the life out of her.

She spotted Annie hanging out the clothes and headed in her direction. Just for something to do, she had started taking cooking lessons from Annie and also helping with her chores. Carrying water and firewood, collecting eggs, and helping with laundry were some of her tasks, but she'd much rather be out wrestling an ornery calf.

Annie's singing reached Bobbie's ears long before she arrived at the line. The sound amazed her. How could Annie be so happy doing something so mundane? She picked up the basket and held it so Annie wouldn't have to bend over and received a brilliant smile for her effort.

"You sound happy this morning."

"It's a beautiful day." Annie resumed humming.

Bobbie looked around, noticing the clear sky for the first time. She stared at Annie. The smile never left her face. "You seem to enjoy your chores."

"I'm taking care of my family. What's not to enjoy?"

Her quick hands pinned up a shirt before pulling another out of the basket.

"It doesn't seem very exciting."

"Not like roping and branding a steer, you mean?"

Bobbie shrugged, and Annie laughed.

"Whatsoever ye do, do it heartily, as to the Lord."

Annie used every opportunity to bring up the Lord and His Word, especially during this past week. Sometimes it worked to draw her into a conversation about the Scriptures. Other times, she ignored the statements as though she hadn't heard a word. Much depended on her mood at the moment. Annie's singing must have buoyed her spirits, because right now, she felt better.

"So you're telling me you find joy in everything you do?"

"Not always. There are some things I dislike more than others, just as I'm sure there are some aspects of your job you don't enjoy, even though you love ranching."

Bobbie nodded her agreement.

"But it all has to do with perspective and attitude."

"Meaning . . . ?"

"Meaning, I could grumble and grouse

about the tasks I don't enjoy, but what kind of impression would that cast? I doubt the Lord would be pleased. I know He's watching and is aware of my attitude. I need to look at it as doing service for Him."

Bobbie thought about her own behavior during the past week and hoped her bad attitude wasn't too obvious. She cocked her head to one side. "You really love God."

Annie's eyes grew wide. "Oh, most certainly!"

"Why?"

Annie smiled at her. "Because He loved me first."

Bobbie studied the look of infinite joy on Annie's face and knew a moment of envy. "How do you know He loved you first?"

Annie turned to her with a look of astonishment. "It says so in the Bible. Oh, Bobbie, have I been so lax in my teachings that you don't even know God loves you?"

She didn't say a word.

"It says in First John, 'We love Him because He first loved us.' John 3:16 tells us, 'For God so loved the world, that He gave his only begotten Son, that whosoever believeth in Him should not perish, but have everlasting life.' God loves each of us, Bobbie. Sending His Son to die for us proves that."

"And you believe what the Bible says is true?"

Annie took the empty basket from her and headed toward the house. "With all my being. Second Timothy tells us that all Scripture is inspired by God. But that's a decision you have to make for yourself. You have to decide whether or not you believe the Bible is God's unerring Word. That will determine how you respond to what you read."

Bobbie matched Annie's steps. "I've been reading the Bible, but it doesn't make much sense."

"That's understandable." Annie held open the door and stepped back to allow Bobbie to enter. She pulled out a chair at the kitchen table and motioned for her to sit. Annie took the chair next to her. "What I mean is, the Bible is written to Christians. Once we accept God's gift of salvation, His Spirit lives within us and helps us understand. That doesn't mean you can't understand, but believers have the Holy Spirit's help, and even then, I don't understand everything."

Bobbie leaned back in her chair with a thump. "So unless I believe, my time spent in the Bible is like wading through water over my head when I can't swim."

"Any time spent in God's Word is worthwhile." Annie leaned toward her and took her hand. "You can have the help you desire. Just reach out to God in faith. Ask and you will receive. Then that hole you're feeling will be filled to overflowing."

Bobbie stared at her. "How did you know . . . about the hole in my heart?"

Annie smiled and patted her hand. "It's what every unbeliever feels until they accept Christ as their Savior."

"You said God loves everyone. But God has His favorites?"

"What do you mean?"

"God takes better care of His family members than He does of nonbelievers."

"God never promised there'd be no more pain or suffering when we become His children. Look at Jace and me. We've been Christians for years, yet we're going through the pain and sorrow of losing our parents. Along with that, Jace has to deal with the loss of cattle. What God does promise is to be with us through the tough times. We don't have to go through the sorrow alone. He gives us the strength and grace to get through it."

Bobbie heard Annie's words but stopped listening at the mention of her parents.

"Can I ask how they died, Annie, or would

it hurt too much?" She had never heard the story but knew from Jace and by some of the men's comments that it had been tragic.

"It still hurts, but time is helping me heal. I think what would help the most is if they found the killer."

Annie stood and poured them each a cup of coffee. When she returned, her blue eyes were rimmed with red.

"I'm sorry, Annie. I shouldn't have asked."

"It's all right. I want to tell you about it." Annie spooned a bit of sugar into her cup and took a sip of coffee. "They were traveling by stagecoach to see a friend who was getting married. The road they traveled had a mountain on one side and a deep gully on the other.

"The sheriff told us a man was waiting for them around a bend. He wore something to cover his face. He started shooting, hitting the driver first. The driver tried to stop the horses but ended up falling off the seat into the gully. That's where they found him. He died shortly thereafter. But he did manage to tell the sheriff what had happened. The horses pulling the stagecoach ended up going over the edge, down into the gully. It rolled over several times before it stopped, killing everyone in it."

Annie paused for another drink. "We

don't understand why the man did this. Nothing was stolen. All the money and jewelry were still on their — bodies." Annie choked on the word. Bobbie reached to squeeze her hand and received a grateful smile.

"I think Jace took it the hardest. He hates to talk about it. He and Dad were very close." Annie's eyes misted over.

Bobbie leaned over and embraced her. "I'm sorry, Annie."

"It's all right. Like I said, it's gotten easier. I think we've both made it through because of our faith. We find comfort in God's Word. I can't imagine how people get through devastating circumstances without Him."

Bobbie blew out a long slow breath. "Thanks for telling me the story." She needed to get out and think about everything. She stood. "I still have some work to do this morning."

"I understand." Annie called out her name at the door. "God won't hide from those who seek Him. He's also waiting with open arms for those who've been running from Him. He can be very patient."

Bobbie smiled and gave a little wave as she walked away. Which one was she doing, seeking or running away? Maybe a little of both?

■ ■ ■ ■

Jace dropped the last bag of oats into the feed barrel and shoved his hat up on his forehead in time to see Bobbie walking from the house. Her boots scuffed small puffs of dust. He thought back on the week. Bobbie had fought against the idea of attending church. She finally agreed, but he felt certain she didn't hear a thing the preacher said. Cade cast several questioning looks, but Jace didn't think Bobbie would appreciate his telling others about her problem, so he kept it to himself.

A voice in his ear interrupted his thoughts. He spun around and saw Coop standing at his shoulder. "What'd you say?"

Coop nodded in Bobbie's direction. "I said, I think she's got reason to be afeared."

"What makes you say that?"

"We-ell . . ."

"Spill it, Coop, or get on with your business." A frown crossed Coop's face. "Sorry. It's been a long week."

"Yep. It sure has." Coop patted him on the back. "I feel for ya."

"What makes you say that?"

"I know ya got to feel bad about picking two bad un's in a row."

He stared at his ranch hand. "What makes you think Bobbie's a bad one?"

Coop shuffled his feet and cleared his throat. "I dint really want to tell ya this, Jace. I like Bobbie much as ever'n else, but I think ya oughtta know."

He gritted his teeth to keep from yelling at Coop again. "Know what?"

"I seen her put lots o' money in Pete's bank. Stacks of it. Ain't no way a wrangler kin get that kind o' money. I oughtta know. An' I even seen her standin' behind the bank one day."

Jace turned and faced Coop. "Are you sure about this, Coop? There's no mistake?"

"Nope. I seen it." Coop shuffled again. "I been thinking, Jace. I hate saying this, but it seems to me that all yer trouble started near the day that young'n showed up."

"You're going to have to explain that, Coop. I had rustled cattle before I hired her."

"That's true enough, but from what I understand, she took her sweet time getting here." Coop scratched his whiskered cheek. "Or mebbe that's just the story she spread when all the while she's been here on yer ranch starting the trouble." Coop gave a woeful shake of his head. "Don't ya see? I heared tell that Bobbie wants her own place.

221

She's made it no secret she likes yer place. Then all sudden like, yer cows'r getting taken." Coop leaned closer, his expression intense. "Ain't ya noticed that she's been the one finding them cows?" He leaned back and spit a thick stream of tobacco juice. He wiped his mouth with his sleeve. "Seems kinda 'spicious like to me."

Jace stared at Coop, unable to believe what he was saying. "What about the last bunch of stolen cattle? She was on the drive with me when that happened."

Coop shrugged. "I was tol' she prob'ly has help, like the ones helping rob them banks. Ya think mebbe it's some young buck from where she used to work? She's purty nuff to bend the heart o' most men."

Jace turned in time to see Bobbie disappear into the barn. She didn't have a deceitful bone in her body. Or did she? Just how well did he know her?

"Onliest reason I said something was cuz I'm looking out for ya, Jace. Don't wanna see ya get hurt again."

Jace clapped the wizened old wrangler on the shoulder. "I appreciate it, Coop. I'll check into everything you said. Would you run into town and pick up my supplies? They should be ready by now."

"Sure thing, Jace. Ya got nothing to worry

'bout with that." Coop spun on his heel and headed for the wagon. He started humming, interrupted by another stream of juice.

Jace turned back toward the barn and rested his arms on the top rail of the corral fence.

Bobbie a bank robber? Could it be possible?

How well could he trust Coop as a witness? Completely. He'd known Coop a long time. He'd worked for his dad for years. He'd never given them reason to doubt his word. The only time Coop gave him any trouble was when Jace made Dew foreman. Coop left the ranch in anger but showed up a week later ready to get back to work.

Jace wanted to believe Bobbie innocent. The stacks of money could be explained if both she and her father saved their earnings. But why would she be standing behind the bank? He ran a hand over his jaw, and the rough stubble scratched at his palm. Open expanse stretched behind the bank, nothing that would need her to go back there. And she'd already told the story of disguising herself to go into town. She could easily do the same for other reasons.

What about the branded cattle? Bobbie did seem to be the bearer of the news. But how was she able to brand them? Did she sneak out at night? *Accomplices.* Even the sheriff mentioned them. If she really were behind it, she'd have to have help. She could meet up with them and keep them informed as to everyone's whereabouts. She could even have told them that Coop would be the only hand around the ranch during the cattle drive. They knew it would be easy pickings.

He groaned and rested his head on his arm. What was he thinking? Bobbie wouldn't do any of this. He'd gotten to know her pretty well over the months. She'd never given any of them reason to doubt her.

The barn door squeaked. He raised his head and saw Bobbie leading Mack out. She had him saddled. Where was she going? Jace scaled the corral fence. His long strides ate up the distance between them as she mounted.

"Wait a minute, Bobbie."

"Jace. I didn't know you were here."

That statement sent alarm through him. "Where do you think you're going? You know you're supposed to stay on the ranch." He grabbed the reins. "Get down, Bobbie."

She stepped down beside him. "Jace?"

"Don't you realize how guilty you look by riding off?"

"I wasn't —"

"Don't tell me you weren't, Bobbie. I've got the proof right here." He shook the reins grasped in his fist.

"But —"

"Go stable your horse. You're not going anywhere."

She reached for the reins. Tears filled her eyes as she gave him a questioning glance. He clenched his jaw and turned away, looking back at her as she led Mack into the barn.

Her head was down, her shoulders slumped. He couldn't tell if she was hurt or just disappointed he'd spoiled her plans. He couldn't let himself care. All that mattered to him now was to prove her innocence or guilt. One way or another, he had to know.

He strode to the corral, mounted his horse, and headed in the direction they first found the branded cow. Maybe he could spot some evidence that might have been left behind. He wouldn't stop there but would check every site where his cows were branded or stolen.

After spending an hour poking around at the first site and coming up empty, he headed at a gallop toward the second. He'd have to hurry if he wanted to be home before dark.

The second site turned out as unsuccessful as the first. Would it be worth the ride to check the last site? He lifted his hat and checked the sky. Only a few hours till dark. He heeled his horse into a gallop.

He neared the area where Bobbie helped birth the calf and slowed. The thought sent the first touch of a smile across his lips that day. He sure would have liked to see her at work. All her efforts had to be quite a sight.

He altered his direction toward the small stand of trees where Bobbie said she found the branded cow. A searing pain stung the upper portion of his left arm just before he heard the sound of rifle fire.

EIGHTEEN

Jace grabbed his rifle and tumbled to the ground. He rolled behind a small boulder, the only protection he could find. Another shot bounced off the rock, sending his scared horse running toward home. He shrunk lower. The sound of the ricochet left his ears ringing. He blew out two long, steadying breaths.

He lifted his hat to wipe his brow, and another bullet pinged against the rock. He set the hat beside him so he wouldn't make that mistake again. The sting on his arm grew in intensity. He slipped his kerchief from his neck and tied it over the wound, using his teeth to help pull it tight. Thankfully, the shot only scratched the skin.

He looked around. *North range.* Hank Willet's place wasn't far from here. Could he be doing the shooting?

Jace rolled onto his stomach, grabbed his hat, and held it just above the ground. He slid it toward the side of the boulder. Another shot rang out. He pulled the hat back and found a bullet hole. Rage ripped through him, followed quickly by fear.

"Hank? Is that you out there?"

Laughter echoed across the plain from the trees.

He lay there stewing. He'd heard Hank's laugh many times over the last year, but he couldn't be sure if this one belonged to him. Who else would be out this far? Bobbie was back at the ranch, but this was the last place she'd found the branded cow. Could it be one of her accomplices?

He raised his rifle far enough to fire a couple shots toward the trees. Two more came right back at him followed by more laughter. The boulder provided the only form of protection. If he tried to move in any direction, the man would have a clear shot.

The sun would be setting before too much longer. Maybe he could sneak off using the darkness for cover, that is, if the shooter didn't sneak up on him first. He sent another shot toward the trees to make sure his attacker didn't get too comfortable. Another blast came back, skipping off the top of the boulder.

He lay for almost an hour, trading a shot

now and then with his foe. The sound of hoofbeats reached his ears. They grew louder. Jace squirmed around trying to find them and spotted two horses and one rider. He grinned when he recognized Dew's horse and figure.

"Look out, Dew. There's a shooter in the trees."

Dew pulled his rifle and sent several shots in that direction. None of them were returned. Jace lifted his hat above the boulder. No bullet came to knock it from his hand. He took a deep breath and stood as Dew stopped next to him. He handed Jace the reins to his horse.

"I knew something was wrong when I saw your horse and you weren't on it." He nodded toward Jace's arm. "You all right?"

"Just a scratch. Let's check out these trees. Maybe he left something behind." Jace mounted and headed toward the stand of trees. He reined his horse to a stop and stuck out his hand. "Thank you, Dew. I think you might have just saved my life."

Darkness fell long before they reached the ranch. While Dew took care of the horses, Jace strode into Annie's house, letting the door slam behind him. He wanted to see the look on Bobbie's face when she saw he was still alive.

Annie slid her chair back. "I'm sorry, Jace. We waited for you before eating, but it got late."

He ignored his sister and watched as Bobbie scanned his face. He knew the moment she saw the blood on his arm. Her eyes grew wide and her mouth fell open as she stood and rushed toward him.

"Jace, your arm. What happened?"

Annie didn't give him time to sort through his thoughts as she bombarded him with questions. She shoved him onto a chair and dressed his wound as he gave a brief rundown.

"You need to tell the sheriff, Jace." Annie's face was only inches from his, so he saw the exact moment the tears formed. "I can't lose you too."

He pulled her into his arms. "It'll be all right. I'll tell him in the morning."

Annie pulled away. "But Jace —"

"I don't want anyone out at night, Annie." He glanced around the table and took in Bobbie's tears before noticing the scared expression on Ben's face. He leaned toward his sister. "It's getting too dangerous. Now let's change the subject."

He pulled his plate toward him and started filling it. "I sure hope this is good because

I'm starved. Ben, you're not eating. Is that your way of telling me your mom's cooking is bad?" He gave the boy a wink and received a smile.

"Nope. Mama's the best cook ever." Ben sent his mother a grin and dug into his food.

Jace forced the food down to keep up appearances. A short time later, Pete took the kids off to get ready for bed. Jace managed to finish the meal without looking at Bobbie again. Then he stood and excused himself.

"Jace?" Annie's voice stopped him.

"I'm fine, Annie. I'll talk to Morgan in the morning, and everything will be all right." He didn't sound convincing even to his own ears, but it was the best he could do at the moment. "Good night."

He took a deep breath of cool night air. *God, help me. I don't know what to think anymore. Who do I believe? Who do I trust?* The verse from Proverbs came to him as if God answered from the stars shining overhead. *Trust in the Lord with all thine heart.* Peace settled over him as he said the verse aloud followed by a prayer of thanksgiving. There was still a long battle ahead of him, but God would be with him every step of the way.

Two days had come and gone since someone had used him for a target. Jace sat on his horse at the top of a rocky butte over-looking a vast portion of range speckled with several of his grazing cattle. The peace-ful scene did nothing to calm the emotions raging through him.

He'd talked to Morgan as promised, but he didn't know what good it had done. After all the questions and snooping around, they gleaned nothing new. Morgan approached Hank Willett about the shooting incident, which only served to produce more animos-ity between Jace and Hank. Morgan ques-tioned Bobbie as to her whereabouts during the week. Jace observed from a distance, but he knew the moment Morgan asked where she was during the shooting. Her gaze seared his flesh. He hadn't been able to look her in the eye since.

He reached up and massaged his shoulder, hoping to ease the tension throbbing at his temples. The effort was in vain. The only way to end the strain would be to find Bobbie innocent.

He gave a snort and shook his head. All his efforts to find evidence for or against her ended in nothing more than getting shot at and a headache. He'd come home to see her sad and questioning eyes gazing at him. She wanted answers. He had none to give.

He turned toward the sound of galloping hooves and found Sonny Marshall heading toward him. He reined in his horse with a skid.

"We've got another branded cow, Jace."

"Does the brand look like the other ones?"

"There's a slight difference. I'll draw it for you when I head back that way." Sonny cleared his throat. "One more thing, Jace. The rumors we've heard about the mountain lion must be true. I just found two dead calves with cat prints around them. The calves' mothers looked a bit beat up too."

"Great. That's just what I need." He played all his options through his mind. Coop, David Lundy, and Dew each rode different portions of his property line. Adam Taylor and Bobbie were at the ranch. He couldn't send Adam to hunt the mountain lion. That boy couldn't shoot a hole in a lake. Most men scattered when he pulled his rifle.

"Ride back to the ranch and get Bobbie. Tell her that she's to go with you to try and spot that cat. Tell her I've already spoken to the sheriff about leaving the ranch site, and it'll be fine. It's better if we go after that mountain lion in pairs, and Bobbie is the only one I can spare right now. Besides, she's a better shot."

"Ain't it the truth."

"I'm going to ride down and see if David's finished checking the south property line. Then we'll both join you."

"Right." Sonny spun his horse around and nudged him into a gallop. Jace stared at his retreating back. He could have sworn he saw a smile on Sonny's face as he turned away.

Bobbie shoved the pitchfork deep, scooping up as much manure as she could before tossing it into the cart. Mucking stalls was one of her least favorite jobs, but it fit her mood. Why couldn't she sing like Annie did during her tasks? Blaring out a tune would help her get through the drudgery, but the music wouldn't come. Would she ever feel music in her soul again?

Two days. She shoved the pitchfork deep. For two days, Jace had avoided her, sending one of the other wranglers whenever he had a message. When they did have to come into contact, his attitude made her scurry from his presence. In all the glances she sent his way, he never once tried to look at her. She could feel his tension no matter the distance between them.

She pitched the refuse into the cart. What had she done or said to make him turn on her? She came up empty. Maybe she should confront him, ask him what was wrong. Bobbie shook her head. Better to leave than face Jace in his present mood.

That thought had crossed her mind more than once. Leaving the ranch sounded like a great idea and yet dreadful at the same time. Morgan would track her down. Jace already seemed to lean toward her being guilty. Riding off would confirm it in his mind, even if she could pull it off. He made it a point to have one of the other wranglers near the ranch. She knew their main job was to keep an eye on her. That started the day after she wanted to race Mack around the ranch site to give him some exercise — the day Jace's foul mood began.

She stabbed the fork into the ground and leaned on it. Jace wasn't the only one acting as if she was guilty. Quite often in the last few days, she'd caught Coop staring, only to see him look away when their eyes met.

Unable to leave the ranch to prove her innocence, she had plenty of time to think. Maybe too much time. Some of the places her thoughts took her left her stunned. What about when she found Coop behind the bank with two other men? The way they had exchanged papers and then split up looked suspicious. Could they have something to do with the robberies?

Bobbie sighed and pulled the pitchfork loose. She wouldn't do the same thing to Coop that others were doing to her. Besides, she liked Coop. He'd always been nice to her.

"Let's go, Bobbie." Sonny stood in the doorway of the barn. "We got work to do."

"I *am* working."

"No, I mean real work. Wrangler work. We got a mountain lion to hunt down and kill. Jace wants you with me on this. He said it'd be fine."

The grin on Sonny's face told her she'd heard right. She dropped the pitchfork, only to have to go back and move it to its rightful place. Neither the pounding in her chest nor her smile as she saddled Mack could be calmed.

Sonny and Bobbie headed out side by side. She heeled Mack into a gallop, anxious to feel the wind in her face. Mack seemed to feed on her exuberance, or maybe he was just as happy to be out on the run. She hated to rein him in, but she had to let Sonny catch up. The two exchanged a grin, and she knew he understood.

They stopped on the way toward the western boundary line where Sonny had found the cat tracks. He showed her where the branded cow was tied and did a quick sketch of the brands before turning it loose. Then he took her to where the mountain lion had killed the calves. After one more quick examination of the area, he led her toward the mountains, following the tracks of the cat.

They kept their horses in a slow walk, alert to any movements or sounds that might help them locate the mountain lion. Their rifles lay across their laps at the ready. It was wonderful to be out and feeling useful again.

Sonny cleared his throat. "Ya know, Bobbie, most of us don't think you're guilty."

Try as she might, she couldn't keep the tears from flooding her eyes. "Thank you, Sonny."

He glanced back at the ground, checking on the tracks before turning to meet her gaze. "Ya might want to dry them tears, else you won't be able to hit the side of the mountain. We need your eyes sharp right now."

Laughter bubbled through her as she swiped at her eyes with the back of her hand.

"He's only acting like that because he's been deceived once before. He didn't take that well either."

She reined in her horse. "What do you

mean, Sonny? Jace thinks I'm betraying him? I thought he believed I was only guilty of robbing banks."

Sonny pulled his hat lower on his forehead. "Oh, there now. I've gone and said too much."

"Well, you'd better keep on talking. How does he think I'm betraying him?"

Sonny took too long examining one of the cat tracks.

"Sonny, you've got to tell me what Jace is thinking."

"He's starting to believe you're playing a part in the cattle rustling. Leastways, that's what Coop told me."

"*What?* How could he possibly think I'd do such a thing?"

Sonny only shrugged and nudged his horse forward. "We'd better keep moving. Jace wants us to find that cat. He plans to join up with us after a bit."

She followed him down the rocky trail, her mind playing over this new information. They came to a large outcropping of stones, skirted them, and moved farther up into the mountains.

"I've got an idea, Bobbie," Sonny said. "There's a good chance that cat may be holed up in that bunch of rocks up there. It may be waiting for nighttime before going down to chew on them calves some more. Why don't you move a little farther down that way while I go up and around them? If I see that cat, I'll fire a shot and try to chase him toward you. If you see it, take your best shot."

"All right. Just be careful up there."

"I will. You too."

While Sonny headed farther up the mountain, she moved down it. When she found a good vantage point, she dismounted and tied Mack to some brush. Then she climbed up to a large rock, hunkered down, and waited.

She sat long enough for her muscles to feel stiff. Even her eyes felt dry from staring up the mountain. She laid her rifle on the boulder in front of her, stretched her legs out, and flexed the muscles, moaning at how good it felt. Then she raised her arms and, one at a time, placed them behind her head, twisting and bending to get her circulation back.

Afterward, she turned back toward the mountain and studied the landscape. Still no movement. So much time had passed, and still no sign of Sonny. He should have made it around the rock cluster by now.

She grabbed her rifle. Something didn't feel right. She stood and pressed against her lower back to relieve the ache. Voices coming from behind an outcropping froze her movements.

"Yer yella, Coop."

Coop? She squatted down and listened.

"I ain't yella."

"No? If you weren't, you'd a taken care o' that girlie as soon as you caught her watchin' us behind the bank . . . or let us do it. We don't need no witnesses."

"I didn't think she needed killing."

A coarse laugh echoed across the rocks followed by a cuss word. "Yeah? Well, yer dumb rumor idea sure didn't work." The man snorted. "A woman bank robber? No way they'd think my long hair'd make her and me look alike. That idea's as dumb as you."

Anger at his lies and betrayal made her want to confront him, slap him, *something* to vent her outrage.

"You jest leave the ideas ta me from now on, Coop. In fact, I'm thinkin' the next time I see that young filly, I'll kill her slow."

By the sound of their voices, they'd be on her in minutes. And from what the man with Coop just said . . .

With the rifle across her arms, Bobbie crawled on her belly to the next rock. She glanced behind her. Scrub brush and rocks

240

still hid her from view. She rose to her feet. Mack was tied down the mountain to her right. If she stayed low, she just might make it.

At her first step, the rocks gave way under her boot. A small screech escaped on her way to the ground.

NINETEEN

Bobbie tried to keep from skidding and ended up rolling several times before she came to a stop. Pain radiated up her arms and along both legs. She lay still for several moments, too stunned to move.

The men. Where's my rifle?

She scanned the ground while she struggled to her feet. The gun had landed only yards from her. She scrambled toward it and grabbed the smooth barrel just as a voice sounded behind her.

"Hold it, girlie."

Amusement tinged the gruff voice. The creak of saddle leather and then the crunch of boot against rocks let her know her captor had dismounted.

"I'll take that."

An unseen hand jerked the rifle from her. Her legs quaked in weakness.

"Now, real easy like, toss yer pistol away."

When she didn't move, the man gave her

head a shove with the barrel of his gun.

"Do it. Use yer left hand."

Bobbie reached for her pistol and heard a coarse chuckle near her ear.

"See, Coop. Nothin' to it."

She twisted to see her betrayer, but the man shoved her head with his gun again.

"Don't move. And toss off that pistol."

The pistol clattered against the rocks before coming to rest in a patch of grass.

"That's better. Now you can turn around."

She turned slowly. Her gaze landed first on Coop sitting atop his horse. Their eyes met for a moment before he looked away. Was that regret she saw in his eyes? She didn't get to think on it long. The man waved the gun in her face.

"Remember me?"

She stared at his whiskered face. He looked familiar.

"No? Well, you oughtta remember the men you shoot at." He flexed the arm holding her rifle, moving it in a wide circle. "All healed up now."

She bit her lip. This was the man who ran into her in Pueblo, almost knocking her down and starting a fight with Sonny. By his comment, he was also the man who jumped her on the cattle drive — the one

Dew said she hit. *Sonny!* Had this man hurt Sonny?

The man smiled, revealing a row of yellow and brown teeth. "Ah! I can tell by your expression you remember." His face moved only inches from hers. "If you weren't so quick with the trigger, you'd o' been dead that night. I aim to take care of that today."

She suppressed a shudder, unsure if it came from his threatening scowl or his maggot breath. Her knees went weak as he pressed his gun to the base of her throat and shoved her back a step.

"I have no problem killin' people. Gives me a feelin' o' power."

She sent a pleading glance at Coop, but he stared at the ground.

The man leaned toward her again. "Did ya tell anyone about it?"

"A–about what?" She hated the way her voice trembled.

He glared at her. "Quit playin' dumb. Did ya tell anyone about seein' us behind the bank?"

Bobbie shook her head. "No, I didn't say anything."

His beady eyes swept her face. He must have been satisfied with what he saw. He nodded and smiled.

"Good." His gaze traveled down her form.

244

Her mouth went dry. Chill bumps broke out on her skin. She crossed her arms in front of her stomach.

"I — I didn't know what you were doing back there. I didn't think anything about it. I never would have connected it to the bank robberies."

"Well, that's a shame now, isn't it?"

She shuddered at the look in his eyes.

"I guess that little mistake of ours will cost ya yer life." He ran the barrel of his pistol along her jaw. "But I think me and you'll have a little fun first."

She stepped back away from him. He reached for her and found the rifle still in his hand. He growled and turned toward Coop.

"Here."

The rifle flew through the air, and Coop looked up in time to grab it.

She shoved him with all her might. The man was a rock. She spun around and started to run. She took two steps before her head snapped back. The man had grabbed her braid. He pulled her against him.

"Now just where did ya think you was goin'? I ain't had my fun yet."

His hot breath trailed across her neck. Bile rose in her throat.

"Easy, Will." Coop spoke for the first time.

"Shut up, Coop. You had yer chance. Now leave me ta mine."

She scratched her nails along Will's cheek. They sunk deep. He bellowed and shoved her away from him. Her body slammed against a boulder, her forehead hitting hard. She groaned and slumped to the ground.

She forced herself to look up. Will glared at her as he wiped his cheek with his sleeve. When he glanced at the blood, Bobbie scrambled toward the pistol she'd tossed away earlier. Will grabbed her foot and yanked her back.

She kicked with her free foot, catching Will in the eye. He roared out a curse as he grabbed her other foot and jerked her toward him. She pummeled him with her fists. He inched her closer, grunting and groaning as each blow landed. With a hard jerk, he pulled her next to him. He rolled on top of her, pinning her to the ground. Will grabbed each of her flailing arms and held them above her head. They were both panting hard from the effort, but she found it hard to catch her breath with him lying on top of her. She squirmed. Will's weight and strength held her tight.

"Well, now. I like this position much better." His eyes gleamed with pleasure.

She tasted her own fear and then realized she had bitten the inside of her cheek. Terror set in. She looked toward her only hope.

"Coop, help me!"

Their eyes met and held for a moment. "I'm sorry," Coop mouthed. He turned his horse around so that she stared at his back. She heard laughter in her ear. The crude sound sent shudders through her body.

"You dint really think he'd help, did ya?"

Dread settled over her like an icy blanket. "Don't do this."

Will nuzzled her neck. Her flesh recoiled until she thought it would turn inside out.

God, help me! her mind screamed. Panic thrummed in her ears, culminating in a loud explosion.

Jace saw Bobbie hit the ground. He spurred his horse into a gallop over the edge of the ridge. His horse scrambled to keep its legs under it while he struggled to remain in the saddle as they hurried down the slope. He heard a second set of hoofbeats and knew David wasn't far behind. When they reached level ground, he pulled his pistol and shot in the direction of Bobbie and the two men.

His heart pounded violently as he raced his horse across the range. The first shot didn't make the man get away from Bobbie.

The second shot had the man rolling off her and racing toward his horse. Jace took careful aim and squeezed the trigger. The bullet knocked the man to the ground.

David raced past him in pursuit of the other rider, who galloped away with the first gunshot. Jace recognized the man's clothing and horse, but his mind refused to believe it was Coop. He yanked back on the reins. The horse skidded to a stop next to the man who had attacked Bobbie. He leapt from the saddle and stomped on the man's arm as he reached for his pistol with a bloody hand. The man howled with pain.

"Don't make me shoot you again," Jace ground out between clenched teeth. He leaned down and tossed the man's pistol away. He holstered his own gun, grabbed the man by his shirtfront, and lifted him from the ground. The man swung at him with his good arm. Jace knocked him back to the ground with one punch. The man didn't move but lay there groaning. Jace reached into his saddlebag, pulled out a length of rope, and trussed him up like a calf waiting for the branding iron.

Satisfied the man couldn't move, Jace ran to Bobbie and knelt beside her. She cowered against a boulder like a frightened rabbit. Blood oozed from a wound on her forehead.

She seemed stunned to see him. Tears flooded her eyes and ran down her cheeks.

"Oh, Bobbie."

Jace helped her to her feet. She wobbled, and he steadied her with an arm around her waist. She clasped his shirt in her fists and pressed her face against his neck. Sobs wracked her body. His throat clenched tightly closed as he fought to keep his own tears at bay.

The shout of men's voices caught his attention. David closed the gap between him and Coop. Sonny appeared out of the mountains ahead of them. He sprang from his horse, knocking Coop from his saddle. Coop tried to scramble away, but David lunged at his ankles. He pulled Coop up by the shirt, only to throw a punch that sent him back into the dirt. Coop attempted to stand and met the solid force of Sonny's fist.

David and Sonny led Coop back to Jace at gunpoint. Blood dripped down Sonny's temple. Blood oozed from an eye and from each corner of Coop's mouth, and he turned to avoid looking at Jace.

"They jumped me up in the mountains, Jace." Sonny touched a finger to his temple. "I didn't know they were there."

Jace nodded, though he never took his

eyes off Coop. Never before had he wanted to thrash a man as much as he wanted to thrash Coop. The questioning would have to wait.

"Tie him up good and tight. Then take these men in to the sheriff's office. Tell Morgan to lock 'em up. Tell him I'll be in as soon as I get Bobbie settled at the house."

"You got it, Jace."

"Sonny." Jace directed a firm look at the young ranch hand. "You make sure they get there no worse off than they are now."

"Yes, sir."

Sonny and David helped the two men into their saddles before escorting them toward town. Jace turned his attention to Bobbie. Never before had he felt so helpless.

"Are you all right, Bobbie?" She nodded slightly but didn't look at him. "Then let's get you home."

He stepped back to let her walk to her horse, but she fell to her knees and retched. He didn't think he could feel any worse than he had earlier, but seeing her in this condition proved him wrong. Waiting until she finished, he pulled the kerchief from his neck and helped her clean her face. Her hands trembled. She looked so weak. His heart moved to his throat at the complete despair he saw on her face.

He picked her up in his arms, set her in his saddle, and swung up behind her. He grabbed one of Mack's reins and then headed for the house. They didn't get far before he heard Bobbie choke. He stopped to let her be sick again. Afterward, he cradled her tightly in his arms as she went limp. He again headed for home, which suddenly seemed much too far away.

TWENTY

Bobbie lay motionless in Jace's arms. Maybe if she stayed still and kept her eyes closed, he wouldn't be inclined to talk or ask questions. She didn't want anything to do with anyone right now. She wanted to be alone. So why did she feel secure in his arms?

The acrid taste in her mouth begged for water. The vomiting had done nothing to purge the foulness of what had happened. Her skin ached to be cleansed, but she knew nothing could wipe away the filth that clung to her from that man's touch. She took a deep breath and fought not to retch again.

Jace's arms tightened around her. Part of her wanted to enjoy the comfort they provided. The other part wanted to lash out at him and all men. But she would forever be grateful to him for saving her from that horrid man. She felt Jace press his cheek to the top of her head. Her thoughts jumbled. The safety and contentment she felt in his arms went directly against all the hurt and anguish his distrust of her produced.

"We're home," Jace whispered.

A door slammed. "Bobbie? Jace, what's wrong with Bobbie? Is she hurt?"

"Let me get her into her bed first, Annie. Then I'll try to explain what happened." Jace took his time dismounting. Bobbie knew he exerted extra effort to be careful with her.

She squirmed to be set down. "I can walk."

He released her legs, only to scoop her up again when they threatened to collapse under her. In moments, she felt the softness of the bed beneath her, but it did nothing to erase the memory of the rocks against her back.

A cry escaped when she felt the unexpected tug of her boots being removed. Annie's cool hand caressed her cheek.

"It's just us, Bobbie." Annie leaned down and gave her a hug. "I'll be right back."

She pulled a blanket over her. Bobbie grasped it and pulled it up to her chin.

Jace's voice ebbed and strengthened from the doorway. "Coop was a part of it." He sounded angry.

"Coop?" More mumbling took place before Annie reappeared at her side. "I'm going to clean that cut on your forehead, Bobbie." A warm rag stung the open wound. Annie went about her task in silence, dipping the cloth on occasion for fresh water. "There. That looks better, but I still want the doctor to take a look at it."

Bobbie's gaze flashed in Annie's direction before looking away. "I don't need a doctor."

"That gash might need a stitch or two."

She didn't argue, but she didn't like the idea either. She just wanted to be left alone.

"Look at me, Bobbie." Her cheek was cupped in Annie's tender palm. She applied pressure until Bobbie looked her way. Love and compassion filled Annie's expression. "None of this was your fault, Bobbie. You can't take the sins of another man on your shoulders. You didn't do anything wrong."

Unable to hold back any longer, Bobbie's tears flowed as sobs wracked her body. Annie gathered her into her arms and held her until the weeping ceased. She took the damp cloth and wiped Bobbie's face.

"Would you like a bath?"

Bobbie nodded and blew into the handkerchief Annie held to her nose. "That sounds good."

"Stay put. I'll call you when it's ready."

"Thanks, Annie. For everything."

Annie smiled but Bobbie couldn't get her lips to return the gesture.

Jace stood in front of Coop's jail cell wishing his hands were gripping the man's neck instead of the iron bars. Coop refused to speak, wouldn't even look up at him. A curse word came from the next cell over. Doc struggled to patch the hole Jace's bullet had made in the other man's shoulder.

"Keep yer mouth shut, Coop. They ain't got nothin'."

"Quiet," Doc demanded, "or I'll shoot you full of morphine until I finish putting you back together."

The man only grumbled and continued his cursing.

"Let me in there, Sheriff," David said. "I'll get them to talk."

"Take it easy, David. They'll talk or they'll hang for what they did to Bobbie. May hang anyway." The sheriff sat at his desk going through wanted posters. Every once in a while, he'd stand and hold a poster up to the man's face, only to return to his seat again.

Still gripping the bars in his hands, Jace turned to his men. "Go back to the ranch, David. You too, Sonny. I'll be along when Doc is finished here. I want him to take a look at Bobbie."

"We can wait with you."

"No, it's already dark, and I need you to go on back and get the chores finished up. You'll have to do Bobbie's too."

They looked reluctant to leave but obeyed without further argument. Once they were gone, Jace went to the sheriff's desk.

"This isn't working, Morgan. Let me in there to talk to Coop."

Morgan looked up from his papers and almost smiled. "Not a chance, Jace. You were mad as a scalded cat when I told you Bobbie was a *suspect* in bank robbery. I'm not sure I can trust how you'll react if Coop still won't cooperate."

He opened his mouth to argue, then clamped it shut. He stood and returned to his position at the bars.

"Talk to me, Coop. Why would you tell me all that stuff about Bobbie, and then turn around and try to kill her?"

Coop looked up. "I didn't —"

"Shut up, Coop!" the man bellowed from the other cell. "They can't hang us if they don't know nothin'."

Coop returned to staring at the floor. Maddening frustration rolled through Jace. "Can't you shut him up, Doc? Knock him out or something."

"I'm just about done, Jace. No need to knock him out now."

Jace pushed away from the bars to pace in front of Morgan's desk. Coop seemed terrified of the other man. Maybe if they could get them away from each other . . .

"Why don't you go out and find my deputy, Jace." The sheriff eyed him with a look of compassion. "I want to talk to Bobbie, and he needs to be here while I'm gone."

"I told you, Morgan, Bobbie's in no frame of mind to talk to you or anyone else for that matter."

"I still gotta try."

Jace headed for the door. "I'll see if I can round up your deputy. I'm not getting anything accomplished here."

Bobbie climbed onto the bed while Annie held back the covers, then she sat on the side of the bed. "Feel better now?"

She couldn't answer. Annie touched her chin, forcing Bobbie to look at her. She had been so kind and loving, even being moved to tears when she saw all the bruises on Bobbie's body. She deserved an honest answer.

"I can still feel him touching me. It seems dirty somehow."

257

Annie leaned over and looked at her long and hard. "But it's *his* dirt, Bobbie, not yours. He had evil on his mind. Don't let that man and what happened steal anything from you. Don't let him change who you are. You're a fighter, Bobbie. I've seen it. Fight these feelings of yours. I know you can beat them."

The kitchen door squeaked open, and the sound of several pairs of boots echoed down the hallway.

"They're here." Annie patted her hand. "I'll go meet them and make sure Doc knows it's just your forehead he's to look at."

"Annie?" Pete called for his wife.

"Coming." Annie met Bobbie's gaze as she tucked the covers up under her chin. "It'll be all right."

Bobbie nodded, and Annie walked out into the hall. She returned minutes later with Doc, Morgan, and Jace on her heels. Bobbie glanced at each of them but couldn't hold their gaze, especially Jace's. She didn't know exactly how she felt about him. The hurt from his distrust clung to her heart.

Doc reached down and squeezed her hand as she gripped the top of the covers. He smiled. "All right, Bobbie, let's see what we have here." His touch to her forehead as he went to work could only be deemed professional. "You did a good job cleaning it, Annie. It looks good. Won't take much to fix up that wound."

Morgan cleared his throat. "Ah, Bobbie? I'd like to ask you some questions, if you don't mind. Coop and the other man aren't talking."

She closed her eyes. Annie squeezed her shoulder. She took a deep breath and slowly let it out, then nodded her agreement.

Morgan smiled and moved to stand behind Doc's shoulder. "Good for you." He winked. "First of all, do you know the man with Coop?"

"Coop called him Will. He never mentioned a last name."

"Have you ever seen him before today?"

She nodded. "He's the one who ran into me in Pueblo."

Jace gasped. "That's right. He almost knocked Bobbie down. He and Sonny almost got into a fight. Maybe that explains why they knocked Sonny out up in the mountains. A bit of revenge."

Bobbie looked back at Morgan. "He also admitted he's the one that attacked me the night I stood watch on the cattle drive."

"Why are they after you, Bobbie? I don't understand," Morgan said.

Bobbie sighed. "They're your bank robbers, Morgan."

Silence filled the room. She could even hear the kitchen clock ticking. Jace collapsed onto the chair behind him and covered his face with his hands.

"How do you know that?" Morgan said. "Did they admit it to you?"

Bobbie nodded. "That and I saw them behind the bank the day I opened my account. That's why they wanted to kill me. They thought of me as a witness."

"Why didn't you tell me that, Bobbie?" Morgan's wiry brows pulled together. "Why didn't you say something before now?"

She looked Morgan in the eyes. "Because it was only speculation on my part. I had no proof." She fought to control her anger. "If I'd said something, I'd have been no better than the person who spread the rumors about me."

Jace stood. "Excuse me." He left the room.

Morgan watched him leave, then turned back to her and nodded. "I understand. Thank you, Bobbie. Ah, maybe we can talk more later about the details?"

"Sure," she said, and Morgan moved to leave. "There's one more bank robber out there, Morgan."

He stopped and turned back, his eyebrows

high on his forehead.

She held up three fingers. "I saw three men behind the bank that day."

"Would you recognize the third man? Can you describe him?"

"I never saw him. Only the head of his horse. The bushes hid him."

"All right. What about the color of his horse?"

"Dark. Because they were in the shadows, I couldn't really tell." Bobbie shrugged. "At a guess, dark chestnut or bay."

"Thank you, Bobbie. If you remember anything else, will you let me know?"

"Yes," she said and turned on her side.

"I'm finished here." The doctor dug in his bag and pulled out a small packet of powder. "If you have trouble sleeping —"

She shook her head. "I don't want it."

The doctor looked up at Annie, and Bobbie followed his gaze. Annie lifted her hands helplessly.

Doc placed the packet on the table beside the bed. "Just in case you change your mind." He stood and followed Morgan out the door.

Annie sat on the bed. "Are you all right?"

The question made tears sting Bobbie's eyes. She nodded.

"You did great. I'm proud of you."

She attempted a smile. "Go, Annie. Go be with your family."

Annie leaned close. "You, Bobbie McIntyre, are a part of my family, and I intend to stay right here with you until you fall asleep."

Her battle with her tears ended. They rolled down her temples into her hair. She sat up, and the two embraced. "Thank you, Annie."

"You're welcome. Now, lie back and get some sleep. You look exhausted."

Annie pulled the chair Jace vacated next to the bed and sat on it with a look of determination. Bobbie reached for Annie's hand and soon drifted off.

Twenty-One

Jace rose from the table when Morgan tapped him on the shoulder and motioned for him to follow. Morgan didn't stop walking until he stood next to his horse.

"She said there's one more man out there, Jace."

"There's three of them?"

Morgan nodded. "You might want to keep her close to the ranch, keep someone nearby. I know she won't like that, but if Coop and his friend were after her, this man might be too."

"Consider it done."

"I'll get Coop off by himself and let him know Bobbie talked. Maybe that'll loosen his tongue."

Jace shook the sheriff's hand. "Thanks, Morgan. Let me know if I can do something."

"Just take care of that little girl in there."

Jace walked back to the house. *Little girl.*

He may have thought as much the day she arrived, but he could think of her only as a woman now. His woman. He stopped at the thought, and then nodded. Yes, he wanted her all to himself. He wanted her heart as well as her help.

"Jace?"

Beans lumbered toward him, a large pot clutched in his hands.

"I figured Annie didn't have no time to cook. Here's some stew and biscuits. It ain't no feast but at least it'll fill your bellies."

"Thanks, Beans. I appreciate that." Jace climbed the porch steps and held the door open. Beans set the pot on the table and peeked toward Bobbie's door. "She all right?"

"I think so. I'm waiting for Annie to let me know for sure."

Beans nodded, clapped him on the shoulder, and slipped out the door.

Jace slumped down into the chair he'd vacated earlier. He propped his elbows on the table and cradled his head in his hands. What a mess he'd made with his mistakes.

Something bumped his arm. He opened his eyes and looked down. Sara had tucked her head between him and the table and peered up at him. Their eyes met, and she broke into a toothy smile. He scooped her into his lap, buried his face in her dark locks, and took a deep breath. She allowed the embrace for only a few moments before she squirmed, turned, and pointed to the pot on the table. He chuckled. This was something he could handle.

Sara clapped her hands when he placed a full bowl of stew in front of her. She took her first bite as Pete and Ben entered the kitchen.

Pete smiled. "I thought I smelled food."

Jace dished up two more bowls for Pete and Ben. *What's taking Annie so long? Is something wrong with Bobbie?*

After they were done eating, Pete cleaned the kids' hands and faces before chasing them through the house on their way to bed. Jace heard them laughing and squealing all the way up the stairs. He smiled. Dad used to do the same thing with him and Annie. Life was so easy as a child. Now, it wore him out.

Pete returned and sat across from him. They waited for Annie to appear, which she did a few minutes later.

"The kids have already been fed and are up in bed," Pete said.

Annie sat in the chair closest to Jace, then reached to put her hand on his arm. "Bobbie's going to be okay. But it'll take time for

265

her to get over what happened."

The three of them sat in silence for a while. He couldn't take it any longer. He had to tell them what had happened.

"It's my fault. She wouldn't have been hurt if it weren't for me."

Pete and Annie stared at him.

"Why, Jace?" Annie said. "What makes you say that?"

He remained silent for a moment as he worked up the courage to say the words. "I was up on the butte with David, overlooking the area where Sonny and Bobbie were hunting. We saw Bobbie with the two men. David wanted to rush down right away to help her, but I wouldn't let him." He stopped and shook his head. "I saw Bobbie down there with them, and all I could think about was that letter to Morgan describing the woman and her two accomplices." Tears welled in his eyes. "If I'd rushed down there right away like David wanted to, that man wouldn't have had a chance to touch her."

Annie reached over and squeezed his arm. Jace drew a deep breath. "How can I ever face her again? I doubted her innocence. My hesitation allowed them to hurt her."

"You need to talk to her about it, Jace," Pete said. "You won't begin to feel better until you do. Until you confess it, it will nag at you until you're miserable."

Jace nodded and took a few deep breaths, trying to regain control of his emotions. "You're right. But I'm going to wait until she recovers from this first."

"Don't wait too long, Jace."

"I won't." He stood to leave, but then stopped. "Do you need me to stay and help tonight, Annie?"

"No. I'll be fine. I want to stay with her in case she can't sleep and needs to talk. Pete's here if I need any help."

Jace nodded, relieved he could delay facing Bobbie, ashamed he felt that way.

Bobbie awoke to find Annie sleeping next to her. Her presence surprised her until she remembered waking during the night to see her trying to sleep in that uncomfortable chair. She had ordered Annie to get into the bed with her or go on to her own. Without hesitation, Annie climbed in next to her.

The first light of dawn peeked through the checkered curtains on her window. For the first time she could remember, the sight didn't bring her any joy. She slid from under the covers, careful not to disturb Annie's sleep. Fresh clothes hung on a hook next to the door. She grabbed them and moved to the washroom to get dressed. Then she slipped out the kitchen door and headed for the privacy of the porch.

Yesterday's events played through her mind and pulled her further back to when she had been accused of bank robbery. Before long, her thoughts drifted to God. If Jace was right about Him being in control of everything, then why did He allow all of this to happen? She had been going to church and the Bible studies without fail.

Footsteps crunched on the stone pathway surrounding the house. She turned and saw Annie headed her way.

"There you are. You were pretty quiet, or else I was very tired." Annie sat next to her. "Do you mind, or would you rather be alone?"

Bobbie shrugged. She no longer knew what she wanted. "You can stay." Annie examined her face, a curious tilt to her head. Bobbie reached over and took her hand. "Thank you for everything, Annie."

"I didn't do anything."

"Yes, you did. You were there for me." She glanced at her and then looked across the ranch. She fought the tears that never seemed far away. "You didn't judge me. Not yesterday or when I was accused of bank robbery. You stood with me as my friend through it all." She swallowed hard and forced out the last. "You did a lot."

Annie smiled and squeezed her hand. The two sat without saying a word. The morning sun shimmered between the trees. How could God create something so beautiful, and then allow something so ugly to happen? It made no sense. Yet Annie loved and trusted Him completely. Why?

"There are a lot of emotions flashing across your face, Bobbie. Care to share some of them?"

A daring blue jay darted out from the trees and stole a bit of corn that lay scattered on the ground for the chickens. She watched mirthlessly.

"Why would God allow this to happen, Annie? What did I do to deserve it? I've been trying to live right — going to church and such. I've tried to learn about Him. I even thought I was beginning to know Him. But now I don't think I know Him at all. I don't understand why this happened. First, He takes my mother from me, then my father, leaving me with no kin to speak of. Now this. I don't understand." Her gaze bored into Annie's, waiting, *pleading* for an answer.

"I don't know the answers to all of that, Bobbie. Sometimes things happen and we don't find out why until much later. Sometimes we never know why this side of heaven."

"Then how can you trust a God like that? How can you trust someone who will put you through terrible things for no apparent reason?"

"There's always a reason, Bobbie. God allows each of us to make choices. We can choose for God or against Him. We can choose good or evil. Free will can get man into trouble." Annie paused. "Or it could be part of God's bigger and perfect plan. There's a verse in Romans that says, 'O the depth of the riches both of the wisdom and the knowledge of God! How unsearchable are His judgments, and His ways past finding out!'

"It's impossible for us mere humans to understand everything about God and His ways and wisdom. He is righteous and sovereign. We can't possibly know or understand His plan. We just have to trust that He knows what's best."

Bobbie pondered that for a moment, trying to soak it all in. "Say that passage again, Annie."

After Annie finished reciting it, Bobbie said, "I like that. It sounds so . . . *immense* is the only word that comes close to describing how that verse sounds."

"That's a good word for it. That's also one of my favorite verses."

"I can see why."

"As for your church and Bible study attendance, Bobbie, they won't save you. Only belief in Jesus Christ as your Savior will do that. And even when we're saved, God doesn't promise that life will be easy or that bad things won't happen. But He does promise to be with us and help us through those times. Wouldn't you rather go through them with God than without Him?"

Annie gripped Bobbie's hand again. "The Bible tells us that God loves us so much that He didn't want us to die separated from Him, so He sent His Son, Jesus, to die in our place so that we could live forever with God. The Bible tells us the way we do that is to confess with our mouth that Jesus is Lord and believe in our heart that God raised Him from the dead, and we can be saved."

Bobbie was quiet at first. Then she sighed. "You make it sound so easy."

"Oh, but it is that easy. It just takes true heartfelt belief to become a child of God. The peace that comes with the knowledge that you are His is incredible. It's a binding relationship. Even more so than that piece of paper you and Pete signed when you

271

placed your money in his care. This relationship can't be torn, lost, or stolen. It's an eternal commitment. *Nothing* can separate us from His love."

Bobbie stared at the sky for several minutes. "I called out to Him." She turned back to Annie. "Yesterday, when that man attacked me. I asked God to help me." Tears welled up in her eyes. "Then Jace showed up."

Annie pulled her close. "Doesn't that show you how much you want and need the Lord? Your thoughts went to Him when you were in trouble. Your soul is crying out to be filled with His presence. You don't have to deny yourself or Him any longer. You can have what you're looking for today, right now."

Bobbie sat back and went over the conversation in her mind. She didn't want to make the most important decision of her life on a whim. She thought back to all the sincere believers she'd ever known. They all had something she didn't — something she wanted.

"I want that kind of peace you spoke of, Annie. I want what my mom had. I want what you, Pete, and Jace have. I want God with me through the good times as well as the bad."

Annie reached over and took Bobbie's hand in hers. "Then ask Him. Step out in faith and ask Him to come and live within you. Admit that you're a sinner and ask Him to forgive you of those sins and to make you His child. All it takes is a prayer."

She looked into Annie's eyes, her heart beating a little faster. Then she bowed her head.

"Dear God in heaven, I've been independent for so long that I've let it blind me to my need for You. I thought I would be fine on my own, putting my trust only in myself, but I was wrong. Lord, I'm tired of walking in that blindness. Take hold of my heart, Lord, and don't ever let go. Forgive me of the sins that I've let build up in my life and wash them all away. Thank You for the chance to become Your child, and help me become the person You want me to be."

She looked up at Annie then, her eyes filled with tears. Annie jumped up and pulled Bobbie into her arms. The women held each other as they wept, but for the first time, Bobbie's tears were of incredible joy.

Jace pulled the outside kitchen door open, but closed it again when he heard the sound of crying. He went around to the porch and cleared his throat to let Bobbie know of his presence, then spotted Annie, who turned with a smile on her face.

"Jace, I'd like you to meet our new sister."

Comprehension came slowly, but he knew of only one thing that would cause the look of joy on Bobbie's face. He flew up the steps to hug her and welcome her to the family of God. Her hesitation accepting his embrace made him stop.

"I've got to tell Pete," Annie said. "He'll be so happy!" She ran into the house, leaving Jace and Bobbie alone.

"I can't tell you how happy this makes me, Bobbie."

"It's an amazing feeling. I'm exhilarated and exhausted all at the same time. My heart is pounding like I've just run a mile, yet I also feel at peace."

"It only gets better. Just wait and see."

Bobbie looked as uncomfortable as Jace felt. He started to suggest they move to the kitchen when she touched his arm.

"Thank you for helping me yesterday, Jace. I don't think there's any way I can tell you how much I appreciate it."

"I'm just glad I was there."

He couldn't breathe. He had so much more to say, but he wasn't prepared. The fact that she still couldn't look him in the eye didn't help, but at least she spoke to him. That was a start.

TWENTY-TWO

Bobbie lifted up on the barn door as she opened it to keep it from squeaking. She'd made it this far without being seen. Sneaking out for an early morning ride had the touch of criminal behavior, but with the way Jace had been hovering, she had no other choice.

He had asked her to stay near the ranch for a while. She thought he was being overprotective. Two days after becoming a Christian, she attended the church service. After the message, many of the members approached her with congratulations. Jace stood at her elbow the entire time. He seemed to be nearby every second as she went about her work on the ranch. If he wasn't in her line of vision, she only had to look around to find him watching. She prayed his protectiveness would wear off soon.

Leading Mack out of the barn, Bobbie

stopped long enough to pat the nose of Jace's stallion, who had stuck his head out of his stall and snorted. If Jace didn't hurry and name the black, she'd do it herself. She dug a treat from her pocket. The stallion loved them almost as much as Mack did.

Hoping to keep Mack silent, Bobbie fed him a treat of his own while she closed the door behind them. Instead of mounting up right away, she led Mack past Annie's house, then Jace's, all the while rubbing Mack's nose to keep him quiet.

Once they were at a safe distance, Bobbie climbed onto the saddle. Mack snorted and pranced, eager to be on his way, waiting for her command that would set him free. She patted his neck. She had wanted to do this for days. A few weeks ago while out rounding up horses, she found a beautiful spot overlooking the river. A perfect place for prayer. The fact that it would take a brisk ride to get there only added to the pleasure of her outing.

She nudged Mack with her heels, and he sprang into action. Within seconds, he stretched out into a full gallop. She whooped and laughed with sheer joy at the feel of the wind skimming across her face. How could she ever describe to anyone how wonderful it felt to be free? Free to move about as she wished, and free from the sinful life that had enslaved her. Her heart felt as though it would jump from her chest.

When they neared the river, she reined Mack to a slow walk. The sun began its ascent and made the dew on the leaves and grass glisten like diamonds. Water ran in the distance as the birds greeted the morning in song.

She stopped and breathed in the beauty of the day. Gone were the solitary days of the past. God had filled her with His Spirit, and she would never be alone again.

She nudged Mack forward. When she found the boulder she sought, she dismounted and tied the reins to a branch. She approached the rock with a sense of reverence.

Bobbie placed the toe of her boot on a lip of the boulder, but her foot promptly slipped off. She tried again, to no avail. The dew she admired earlier now became a hindrance. She walked around the rock looking for a better foothold, carefully avoiding the drop-off to the river only feet away. None could be found. Not about to be deterred, she walked back to where she started. She pulled off her boots and placed her foot, now only in stockings, on the lip and pushed herself on top. She grinned at her success — and her wet feet. The smile turned to a frown at the idea of a wet bottom.

She looked up and whistled. "Come here, Mack." When the branch pulled at his rein, he stopped. She called him again, and he tugged until the branch snapped. She released the blanket from the saddle, then sent Mack away, not liking him so close to the drop-off.

She placed the blanket on the rock, sat, and gazed around. The view looked just as she remembered only now it seemed more beautiful. She bowed her head and praised God for His goodness and love. Time stopped as she poured out her heart.

Jace jumped out of bed. The sun hovered near the top of his window instead of at the sill. He shouldn't have stayed up late praying and thinking. Now, he wasn't sure when he'd be able to find Bobbie alone. He needed to talk to her.

He threw on his clothes and hurried to Annie's, hoping she still had some breakfast. His sister's eyebrows went up when he rushed into the kitchen.

"I overslept." Bobbie's bedroom door was still closed. He jerked his head toward it. "She's not up yet?"

"I guess not. I figured she had trouble sleeping." Annie stopped scrubbing the pot long enough to look at him. "Is something wrong? You look, I don't know . . . anxious I guess."

"I need to talk to Bobbie."

"Then go ahead and knock."

He tapped on Bobbie's door but didn't hear a response. Tapping again, he turned the knob while calling her name. "Bobbie?" Inside, her bed lay neatly made. He returned to the kitchen. "She's not in there."

Annie stopped scrubbing and looked at him.

He read concern on his sister's face and shrugged. "She must be out watching the sun come up. She likes the sunrise. I'm going to look for her."

Jace checked the porch before heading toward the barn. Maybe she was getting Mack saddled for the day. When he found the stall empty, he ran back outside and scanned the ranch site looking for her big bay. Nothing. He headed back to Annie's house, stepped inside the kitchen, and let the door slam behind him.

"Mack is gone. Did Bobbie say anything to you about going for a ride this morning?"

"No." Annie walked into Bobbie's room

and checked the dresser. Her clothes were folded in neat piles inside. Annie slid the drawer shut, the worried frown gone from her face.

"Why did you look in her dresser?"

"I don't know, Jace. I guess I needed to know for sure. She seems happy enough, but she's never done anything like this before. I just wanted to check."

"Well, her bed's made so I don't think anyone took her from here."

"What? What do you mean, Jace?"

He could have torn out his tongue when he saw the alarm on his sister's face. "Now, Annie —"

"You think someone's still after her? She said there's one more robber out there. Do you think he's trying to kill her? Is that why you're making her stay close to the ranch?"

Jace ran his hands through his hair. "I'm not sure."

"Jace!"

He pulled Annie toward him to calm her down, but she pushed away.

"Why are you still standing here? Go find her!"

He ran for his horse and was about to climb onto the saddle when he saw his cook walking with a purposeful stride toward him.

281

"What's up, Beans? I'm in a bit of a hurry."

"You going to look for Bobbie?"

Jace nodded, and Beans pointed to the mountains toward the west. "I saw her head off in that direction." When Jace moved to leave, Beans grabbed his arm. "You tell her whatever it takes to make her stay."

"What're you trying to say, Beans? You think she wants to leave?"

Beans shuffled his feet, eyes downcast. "I don't know, Jace. I just know she's acting different." He shrugged. "I know she wants her own place. Maybe she thinks it's past time to be looking for it."

His old friend may as well have stuck a knife in his gut. "Thanks for the help."

"You know, she's quite a girl, boss."

Jace smiled. "That she is, Beans."

He mounted his horse and headed toward the mountains. He rode for over an hour and still hadn't found her. Twice he thought he'd seen her, only to come up empty. He headed toward the river, though he could think of no reason why she would need to be in that area.

He was about to head east when he spotted Mack in the distance. He peered around trying to get a glimpse of Bobbie as well. She sat on a large rock, her back against another one overlooking the river flowing below. He left his horse behind a thick cluster of bushes.

A twig snapped, and Bobbie grabbed for her pistol. A deer stepped into an opening between them. Bobbie smiled as the buck sniffed its surroundings. The tail flipped up into the air, and the deer ran off into the woods. Bobbie drew her legs up and rested her forehead on her knees, her hands folded in front of her.

He walked up to where she sat, trying to be as quiet as possible. He leaned on a nearby rock and watched her. After several minutes, her head came up, and she stared straight ahead with a peaceful look on her face.

"You're a tough lady to find."

Bobbie jumped, her head snapping in his direction.

He smiled. "Hi, Bobbie."

"Good morning, Jace. How'd you find me?"

"It wasn't easy. In fact, I probably wouldn't have found you at all if Beans hadn't pointed me in this direction. Were you trying to hide?"

She looked straight ahead again. "No. I just wanted some time alone. I left a note on the bed."

"It must have blown off. We didn't see it."

"We?"

"Annie didn't see it either."

Bobbie nodded, then motioned to her surroundings. "I found this place while rounding up your horses. I thought it was pretty."

"It is." He paused. "Do you still want some time alone?"

"No. I was about to head back."

Jace leaned on the boulder and waited in silence for her to look at him. In a few minutes, she turned to him, her eyebrows raised. He glanced away and cleared his throat, then removed his hat and twisted it in his hands.

"I need to talk to you about something." He could feel her staring, waiting for him to continue, but he didn't return the gaze. He cleared his throat again. "Well actually, I need to tell you something. Confess really."

"What is it, Jace?" Her voice was all business.

He rubbed the back of his neck and took a deep breath. "I could have stopped that man from touching you, Bobbie." He looked up when she didn't respond and could tell by her expression he had her full attention.

Bobbie shook her head as though he'd slapped her. "What?"

He stared into the distance. "David and I

were about to ride from the butte into the valley when we saw you talking to those men. David wanted to race down there right away, but I . . . I stopped him."

Silence.

"Why, Jace?"

He couldn't get the words past his tight throat.

"Why did you stop David?" The pitch of her voice sliced him to his core.

He forced himself to face her. "Because . . . when I saw you with those men, the only thing I could think of was the letter to Morgan about the woman robber and her two companions. In my eyes, it confirmed your guilt."

Bobbie gasped, and he knew he had hurt her more than he'd feared. If only there was a way to take everything back. Start over.

"I'm sorry, Bobbie. I'm sorry I doubted your innocence. Can you ever forgive me?"

She turned away from him and swiped her sleeve across her eyes. He remained silent. There were no words.

"Why did you think I was guilty? What made you turn on me, Jace?"

The pain in her voice tore at his heart. "It was my own fault. I allowed someone's suspicions to sway what I knew to be right. I'm the only one to blame."

"What'd Coop tell you?"

Jace shook his head. "That's not important anymore. I just wish I had figured out the lies before it was too late. I'm sorry, Bobbie. I hope one day you can forgive me."

"I already have."

Her words gave him the courage to finish saying what he'd come for to begin with. "I need to tell you something else."

She turned to look at him, a look of unease in her eyes. He set his hat on the rock. He'd tortured it enough.

"I care about you, Bobbie." Jace stopped. "No, that's not right." He looked into her eyes. "I'm in love with you, Bobbie."

Her brow furrowed, and she dipped her head so he could no longer see her face.

"I know that doesn't make much sense after the way I treated you the last couple weeks. Maybe my feelings for you scared me, and I needed an excuse to turn them away. I'm not really sure right now. What I am sure of is how I feel about you. I don't ever want you to leave this ranch. I want you here by my side for the rest of our lives."

It was time to stay silent for a while. After several moments had passed without a response, he took her chin in his hand and turned her face toward him. Bobbie didn't pull away, and hope rose. "You didn't react when I told you I loved you."

Bobbie smiled, but the sadness in her eyes remained. "I guess that's because love for you is different than what I call love."

"Love is love, Bobbie. Don't make this difficult for me."

"I wouldn't do that, Jace. Honestly." Her tone was calm, almost sympathetic. "As far as I know, love grows from friendship and trust."

"Haven't I been a friend to you?" He kept his eyes trained on her face.

"Hey, I admire you for giving a woman a job as a wrangler. But if you couldn't trust me as a ranch hand, you'd never trust me with your heart."

"You said you forgave my mistake. Are you telling me different now?" Jace reached for her arm, but she twisted away from him.

"I told you the truth." Bobbie slapped her hand over her heart. "I do forgive you, Jace, but I'd always have to prove myself to you." She shrugged and kicked at the boulder. "I'm used to having to prove myself. You did no different than the rest, so don't feel bad or —"

"No different than the rest?" Jace grasped her hand and pulled her close. "Do you have any idea what you do to my heart? How it threatened to pound through my rib cage when you ran your fingers through my hair while you were cutting it? Or the way it begs for you to send a smile my way?"

Bobbie tried to pull free, her tongue wetting her lips. The sight sent a shock through his nerves. He wanted to kiss her. He leaned in further until their lips were a breath away. She pushed against his chest.

"Don't, Jace." Fear and apprehension clouded her eyes.

"I'm sorry." He raked his fingers through his hair as he turned away. "I shouldn't have let that happen."

A moment of silence passed before she touched his arm. "Maybe I just need more time."

He held out his hand. She put hers into it and let him help her down from the rock. She leaned against it to replace her boots while he reached to grab her blanket. He thrust his crumpled hat on his head.

Her hand settled like a feather on his arm. "Thank you for coming to talk to me, Jace. It helped ease a lot of hurts."

"I should have done it sooner."

She sent him a tentative smile and climbed into the saddle. "It's enough that you did it."

They rode at a slow pace until they reached the clearing. Then Bobbie grinned at him. Before he could react, she and Mack took off at a gallop. He gave a whoop and spurred his horse after her. Her laughter floated back to him and he smiled. Maybe he wouldn't have to wait as long as he thought.

Right about the time he wondered if he'd ever catch up to Bobbie, she reined to a stop. In seconds, he reached her. He followed her gaze — and saw the buzzards circling.

TWENTY-THREE

Bobbie stared at the circling buzzards a moment longer before her gaze dropped to her hands. Jace realized she wasn't a bank robber, but did he still think her capable of rustling his cattle?

"Let's go see what the rustlers have been up to this time." Jace's voice sounded flat, tense.

He nudged his horse forward and she followed, staring at his broad back. Mere minutes ago, he laughed as he chased her. She didn't know what came over her to challenge him like that. What she did know was the immense pleasure she felt when he sought her out to apologize and declare his love. She could still sense the warmth of his touch on her face . . . and his attempt to kiss her. Part of her wanted it like nothing else. The other part recalled the nauseating touch of another man. His lips . . . How long would that part hold reign over her emotions? She also had to question the wisdom of returning the feelings of a man who could be turned against her so easily. How could she trust someone who didn't trust her in return?

She nudged her horse up next to his as they neared the area where the buzzards flew. Reining Mack to a stop, she stepped from the saddle, almost sagging to her knees at the sight of Jace's favorite breeding mare lying before them. She forced her feet to carry her to the animal. Jace still sat on his horse. Their gazes met for a moment before he finally dismounted.

"Oh, Belle." She knelt to caress the horse but drew her hand back when the head rose then flopped back to the ground.

Jace dropped to his knees and ran a hand over Belle's protruding stomach. "We'll have to help her or lose her foal. Maybe her too." He ran for his rope. "Which end you want to work?"

"I'll take the head."

She laid across Belle's neck as Jace reached in for the foal. He shook his head. "It's tangled in the cord."

After a few moments of maneuvering, Jace pulled out first one leg then the other. He tied the small rope around the hocks and gently started to pull. The small, cream-colored foal emerged in one smooth motion. Jace shoved a finger in each nostril to make it sneeze. Two snorts later, the foal struggled to lift its head.

Jace did a quick examination. "A colt. Belle almost always gives me a strong, healthy colt."

Bobbie stood to allow Belle to rise. The mare remained on the ground though she nickered from time to time. After several minutes, Belle rose and tended to her newborn. As mother and son got acquainted, Bobbie couldn't stop the moisture in her eyes.

Jace leaned down. "Are you crying?"

"No." She looked away and swiped her sleeve across her face. "Just leaking happiness."

He laughed, put his arm around her shoulders, and pulled her close. "I know the feeling." He gave her another squeeze, then moved to Belle's side. "I thought Belle was dead, another casualty of a sick and cruel enemy."

Bobbie stood on the opposite side of Belle. "And who do you think is your enemy?"

He didn't answer. Didn't even look at her. "You think it's me."

Jace's head came up. "Of course not."

"Then who?"

"Hank Willett, and I plan to get a confession out of him. I don't know how yet, but I will."

"Are you sure of this? I mean, do you know for a fact it's Hank or is this an assumption?" He stared at her as if he didn't understand. "I know what it feels like to be accused of something I didn't do. I remember all the emotions raging through me, and I had no control over them." She sent Jace an imploring look. "I'd rather be trampled in a stampede than go through that again."

Jace took her in his arms. "I'm sorry, Bobbie."

She allowed the embrace, then took a step back so she could look into his eyes. "All I ask is that you find proof before you confront Mr. Willett. It may save both of you some grief."

"You're right." He tucked a piece of her hair behind her ear, letting his fingers trace her jawline before sliding his hand down her arm to grasp her hand. "Thank you for the reminder."

Her skin tingled where he touched her. She squeezed his hand before stepping past him toward Belle.

"I'll help you get Belle and Beau home."

"Beau?"

She smiled. "Sure. It fits. He's a handsome little guy, don't you think? He'll have all the girls' attention before long."

He moved up close behind her. She could feel his breath on her ear. "I'm not sure about that, but you've certainly got mine."

Chills raced over her skin again. Did he know what he was doing to her? She moved to the other side of Mack and looked at Jace over the saddle.

"Would you —" She stopped and cleared her throat. "Would you prefer I send one of the men back here to help you?"

He looked from the mare to her. "No. I'm riding back with you."

She sighed. "I'll be fine."

He acted as though he didn't hear her. He strode to his horse and mounted, waiting for her to do the same.

"Jace —"

"Bobbie, Belle's a great breeding mare, and I think the world of her, but she's an animal. You're the woman I love, and I'll do everything I can to protect you. We'll come back for Belle when she and Beau have had a chance to rest and gain some strength."

Her throat clogged with emotion. All arguments faded, and she climbed onto her saddle without another word.

"Dew, where's Bobbie?" Jace had been searching for close to 15 minutes. The woman could disappear faster than his sister's hot cakes.

Dew was checking one of his horse's shoes. He let the leg drop. "One of the mares didn't show up with the rest. Bobbie said she thought she knew where to find her."

"Which mare?"

"The one due to foal."

"I oughta get rid of her. She does this every year. Picks a new spot each time too." Jace shook his head. "Bobbie say which way she was headed?"

Dew pointed a thumb over his shoulder as he grabbed another of his horse's legs. "Toward the bluff. She said she shouldn't be long."

Jace stood in indecision as he watched Dew clean the mud from around the horse-shoe, then made up his mind. "I'm going to check on her. If that mare foaled, Bobbie may need some help. She shouldn't be alone out there anyway."

"Right. I had that same thought, but she insisted she'd be fine."

He could just hear her saying those very words. He threw his leg over the rump of his horse and urged him into a gallop. The message he had to give Bobbie wasn't urgent. He could tell her they had an invitation to supper at the Cromwells when she returned, yet he couldn't resist the desire to track her down. He chose the shorter route. Though it had more obstacles to traverse, the view made it worth the effort. He rode past the edge of the pond, ascended along the rocky face of a small cliff, and headed toward a tiny grove of trees. He cut through the dense growth of the grove, which put him only minutes from the bluff.

He reined to a stop. Several yards away, Bobbie and Mack pranced in the grassy meadow at the base of the slope. *What are they doing?* Bobbie turned Mack in a circle one direction. In the blink of an eye, she turned him to go in the other. He dashed ahead, only to stop and spin in the opposite direction. If Jace didn't know better, he'd think they were dancing. The next moment, Mack bounced back and forth as if sorting a calf for branding.

Bobbie scrambled from her saddle to the ground. Jace stood in the stirrups for a better look. She jumped up and raced in circles. She'd grab at the ground, run farther, and grab for something again.

Jace nudged his mount down the slope and came up behind her. Her head was down. She appeared to be working on something.

"What are you doing?"

She gasped and spun around. Her chest heaved and her hands clutched at her stomach.

Jace jumped from his horse and hurried toward her. "Are you hurt?"

"Uh, no." She buttoned the bottom of her shirt. "What brings —" She grabbed at her side.

"Bobbie, tell me what's wrong."

"Nothing. Really." She squirmed and giggled.

"Bobbie —"

She gasped and looked down at her shirt. "Oh, for pity's sake!"

"All right, Bobbie. Start talking."

She looked up at him. "It wet on me."

He suppressed a laugh. "Would you care to explain that?"

Bobbie pursed her lips and undid her bottom button. She reached in and pulled out a small handful of fur and held it out to him. "I thought the kids might like to see a baby rabbit."

"Is that what you and Mack were after?"

She nodded. Her cheeks flushed pink. "I thought it was cute."

She was the cute one. "You're full of surprises. You go after a horse and round up a hare." He shook his head. "Well, it never hurts to start small."

She stuffed the bunny back inside her shirt, then headed for Mack and pointed toward the southwest. "The mare should be right up there."

"Wh–you're still going after the mare?"

"Why not?" Bobbie swung up onto the saddle and patted the bunny hiding in her shirt. "He's safe."

She flicked the reins and shot off. He hurried to mount up and galloped after her. Life would be different with her around — if she chose to stick around.

Bobbie stopped and pointed. "She's foaled. I'll go up around and rope her. You can run in and grab the baby."

"Oh, well thanks. Just make sure you don't let her get loose. I sure don't need an angry mama after me."

"She's pretty tame, Jace. She'd probably only hurt you a little. A lot less than that stallion you tried to break." She grinned at him and urged Mack farther up the bluff.

He followed her progress up and around the mare. The horse watched her, too, as she stood her ground over her foal. Bobbie swung her lariat a few times and let it go with a quick flick of her wrist. The noose landed right on target. She jerked the rope and looped her end around the saddle horn. Mack moved back. The mare fought against the lariat, bucking and swinging her head in a wild rhythm.

Jace spurred his horse toward the foal. He jumped down, scooped it into his arms, and mounted up again.

The barn door stood open when they arrived home. He carried the foal into a stall and stood back. Bobbie released the mare. The horse trotted inside, sniffed the air, and ran to her baby.

Once Jace closed the stall door, Bobbie turned and headed toward the house. He followed close behind. He wanted to see this. Ben faced Bobbie as she squatted down and maneuvered the rabbit toward the opening of her shirt. Jace moved so he could watch both of their faces.

When she pulled the bunny out, Ben gasped and his eyes grew big. "How did you do that?"

"I caught him out on the prairie."

"You did?" Ben's voice squealed.

"Touch him. He's so soft, you can hardly

feel the fur."

Ben reached out and ran his finger along the head, imitating Bobbie's movements. A grin stretched across his face. "He *is* soft."

Annie entered the room with Sara. Ben beckoned them over.

"Feel it, Mama."

Annie sat on the sofa and ran a finger over the fur.

"Isn't it soft?" Ben said.

Annie smiled and kissed him on the nose. "Yes, very."

The bunny squirmed, and Sara took a step back. Ben took her hand. "Touch it, Sara." Sara took another step away and gave a vigorous shake of her head. Ben moved to his mother. "Can I keep it, Mama?"

Annie sent Bobbie an incredulous look. It was all Jace could do not to burst into laughter.

"Ah, Ben?" Bobbie tucked the bunny against her as she touched Ben's shoulder. "I don't think it's a good idea to keep it."

Ben reached to pet the rabbit. "Why not?"

"Well, because he wouldn't be happy here."

"Why not? I'd care for him real good."

Bobbie pulled Ben closer. "But he wouldn't be home, Ben."

Ben frowned. Bobbie sat on a chair and

pulled him onto her lap. The bunny squirmed, and she struggled to get it under control. When it was quiet again, she turned back to Ben.

"He squirms because he doesn't like being here." She dipped her head to look into Ben's face. "If I were to take you into town and leave you with a very nice family, like the Cromwells for instance, would it be all right with you if they kept you and raised you?"

Ben's eyes widened. He shook his head. "I wanna be home."

"That's just like this bunny. He might think you're real nice, but he wants to be home. Do you understand?"

Ben nodded and touched the bunny's ears.

Bobbie hugged him and kissed his cheek. "You're such a good boy, Ben." She shot an apologetic look at Annie. "I need to go back and turn him loose. Maybe your mom will let you ride with me to let him go?"

Ben whipped around to look at his mom. "Can I, Mama? Can I ride with Bobbie?"

Annie reached around Ben and pinched Bobbie's arm. Then she started to say something, but stopped herself and sighed. "I guess that would be all right, Ben. Maybe you can talk your Uncle Jace into riding out there with you."

Ben jumped from Bobbie's lap and ran to Jace, who scooped him up in his arms. "Will you, Uncle Jace? Will you ride with us?"

Jace tapped his own cheek with his forefinger. Ben grinned, threw his arms around Jace's neck, and gave him a loud, smacking kiss.

"You just talked me into it," Jace said.

Ben cheered and kicked his feet to be let down.

Jace walked over to Bobbie as she stood. "That was very smooth. I wondered how you were going to wiggle your way out of that one."

"It never occurred to me he'd want to keep it. I just wanted him to see it." Bobbie turned to Ben. "You ready to go?" He bobbed his head. "Would you like to carry him inside your shirt, or should I put him back in mine?"

Annie craned her neck and wrinkled her nose. "Inside the shirt?"

Ben nodded then leaned down and, with his tongue tucked at the corner of his mouth, fumbled with his button. Bobbie bent to help him get the bunny inside. Jace lifted Ben into his arms and carried him out to the horses. After Bobbie climbed astride Mack, Jace handed the boy to her and mounted his own horse.

They headed back toward the bluff. Ben talked the entire ride out about how he would have played with and taken care of the bunny if he could have kept him. Jace exchanged many amused glances with Bobbie. She dropped kiss after kiss on the top of Ben's head. Jace envied the boy.

She reined to a stop. "This looks like the place."

Jace jumped down and lifted Ben to the ground. He helped Ben with the button, and Bobbie removed the bunny.

She held it in front of Ben's face. "Do you want to kiss it goodbye?"

He leaned down and pressed his face into the fur.

She smiled. "All set?"

Ben nodded. She placed the bunny on the ground and loosened her grip. It didn't move. She bumped it with her thumb, and the bunny scampered off.

"Bye, bunny," Ben called after it, then bowed his head. "Please, God, keep my bunny safe. Make him strong. Amen."

"Amen," Jace echoed, but he'd never closed his eyes. The outline of a man on a horse stood out against the sky. He inched toward the others.

"Bobbie, I think it's time we get Ben home."

She stood next to him and followed his gaze. In seconds, she held Ben in her arms.

"You two go on," Jace said. "I want to check this out."

He headed toward his horse, and Bobbie grabbed his arm.

"I think we should go home together."

He ignored the pleading look in her eyes and placed his foot in the stirrup.

"Ride home with us, Jace. It would be better if you came back here with Morgan and some others." She flashed her eyes toward Ben and motioned with her head.

He looked at Ben. The boy's gaze dashed between the two of them, and anxiety tinged his freckled face.

Jace touched Ben's cheek and nodded. "You're right. You ready to go home, Ben?"

"Yep."

Jace mounted and looked back toward the bluff. The man was gone.

They wasted no time getting back. Jace called out to Dew and Sonny, and the three hurried back to the bluff. While Sonny followed the man's trail, Jace scanned the area. He saw no other movement.

Sonny motioned to him. "The trail ends in these rocks, Jace. It's like he knows this land as good as we do. He knows how to disappear."

Jace ran several men through his mind as they headed home. Who knew his land as well as he did? Any number of people could qualify. He'd have to be patient a while longer and hope the man made a mistake that led to his downfall.

TWENTY-FOUR

Jace and Bobbie headed into town early for the Bible study with plans to eat supper with Matt and Rebecca Cromwell, Cade Ramsey, and Cade's mother. Cade had confessed to finagling an invitation for Jace and Bobbie in order to see the two together. Jace threatened his friend with a severe beating if he did or said anything to embarrass Bobbie.

Jace had offered to drive the buggy in an attempt to be close to Bobbie, but she insisted on riding Mack. He glanced at her. She looked good for having only half an hour to get ready. With all that had happened that afternoon, he'd forgotten to tell her about the invitation.

She looked deep in thought. Jace nudged his horse closer to hers, and her gaze now met his instead of looking at the ground.

"Are you all right, Bobbie?"

Bobbie's brows shot up. "Yes. Why?"

"I just want to make sure you aren't still suffering in any way from that attack."

"I'm fine, Jace. The men are behind bars where they belong, and I hope they stay there. What more could I ask?"

Jace smiled when he heard that.

"What's that smile for?" Bobbie said, returning it with one of her own.

"It's just good to see you doing so well after something that awful."

"Well, you know who I have to thank for that."

"I sure do. God's love can do amazing things in us."

"Oh, Jace, I had no idea a person could feel like this." Bobbie's face beamed with joy. "I've never felt so loved. I know my parents loved me, and it felt good. But this is almost indescribable."

Jace's heart filled from the joy he saw on her face. A thought occurred to him.

"Bobbie, the town always has a picnic and celebration for Founder's Day. Would you allow me to be your escort?"

"My escort?"

"Yes. I wanted to make sure I was the first one in line to ask."

"Well, since you're in a line of one, you have nothing to worry about."

"Maybe, but that line will grow. So?"

"All right. Sounds like fun."

They rode a ways in silence, then Jace said, "Let's walk the rest of the way. It's not much farther from here."

She dismounted without a word. He took her reins and led both horses.

Upon their arrival at the Cromwells, Matt pulled Bobbie into a warm embrace. "How've you been, Bobbie? Rebecca and I have been praying for you."

"Thank you, Matt. I appreciate that. I've been fine. Maybe that's because of your prayers." Bobbie looked around. "Is Rebecca in the kitchen?"

"She sure is, along with Ella Ramsey. Just go on in."

Cade walked in from the kitchen and heard the tail end of the conversation. "The meal's almost ready, Bobbie, so it's safe to help." He grinned as he pulled her into his arms.

Bobbie stepped back and gave him a playful slap on the arm, then shook her finger at him. "I'll have you know that I've learned a lot since that night. Haven't I, Jace?"

Jace pretended to be examining something on the ceiling as he rocked on his heels.

She swatted his arm too. "You're a big help."

"Well, I'm waiting for an invitation to find that out for myself," Cade said.

"All right. Next Wednesday. You come out and eat, and you can ride back to the study with us."

"And you're doing the cooking?"

Bobbie planted her hands on her hips. "Of course."

"Done. I've got to see this for myself."

Bobbie made a face at him before she headed for the kitchen. Cade laughed, then he and Jace followed Matt into the living room. Cade plopped down on a chair, leaving Jace the sofa.

"So, Jace?" Cade grinned at him.

"So what?"

"So, does Bobbie know you're in love with her?"

"Cade!" Matt sent him a scolding look.

"What? I think everyone knows how he feels, except for Bobbie."

"That's still none of your business," Matt shot back.

"Sorry, Jace." The grin remained fixed to Cade's face.

"Are you two planning on getting to the picnic sometime today?" Pete called up the stairs.

Bobbie stood at the top of the steps wearing one of the new dresses Annie made for her in her favorite color of green. She glanced at Annie and grinned. "Men!"

"I'd like to try to get there before all the food is gone." Pete turned to Jace. "Women. Waiting on one is bad enough, but when you put two of them together, it's a nightmare."

"I heard that," Annie said as she led Bobbie down the steps.

Pete gave his wife a hug before herding his family out the door. Bobbie heard him inform Annie that he had already loaded the wagon with all the food and baskets.

Bobbie eyed Jace as she came down the steps. He looked distracted. She knew he hated the idea of leaving the ranch site unattended and had managed to convince Dew and Beans to take turns watching the place. The plan probably relieved only a fraction of his worry.

When he glanced up and saw her, a slow smile spread across his face. "You look beautiful, Bobbie."

"Thank you." She found herself tongue-tied as he lent her his elbow and escorted her to the wagon. "So what all will be taking place today?" she finally managed to say.

"The first thing we do is eat," Pete said.

Annie turned around. "After that is a pie-judging contest followed by a pie-eating contest. Needless to say, the men who participate are so full, they're quite useless for the next two or three hours." Annie paused before turning to Pete. "So dear, are you planning on participating in the pie-eating contest again this year?"

Pete sent a playful scowl toward his wife. "I wasn't useless for three hours last year."

"No, your uselessness was closer to four hours."

"What's after that?" Bobbie asked.

"Then there are various games that everyone can participate in, like sack racing and horse racing. There's even a greased pig for the kids to try to catch. That's usually hilarious."

"They have a shooting contest that you ought to compete in, Bobbie," Jace said. "You're sure to win."

"I'm not dressed for that."

"What makes you think you have to be wearing trousers to shoot a gun?"

Bobbie's mouth opened and closed a few times as she tried to come up with a good answer, but words failed her.

They arrived in town, and Pete helped Jace unload the food and baskets before taking the horses and wagon to the Cromwells' for the day. When he returned, they all joined the growing line of people loading their plates from the tables set up with so much food Bobbie expected them to collapse.

After they were done eating, Bobbie followed Annie to the pie-judging contest and examined the pastries laid out on the table. Jace came up behind her. "Think you could make a pie that looks like one of these?"

She elbowed him in the stomach before turning to smile up into his face. "You know very well that Annie's been teaching me how to cook and bake. In fact, the meal I made for Cade turned out pretty good, if I do say so myself. And look, you're still alive."

When Jace chuckled, Bobbie realized how much she enjoyed making him laugh. She expected him to wander off to find the other men. Instead, he continued to follow her as they moved down the table.

They were just leaving the pies when two young women approached. The taller of the two had long blonde hair twisted into tight curls. She wore a flamboyant lavender dress much too fancy for a picnic. The other girl was dressed much plainer, but to Bobbie, she was prettier than the blonde because she didn't wear an air of superiority. The girl walked behind the blonde as though accustomed to standing in her shadow.

"Hi Annie . . . Jace." The blonde's gaze never left Jace except for a quick glance at Bobbie.

"Hello, Cassie. How are you, Sondra?" Jace sent them both a warm smile.

Sondra returned his smile and nodded. Cassie linked her arm through Jace's and began to walk. That left her friend and Bobbie to follow behind. Jace glanced back at her but continued walking with the young lady.

Bobbie wasn't a betting woman, but if she were, she'd be willing to wager her ranch money that Jace Kincaid would never accuse that delicate flower of stealing his cattle! She wanted to run away from the torment of seeing Jace with another woman and the way he looked down into Cassie's upturned face.

"I was disappointed that you didn't come by to ask me to this party, Jace. I thought after our conversation a few months ago that you planned to escort me to this celebration like you did last year."

Jace stopped and turned to Bobbie. "Cassie, Sondra, have you two met Bobbie?"

"I've seen her in church," Cassie said, still holding fast to Jace's arm. Her haughty gaze started at the top of Bobbie's head and traveled all the way down to the hem of her dress. "Where are your trousers?"

Bobbie's mouth went dry. The look of shock on Jace's face at Cassie's rude and malicious question helped keep her calm. She took a deep breath and smiled. "I decided to leave them at home today. But you sure have a beautiful dress."

Cassie's brows rose. "Thank you," she said, though her thankfulness didn't show on her face.

Jace stepped away from Cassie as he pried her fingers from his arm. "It was good to see you and Sondra again, Cassie, but if you'll excuse us, we need to be moving along."

Cassie grimaced and stomped her foot. She grabbed Sondra's arm and pulled her along as she flounced away.

"I'd understand if you wanted to go after her, Jace," Bobbie said. "I don't want to come between the two of you."

Jace smiled. "That's nice of you, Bobbie, but there's nothing between the two of us. I'm perfectly happy right where I am."

She inclined her head before turning away. He had no idea what his comment did for her heart.

Rebecca Cromwell walked up with Ben and Sara and announced that the pie eaters were getting seated to begin the contest.

They all wandered over to watch the fun. Several pies lined the tables, and Pete sat in the center with Matt Cromwell right beside him. There were still two empty seats. They tried to get Jace to join them, but he refused, stating that he couldn't possibly eat another bite. They turned to Pastor Robbins and to Cade and convinced the two to join them.

Sheriff Thomas officiated the contest. Once all the men had their arms behind their backs, he fired his gun into the air, and the men dropped their faces into the middle of the pies. Pete briefly came up for air before stuffing his face back into the pie.

"Oh my goodness!" Bobbie exclaimed. "Did you see Pete's face?"

"Well, at least this year he chose an apple pie," Annie said. "Last year, he chose blackberry, and his face and shirt were all purple. Now *that* was a mess."

Bobbie jumped when the gun went off again, informing everyone the contest was over. Sheriff Thomas walked over and held up Matt's arm. "The winner!" Everyone cheered and applauded as Matt stood and accepted his ribbon, wiping his face on a towel the sheriff offered.

How long had it been since she'd had such fun? Sadly, she couldn't remember.

The crowd moved off toward the next

competition while the members of the study group followed at a slower pace, enjoying their time together. They arrived at the sack race just as it ended.

"You know, Bobbie," Matt said, "there's still time to enter the shooting contest. Jace tells me you're quite good."

"No thanks, Matt. I'm just here to enjoy myself today. Shooting is a small part of what I do for a living, and I don't plan on doing anything even remotely like work today."

Jace leaned down to Bobbie's ear. "That's a better excuse than the one you gave me."

Surprised, she looked up at him. "I'll tell you what, Jace. You catch that greased pig, and I'll join the shooting contest."

Jace gave her a fiendish look and turned toward the pig contest. She ran after him and grabbed his arm.

"Where are you going?"

"To catch a pig."

"But you'll get all dirty."

"It'll be worth it."

"Jace!"

"Yes?" Jace finally stopped walking and turned to look at her.

"You're not really going through with this, are you?"

"You gave me a challenge and I accepted."

Bobbie blocked Jace's path and looked up to find him trying to withhold his laughter.

"What's so funny?"

"You. Quite a predicament you're in, don't you think?"

She made a face. Maybe if she stomped on his toes hard enough, he wouldn't be able to run very fast, not to mention it would sure make her feel better. The only other thing she could think of was a kiss on the cheek. The gesture worked on Beans. But this was Jace.

He placed his hands on her shoulders. "Bobbie, if you don't want to be in the contest, just say so. You don't have to make up excuses."

Bobbie glanced at his cheek then looked down at his toes. She shook her head. "I don't want to be in the contest," she said as she peered into his face.

"All right. Now, wasn't that easy?"

A sudden warm breeze blew some of Bobbie's hair across her face. Jace reached up to tuck it behind her ear. "You really don't like to draw attention to yourself, do you?"

Bobbie shivered at the tenderness in his voice and shook her head. He leaned toward her until they stood inches apart.

"Well, you'd better get used to the attention, Bobbie. You're so beautiful, people can't resist looking at you."

Bobbie tried to deny his comment, but what she saw in his eyes stole her ability to speak.

"Come on, you two," someone yelled. "You'll make us late for the greased pig."

Bobbie looked over to find the entire group watching them with interest and amusement. Jace extended his elbow, and Bobbie hesitated only a moment before she accepted. The day had just taken an interesting turn.

As they stood waiting for the pig to be released, Jace leaned down to her ear. "I see someone I've been wanting to talk to, Bobbie. Do you mind if I leave you for a minute or two?"

"Not at all. I'll be right here."

Was she a fool for trying to resist him? The hurt he caused with his doubt and mistrust was still fresh. Each time she tried to bury the pain, the memories resurfaced and her fears were rekindled, but her feelings for him couldn't be ignored.

She turned back at a cheer from the crowd. Someone standing in front of her blocked her view, so she moved away from Annie and the rest of the group until she could see the kids running after the pig. She couldn't help but laugh as the pig continually slipped away from the children's grasp. The kids fell down and rolled in the straw, most of it sticking to their clothing when they stood.

She felt a tug on her arm and turned, expecting Jace. Instead, Cassie's gaze bored into her.

"Excuse me," Cassie said in a polite voice. "Sonny sent me to find you. He said he needs you right away. He looked rather upset."

Bobbie examined Cassie's face for signs of a trick, but the girl looked sincere — even a little upset. She looked around for Sonny but didn't see him.

"Where is he?"

"Over by the livery. He looked like he was in pain. I think you should hurry."

Bobbie took two steps, then stopped. "I need to tell Jace where I'm going."

"I'll tell him for you. I don't think you should waste that much time. Sonny looked like he wanted you right away."

Bobbie turned on her heel and walked as fast as her dress would allow. A sense of dread grew with each step. What had happened to Sonny? Why would he want her instead of Jace?

"Bobbie!"

She glanced to her left. The sight of Sonny smiling and waving stopped her cold. He didn't look or act like he was in any pain.

Bobbie turned back to see if she could spot Cassie, but she couldn't find her anywhere. She spun toward the livery and saw someone peeking around the corner.

TWENTY-FIVE

Bobbie turned to call to Sonny, but he'd disappeared. A look back at the livery let her know the man peering from behind had also vanished.

O Lord, what is happening? Why did Cassie send me back here?

Someone grabbed her arm. Bobbie screamed and tried to pull free. "Let me go!"

"Bobbie. It's me!"

Jace?

He turned her around. Sheriff Morgan Thomas stood at his side.

"What's going on, Bobbie? You said you were going to wait —"

Bobbie threw herself into the safety of Jace's strong arms.

He pulled her close and pressed his cheek against her hair. "What's wrong, Bobbie? What has you scared?"

Her finger shook as she pointed toward

the livery. "Back there. I think he's here."

"Who?"

"The third man."

Morgan raced off, sidearm in hand.

"And you were going after him yourself?" Jace said.

She shook her head.

"Then what were you doing over here, Bobbie?"

"Cassie. She . . . she . . ."

"What about her?"

Bobbie looked around and then pointed at Cassie as the young woman slipped into the gathering crowd. "Cassie told me Sonny was here and needed my help."

"Grab her!" Jace yelled.

Jace put his arm around Bobbie as the crowd closed on Cassie. Morgan returned, asked Jace what was going on, then walked over and took Cassie by the arm. "Let's continue this in my office."

"Bobbie?" Annie hurried toward Jace and Bobbie, her brow furrowed.

"I'm all right, Annie," Bobbie said as the two embraced. "A little scared maybe, but I'm not hurt."

"Why don't you take your family home, Pete," Jace said. "I'll get a buggy from Matt when we're finished here. We'll explain everything when we get home."

"Good idea. We'll see you at the ranch." Pete put his arm around Annie and led her and the children away.

Jace and Bobbie walked into the sheriff's office and found Morgan glowering at Cassie as she sat chewing on a fingernail. Jace led Bobbie to a chair far enough from the door where she couldn't run off without his being able to stop her. She looked ready to bolt at the first sign of trouble.

"Will you be all right?" he whispered. When Bobbie nodded, he patted her arm and moved next to Morgan. "Start talking, Cassie," he said as he perched on the corner of the desk.

She looked at him, rolled her eyes, and looked away.

"Throw her in a cell, Morgan."

Cassie's gaze snapped back to him, her eyes like those of a rabbit cornered by a coyote.

"What? But I didn't do anything."

"No? What about leading Bobbie into a trap where she could've been killed?"

"No! I — no," she said in a weak voice.

"If you don't want to end up behind bars, Miss Chatham," Morgan said, "you'd better tell us your side of the story."

Cassie fidgeted, twining her fingers. "I . . .

he . . . he said he just wanted to meet Bobbie."

"Who? Who is *he?*" Jace said.

Cassie shook her blonde curls. "I don't know."

"Cassie!"

"I swear! I never saw his face. He stood around the corner of a building and told me to look away while he talked so no one would suspect he was there."

Jace examined her face. She appeared to be telling the truth. "What did he say?"

Cassie glanced at Bobbie, then looked at the floor. "He said he saw our little, uh, altercation by the pies. He said if I helped him, he'd get Bobbie out of the way for me . . ." She looked up at Jace. "So I could have you all to myself. He said he'd pay me to help."

"What did you think 'out of the way' meant, Cassie?"

"I didn't know. I just thought he'd distract her so I could be with you."

Jace blew out his breath in disgust. He started pacing. "What else?"

"Nothing really. He suggested I tell Bobbie that Sonny was looking for her, that she cared enough about him to come running."

Jace turned to Bobbie.

Her face held little expression, but her

mouth dropped open. "But Sonny was there at the livery. I saw him."

Morgan frowned, sat in thought for several seconds, then leaned over his desk. "How do you know it wasn't Sonny doing the talking?"

The corner of Cassie's lip rose in a sneer. "I think I'm smart enough to recognize Sonny's voice. We've met, you know." Cassie shrugged. "I couldn't identify this man's voice, but he thought the only way to get Bobbie to leave Jace's side was to use Sonny."

Jace stopped and met Morgan's gaze. "Are you sure you didn't recognize his voice, Cassie?"

"Yes."

Jace leaned down into her face. "Are you sure?"

"Yes, I'm sure. And I'd appreciate it if you'd stop treating me like I'm some kind of criminal, Jace." She batted her lashes. "It's not a crime to want your attention, is it?"

Jace snorted. He moved to Bobbie's side and squatted down. "Do you want to say anything?"

Bobbie shook her head.

"Do you have any questions you want to ask?"

"No. I'd like to go home now, though."

"We're almost finished."

Morgan strode to the door, opened it, and called to his deputy. "Marcus, I want you to escort Miss Chatham home." He turned back to Cassie. "Stay close to home, Cassie. I may not be finished with you yet."

He shut the door as she tried to protest on her way out and headed back to his desk. He waved Bobbie into the chair Cassie vacated. "All right, Bobbie. Tell me your side of this."

"There's nothing to tell, Morgan." Bobbie's voice sounded weary as she sank onto the chair. "I told you all I know."

"Tell me again. Why did you think that was the man with Coop?"

Bobbie shrugged. "Seemed logical. I figure he's the only other person who meant me any harm."

"Makes sense. Then what?"

"Then he disappeared and Jace grabbed me."

Morgan sat back in his chair with a thud as he rubbed his chin. "What about the fact that you saw Sonny there?"

"I doubt he's the one after me."

Jace squatted next to her. "Why do you doubt that? You saw him there. It could have been him." He wouldn't be the first of his hired hands who'd not been the innocent person they'd claimed to be.

Bobbie ran her hand over her face, then let it fall back into her lap. "I've gotten to know Sonny pretty well. He's not the type of person who'd hurt me."

Morgan crossed his arms. "All right, Bobbie, I guess that's all for now. You'd be wise to stay around the ranch, maybe even inside the house until we catch this man."

Bobbie stood and shook her head. "No, Morgan. I'm not going to let this man determine what I do or where I go."

Jace stepped toward her. "Bobbie —"

"Don't you start too." She shook her finger in his face. "I spent almost two weeks locked up at your ranch. I won't do it again. I'm not the one who did something wrong."

Jace held up his hands. "All right, Bobbie. But would you at least make sure someone is with you at all times?"

"I won't make any promises. I've had enough of being a prisoner. And don't push this, Jace. I'm about fed up with the whole thing."

"All right. I won't say another word about it." He turned his head. "Are we through, Morgan? I'd like to get Bobbie home."

"Sure." Morgan stood. "And Bobbie?" She looked up at him. "Please be careful."

"I always am, Morgan."

They stepped out onto the boardwalk before Jace stopped her and pointed to the bench in front of the sheriff's office. "Why don't you wait here, Bobbie? I'll get a buggy for us."

She dropped down on the bench without an argument.

As Jace's long strides carried him toward the livery, his thoughtfulness made Bobbie's heart swell. He had yet to repeat the words aloud that he loved her, but his every action toward her showed his feelings.

He seemed to be doing everything in his power to prove he deserved her trust. Did she love him? She wasn't sure. But maybe it was time to open her heart and attempt to trust once again, come what may.

Intent on talking to Jace about her thoughts, Bobbie decided to leave the bench and head toward the livery.

Voices floated out of the doorway to the livery as she approached. They sounded excited, and one of the voices belonged to a woman. Bobbie peeked around the corner, and a gasp stuck at the back of her throat. Jace was hugging another woman, holding her in a way he'd never held her, and the look on his face told her all she needed to know.

Bobbie pulled back and leaned against the side of the livery to get her bearings. Then she turned and headed for the post office in search of a newspaper. She prayed there would be a listing for a ranch up for sale.

TWENTY-SIX

Bobbie found a newspaper and managed to return to the bench in front of the sheriff's office before Jace arrived with a buggy. Without a word, she climbed onto the seat, not waiting for or wanting his help. She ignored the questioning looks he sent her way. He stayed quiet most of the way home, and Bobbie was grateful not to have to speak.

She jumped from the buggy as soon as it stopped at the house and threw a thank you over her shoulder.

"Bobbie?"

Jace's voice stopped her. She didn't turn around when he came up behind her because she couldn't bring herself to look at his face.

"Are you all right? Did something happen at the sheriff's office after I left? You were awfully quiet on the way home."

"I'm . . . just tired."

He placed a light touch on her shoulder. "Go get some rest," he whispered.

Bobbie nodded and entered the house without looking back. She kicked off her shoes and fell onto the bed. The tears she'd managed to hold in check now made paths down her cheeks.

Help me, Lord. Ease this pain in my heart. She crumpled the paper to her chest. *Please, Lord, let there be a listing of a ranch for sale. I can't stay here. I can't watch Jace with another woman.*

These tears! They came so easily of late. Bobbie turned to her pillow and let the clean, crisp smell of the sheets soothe her. Maybe she'd rest a bit before tackling the sale ads. Her lids grew heavy.

The sound of laughter yanked Bobbie from her slumber. The moon cast an eerie glow in her room. She reached to light the lantern. As she sat up, a blanket fell from her shoulders. The laughter and happy chatter continued outside her door, but Bobbie wasn't in the mood to join them. She changed into her working clothes and set about removing the tangles from her hair. A tap sounded on her door, and Bobbie turned as it opened.

"Bobbie, you're awake," Annie said as she entered. "There's someone here I'd like you to meet. Will you come out and join us for supper?"

Bobbie followed Annie into the kitchen and hoped the smile pasted on her face didn't look as fake as it felt. Her feet came to a halt and refused to move when she saw the woman seated next to Jace at the table — the same one Jace had held in his arms at the livery.

The woman's hand laid possessive claim to Jace's arm as she leaned toward him. The desire to tear the woman's hair out washed over her.

Annie took Bobbie by the arm and led her further into the kitchen. "Bobbie, I'd like you to meet a long-time friend of ours, Kim Harbough. We grew up together. She's like a sister to Jace and me."

Bobbie forced the smile back on her face as she greeted the woman. Why did the name sound familiar? Her mind clung to the word *sister,* and she almost laughed. Kim's manner toward Jace didn't appear sisterly.

"Hi, Bobbie." Kim approached and gave her a hug. "Annie and Jace have been telling me all about you. I'm delighted to meet someone so important to this family."

Bobbie felt her mouth hanging open and

clamped it shut. "Thank you," she managed to say.

Kim gave her another quick hug before returning to her chair. Annie stepped in front of Bobbie.

"Are you feeling all right, Bobbie? Do you need to go back and get more rest? I know today was hard on you."

Bobbie almost laughed. *If you only knew.* "I'll be fine. I'll get a bite to eat and then go back to bed."

"Great. Have a seat, and we'll get started."

Bobbie hadn't noticed the rest of Annie's family sitting around the table. She now smiled at each of them before bowing her head while Pete blessed the meal. She latched onto something Pete said and mulled it over while the food was passed.

"Let Kim's short stay with us be filled with fun and laughter while we renew our friend-ship."

Short stay? That sounded promising. *What am I thinking?* If he could be so fickle as to turn his feelings on and off at will with two different women, then he wasn't to be trusted.

"Bobbie?" Jace gave her quizzical look.

"Yes?"

"You didn't answer Kim's question."

"I'm sorry. Could you repeat it for me?"

"What's your favorite part of ranching?" Kim said.

"Oh, the horses. I find them very intelligent, and once they're trained, they seem to want nothing more than to please their owner."

Jace snorted. "She's talking about her own horse, of course. They're not all like that. Mack and Bobbie are so close, I think they can read each other's minds."

Bobbie stared Jace in the eyes. "I know I can trust him. He has never hurt me or let me down in any way."

Jace's gaze didn't flinch from hers. He tilted his head and lifted an eyebrow.

"So," Bobbie said, "you all grew up together." She looked at Kim. "Were you neighbors?"

"No. My parents loved to travel and hardly ever stayed home." Kim made a face. "They thought that would be bad for me, for my education, so they left me with my aunt and uncle, Frank and Dorothy Ashton. I'm sure you've met them. They run the mercantile."

Bobbie nodded, the name finally falling into place. This was the Kim that Cade Ramsey loved. Apparently, Kim's interest had changed targets.

"Well, Mrs. Kincaid was nice enough to

invite me to stay with them during the summers. I enjoyed getting out of town for a while." Kim reached over and touched Annie's arm. "Not to mention spending so much time with my best friend. We used to stay up late some nights telling each other our hopes and dreams."

"And giggling until Mom hollered for you to be quiet and go to sleep," Jace said.

"That too." An impish look came over her face. "I remember when Annie met Pete. Oh, the long hours of dreaming we did then."

"Now, Kim," Annie said, "some conversations were meant to stay secret."

Pete's fork clattered against his plate. "I think maybe I should hear some of what you said about me."

Kim opened her mouth to speak. Annie cut her off. "Well, if we're going to reveal secrets, I could mention a few nights spent mooning over another certain young man." All eyes went to Kim, who blushed a pretty pink as she dropped her gaze.

"All right, Annie," she said. "You win."

What little appetite Bobbie had disappeared. She slid her chair back and stood.

"If you'll excuse me, I think I need a little more rest. It was nice meeting you, Kim. I hope you enjoy your stay."

Bobbie retreated to the safety of her room. She thought she'd have to ask forgiveness later for her abrupt departure, but it would have to wait until her frame of mind improved. She plopped on her bed and snatched up the newspaper.

Jace stared at Bobbie's closed door for several long moments. What happened between the questioning at the sheriff's office and the ride home? Bobbie went from a person clinging to him and looking to him for comfort to being withdrawn and prickly. Kim's presence couldn't be the cause. Bobbie started acting funny before the two women met. Much as he wanted to confront her about it, he'd have to wait. He pulled his attention back to the conversation between Annie and Kim, something he found himself having to do many times over the course of the night.

He woke the next morning with the intent to find a moment alone with Bobbie. Did she remember something about her attacker? Was it something Cassie said? *Women!* He'd never figure them out.

Annie and Kim bustled around the kitchen making breakfast. Bobbie wasn't there. Jace peeked into her room and found it empty. Had she gone off riding again? If so, he knew where to find her. Then he'd wring her neck for going off alone.

Annie turned and smiled. "Good morning, Jace. Bobbie wanted me to tell you that she and Sonny went after that cat again. Sonny thought he saw some tracks along the creek."

Jealousy fought with alarm at the thought of Bobbie and Sonny together. "How long ago did they leave?"

Annie glanced at the clock. "About half an hour ago, I guess."

He turned to leave.

"You're not staying for breakfast? Kim's leaving for town this morning, and we won't get to see her again until Sunday. She might be leaving shortly after that."

"I guess I've got a few minutes."

He pulled out a chair and told himself to be patient. It didn't work. Being polite and attentive took every bit of his effort. When Kim finally said her good-byes, he blew a sigh of relief.

Dew pointed the way Sonny and Bobbie had headed. Jace took off at a gallop after them. They had an hour head start, and he guessed it would take him at least half an hour to find them.

The crack of a rifle echoed back to him from the east ridge. He reined to a stop and listened for another shot. It never came. Heart pounding, Jace urged his horse back into a gallop, praying for Bobbie's safety. He found her and Sonny squatting down where a mountain ravine ran into the creek.

Sonny turned and waved him over. "Jace, you've got to see this. Bobbie hit that mountain lion right in the heart."

Relief rolled through him with such force, he felt weak. After a quick glance at him, Bobbie turned back and continued examining the cat, exhibiting no more warmth than she had last night. The woman drove him to distraction.

Jace squatted next to her. "That's a big cat." She didn't say a word. "Nice shot."

"Yeah, I'm good for some things," Bobbie said.

Jace studied the woman he loved before he stood. "Good work, you two. I guess we won't have to worry about this critter killing any more cattle. Now we only have a bigger one to catch."

Sonny grinned and shook his head.

"Why don't you head back, Sonny. I'm taking Bobbie with me for a while. We won't be long."

Sonny looped his thumbs in his belt. "Need help with anything, Jace?"

"No thanks. I think I can handle this job."

Sonny hunched his shoulders and shoved his fists deep into the pockets of his denims.

Jace winked. "Thanks for all your help."

"You bet."

Bobbie headed for her horse as soon as Sonny left. She shoved her rifle in its sheath and tied it down. "What's the job?"

Jace followed close behind. "It has nothing to do with ranching." His hand closed around hers. "What's wrong, Bobbie? You've been acting cool and withdrawn since our meeting with Morgan. What happened?"

Bobbie spun away from him, but he took her by the arms and turned her back.

"Talk to me, Bobbie."

"There's nothing to talk about, Jace."

"Everything about you is important to me."

Bobbie's lips thinned into a straight line, and her chin jutted forward. Jace held her in silence, waiting for her to speak her mind.

"How long is Kim staying?"

Confusion jumbled his thoughts. "I don't know. It depends."

Bobbie snorted a laugh. "On what?"

Jace wanted to shake her for changing the subject. "On what kind of response she gets from Cade. Why does this matter?"

"Cade?"

Jace's grip loosened. "Yes, Cade. If she

339

gets the reaction she's hoping for, she might stay a little longer, maybe indefinitely."

Bobbie looked away, tucked her hands in her pockets, and kicked at the soil with her boot.

"I told you about the two of them in school," Jace said. "Did you think she was here for me?"

Bobbie's gaze dropped to her feet as she shrugged. He put his fingers under her chin and lifted until their eyes met.

"Would it have bothered you if she was?" he asked in a whisper. She didn't answer. "Is that what all this has been about?"

She stepped back, and he had to release her.

"I saw the way you held her in the livery. What else was I supposed to think?"

"You could have asked me about it instead of jumping to conclusions. Granted, I made the same mistake about you not all that long ago when I thought you were a bank robber." He took her by the arms again. "But I thought we'd both learned from that."

Bobbie shrugged. Jace smiled down at her. He ran a finger along her jaw line. "Were you jealous?" She tried to look away but he cupped her face in his hands. "Tell me, Bobbie," he whispered. "Were you jealous?"

"I . . . ah . . ." Her tongue darted out to

wet her lips. "Maybe."

Jace traced her lips with his thumb. When they parted, he leaned down. "Bobbie," he whispered.

Rifle shots echoed across the plain for the second time that day. Jace lifted his head and looked into Bobbie's eyes before turning toward the sound. In seconds, they were both in their saddles, crossing the creek and racing across the wide, open flat.

Twenty-Seven

Jace and Bobbie rushed toward the source of the gunfire. Cattle scattered every direction. Jace reined in his horse to avoid hitting a calf. Several more bawled as they scrambled around in search of their mothers. Further west, back toward the river, more shots rang out.

Jace heeled his horse back into a gallop. Bobbie followed at a slower pace, looking as though she wanted to stop and help the youngsters. He slowed to let her catch up.

When Jace saw Bobbie jump from her saddle to check a limping calf, he stopped and turned. The calf managed to avoid her and ran to its angry mother. Jace prepared to run interference if the cow decided to do more than shield her baby. Bobbie looked up at him, her eyes stricken.

Another blast sounded in the distance. Jace spun his horse around.

"Let's go, Bobbie." He took off at a gallop.

Bobbie caught up to him. Tears stained her cheeks. She met his gaze, and he saw the determination in her eyes. She wanted these men as bad as he did.

He raced toward another mound in the distance. A horse with no rider galloped away. Dread filled Jace as they drew nearer and saw Sonny on the ground, the grass around him crimson. Jace reined to a stop, jumped to the ground, and knelt beside him.

"Sonny?" Jace looked Sonny over. Blood ran the length of his leg from thigh to ankle. "You've been shot?"

Sonny nodded. "The bullet went right through my leg." He looked up at Jace. "I heard a shot and followed the sound. A man on horseback came hightailing it over that ridge straight toward Lookout Peak. I went after him, but he kept shootin' to get the cattle stampedin' as he went by. I never saw anythin' like it. He didn't start shootin' at me till I got close."

"Do you know where he went?"

Sonny jerked a thumb toward the northwest. "Headed into the mountain."

Jace climbed into his saddle, and Bobbie moved to do the same.

"Stay here, Bobbie."

"But Jace —"

He looked her in the eyes. "Stay here."

He spun his horse around and raced toward the mountain. Hoofprints dotted a dry ravine bed. Jace followed them, determined to bring the man's game to an end.

He came to a steep incline. The hoofprints he'd been following no longer showed, but the last he saw, they were still headed in this direction. He nudged his horse on, and they continued up the mountain.

A bullet whizzed past his ear and ricocheted off the rock behind him. He reined his horse behind a boulder. No other shots followed. Resigned he'd never catch the guy on his own, Jace turned back. Besides, Sonny needed a doctor. Wasting time in the mountain wouldn't help at all.

Bobbie tied her kerchief around Sonny's leg just above the wound and pressed her hand against the opening to stanch the flow. Hearing more gunfire, she kept up a steady prayer for Jace's protection.

She didn't know how long they waited, but she was thankful to hear galloping horses headed their way. Bobbie glanced toward the ranch. Dew and David approached, Sonny's horse in tow. She looked toward the mountain and spotted Jace returning. They arrived about the same time.

Jace jumped down and examined Sonny's wound. "How're you doing, Sonny?"

"I'm all right. Got a right nice nurse, here." He grinned and winked at her.

Jace met Bobbie's gaze and mouthed, "Thanks."

"You heard the gunfire?" Jace asked Dew.

His foreman nodded. "Sounded distant, but we came at a run."

Jace looked around. "Where's Adam?"

"Didn't see him. Haven't seen him all morning."

Jace stared at Dew before he looked back at the mountain, then back at Dew.

"Aw, now, Jace," Dew said.

"Where was Adam the last time this happened?"

"I don't know. But Jace, it couldn't be him."

"Why not?"

Dew waved his hand. "He's just a kid. Besides, he was on the drive with us. He'd have no part in something like this."

"We thought the same thing about Coop." Jace laid a hand on Dew's shoulder. "Look, I've got to get Sonny to the doctor. I'd like you to start rounding up the rest of the cattle. Drive them up close to the ranch site.

I've got to save what precious few I have left." He glanced toward the mountain. "That man's getting mighty brave to try stealing them in broad daylight."

"It's near time for fall roundup anyway," Dew said.

Jace helped Sonny onto his horse before climbing onto his saddle. "Let's go, Bobbie."

Bobbie had stood by, silent as she listened to Jace, but now she shook her head. "I'm going to help Dew."

"I'm in no mood for arguments, Bobbie."

"You need my help, Jace, and I'll be more help here than riding into town with you." He wasn't convinced and showed it by the skeptical tilt of his eyebrow. "I'll stay next to Dew or David. I won't go off on my own. I promise."

"All right. Just be careful."

Dew moved to her side. "She'll be fine."

Another horse approached, and they all turned. Adam arrived with his horse in a lather. Jace dismounted, pulled Adam from his saddle, and held him by his shirtfront.

"Where've you been?"

"I got here as quick as I could."

"That didn't answer my question. Dew said you haven't been around all morning. Now Sonny's hurt and I've got cattle scattered everywhere."

Adam's eyes grew large. "It wasn't me, Jace. I swear."

"Where were you?" Jace gave him a shake.

"All right." He raised his hands. A fine sweat covered his top lip and brow. "I snuck off and spent the night with a . . . a woman."

Jace snorted.

"I swear, Jace."

"Who?"

"One of them saloon girls." Adam dropped his hands and his chin fell to his chest. He wouldn't meet anyone's gaze.

Jace let go of his shirt. "She'll verify your story?"

Adam nodded.

Jace lifted his hat, ran his fingers through his hair, and clamped the hat back on.

"I need to get Sonny to town." He looked at Dew before meeting Bobbie's gaze. "I'll get back as soon as I can."

Jace didn't leave Bobbie's thoughts the entire time she spent rounding up the cattle. The number of head they gathered was pitifully low. How would Jace make ends meet through the winter? They still had the remainder of the ranch to search, but she didn't hold out much hope for what they'd find.

They needed help, but no one came

around looking for work. Why? Ranch hands usually came and went all the time, yet none came to the Double K. Did the men stay away because they heard about the trouble, or was it possible someone threatened them if they tried to hire on? Whatever the reason, she worked all the harder trying to make up the difference.

When Jace returned, Bobbie moved next to him as they continued driving the cattle toward the ranch. "Sonny okay?"

Jace nodded. "I left him in town with Doc. He'll probably come home tomorrow. Doc said it was a clean wound."

She reached out and touched his arm. "How about you, Jace? How are you doing?"

He took her hand in his and gave it a brief squeeze before letting go. "I don't know what's going on, Bobbie. I don't understand why this is happening." He shook his head. "At this rate, I'll be out of business by winter. Worse than that, my ranch hands might get killed." He blew out a long, slow breath. "Maybe I should just quit. End this before anyone else gets hurt."

"Then you'll be playing right into this guy's hands, doing just what he wants. Don't let him win, Jace. You love ranching. You're good at it. Don't let him take it away from you."

Jace looked into her eyes. He reached out and cupped her cheek. "I love you, Bobbie."

Bobbie smiled, then dropped her gaze, unable to meet the intensity of his.

"Jace!" Dew called out. "Do you want some of these cattle corralled?"

Bobbie looked back up at Jace. He winked before moving off to meet with his foreman. Bobbie stared at his wide shoulders and recalled the strength she felt there. Her gaze traveled up. It was long past time for another haircut.

TWENTY-EIGHT

The next few days were spent rounding up all the cattle and horses. Every corner, thicket, and crevice was checked for any animal trying to hide. Bobbie fell into bed each night exhausted from the strain. The work was strenuous, but also the fact that each new area posed a potential threat, a possible bullet heading toward them, caused additional stress.

Jace worried about her. Bobbie saw it in the way his gaze followed her every move. His orders were short and specific. Stay near the ranch. Keep someone with you at all times. Sort through and work with the horses.

She shook her head at the last as she headed back to the corral. The horses could be sorted another time. But Jace didn't need any more to worry about, so she didn't give him a fight. Besides, Bobbie enjoyed working with horses. She found them much more rewarding than herding cattle.

Bobbie led some of the horses into the corral nearest the barn and turned them loose. She latched the gate and headed to the farthest pen to get the stallion. She needed the enclosure for the next bunch of mares.

Her heart stopped when she found the gate open and the black nowhere to be found. Jace was relying on the stallion to help him rebuild his herd and bank account. She'd heard him say as much the night before.

Bobbie checked for tracks. The skid marks in the dirt told Bobbie the stallion had made a sharp turn to the west after leaving the corral — toward the mountains. *Of course. The most difficult place to find him. Why am I not surprised?*

She grabbed Mack's reins and jumped onto the saddle. "Come on, Mack. We've got work to do."

They raced across the flat. Bobbie stopped from time to time, checking for tracks. Most were deep, telling her the stallion fled at a high rate of speed. The hoofprints disappeared as soon as she started into the mountains. The stallion seemed to be going in a straight line so she continued in the same direction.

Nearly an hour later, Bobbie reached an area she'd never been to before. Was she still on Kincaid property? The ground leveled off and the shrubs and bushes grew thicker. She skirted them, certain the stallion wouldn't have run through the copse of trees. She scanned the distance but saw nothing. The unfamiliar territory made her jittery, but she refused to turn back. Not yet.

Mack snorted and tossed his head. The stallion must be nearby for Mack to act so skittish. The farther they moved forward, the more her horse acted up. Bobbie reined him in and dismounted.

"All right, Mack. I won't make you go any farther." She tied him to a branch and patted his neck. "Good job, boy."

She grabbed her lariat and continued walking, taking great pains not to make any noise. The trees thinned, showing her a wide flat of land. There, in the middle of the plain, stood the stallion.

"You rascal."

He couldn't have chosen a worse place to graze. Under normal circumstances, she would have tried walking right up to him. Now that he'd had a taste of freedom, he was sure to be wary, running off at the slightest reason. She checked the direction of the wind. *Perfect.* If she stayed close to the edge of the trees, she could move to his backside and try to sneak up from behind.

She bent at the waist and scooted along the tree line. The stallion looked up from his grazing. Bobbie froze mid-step and stood motionless until he went back to munching on grass. Then she dashed the last bit of distance before squatting down. She'd need to catch her breath before going after him.

The stallion looked as if he belonged in this place. His tail swished at the flies in a peaceful rhythm, and it seemed a shame to remove him. But it had to be done.

Bobbie stood and loosened her lariat, praying she would be able to rope him without any difficulty. She wanted to get home. This whole situation and unfamiliar area had her nerves stretched tight. She took a deep breath, squared her shoulders, and started out toward the stallion.

"That's my horse you're aiming to steal."

Bobbie froze. Her skin prickled from her scalp to her toes.

"You know we hang horse thieves in these parts."

Bobbie turned with slow and steady movements. She saw the man and the lariat fell from her grasp. "Grant!"

"So you remember me. I'm glad."

Bobbie's throat constricted as a band tightened around her chest. "I thought you went to Texas."

He snorted. "Nope."

A rifle lay propped across his arms as he leaned against a tree, his hat tipped back on his head and a piece of grass hanging from his lips. She'd never be able to reach her pistol before he shot her.

"You've sure caused me a lot of trouble, Miss McIntyre." He motioned toward her waist. "I want that sidearm."

A tremor moved through Bobbie's weakened legs. Could any good come from someone whose eyes held such a look of evil?

"Now!"

She flinched at the sharp command. He took a step toward her, and she reached for the pistol.

"Slow and easy. Use your left hand. I've seen you shoot, remember?"

She stared at him as she pulled out the gun.

"Toss it at my feet."

She obeyed.

"Now, turn around."

Bobbie eyed the piece of rope in his hand.

"Why did you try to take me at the celebration?"

Grant laughed. "All in good time. Now, turn around."

When Bobbie complied, he slipped a loop around her wrist and pulled it tight.

"Give me your other hand. Don't fight me if you don't want to get hurt."

Another shudder traveled through her. He grabbed her arm and tied her hands behind her back. He yanked on the rope. Pain radiated through her wrists. He pulled her backward, knocked her to the ground, and tied her to a tree.

He hunkered down in front of her and grinned. "If you'll excuse me, I gotta retrieve my horse."

Bobbie's anger flared at his cocky attitude. She resisted the urge to give him a kick and send him rolling in the dirt.

When he turned and walked away, Bobbie struggled to get loose. The rope bit into her flesh with each twist and tug. The pain grew too great for her to continue.

Grant bent down and removed the hobbles from the stallion. He'd put the horse out there as a lure. The fact that it had worked tore at her insides.

He returned and tied the stallion near her. "Let's see. I believe your horse is tied on the other side of these trees." He winked. "Don't get up. I'll get him for you."

Grant's laughter drifted back to her, and Bobbie wanted to scream. He returned with his horse and Mack, then squatted next to her and untied the rope.

Grant clicked his tongue. "You should have known better, Bobbie. You can't get away from me again. Now, your pretty wrists are all red and raw. Such a shame."

He lifted her from the ground and set her on Mack. Bobbie glanced around and toyed with the idea of spurring Mack into a gallop. How far would she get?

Grant spat in the dirt. "Don't even think about it."

He took the reins, climbed onto his saddle, and leaned to untie the stallion. He appeared to be enjoying the power he held over her, taking his time as he led them along the tree line.

"Where are we going?"

"My cabin. And don't be asking a lot of questions."

"Where is it?"

"Up ahead a ways." Grant glared at her. "Now, be quiet!"

"Why'd you steal Jace's horse?"

"It got you here, didn't it?" He laughed. "I knew you or Jace would come for it. If it

was you, I knew Jace would come after y
I needed to kill ya both, and you fell rignt
into my plans."

"Why do you need to kill me?"

"Wouldn't have to if you'd kept your nose
out of our business."

"So it *is* you that worked with Will and
Coop."

"Nope. They worked for me."

Bobbie mulled that over. How had Coop
managed to fall in with such a wicked man?
"Why do you need to kill Jace?"

"I'll explain the rest when I'm good and
ready. Now just shut up."

The man was maddening — and scary.
He led them through another set of trees.
Up ahead, a shack sat framed by wild shrub-
bery. They stopped in front of it. He pulled
her from the saddle and steadied her when
she almost fell. He pulled her into the shack
and shoved her against the wall.

"Don't move."

A match flared, and the flickering light allowed her to catch a glimpse of this man's
home. She shuddered. Filth filled every
corner, and cobwebs draped the windows.
He lit a lantern and turned the flame high.
The furnishings were meager with only a
cookstove, cot, and a small table with two
chairs. A pole in the center of the room

seemed to sprout from the floor and ran all the way to the roof. Was that all that kept the roof from falling in on them?

Grant grabbed her arm, led her to the pole, and shoved her to the floor. He untied her wrists, only to wrap her arms around the pole before retying her. At least this time, her arms were in front of her, though it didn't give her anything to lean against.

At first Bobbie thought she sat on a dirt floor, but when she scuffed at it with her boot, she found wood that hadn't been swept in a long time. She imagined all the critters that could be crawling through the grime and shuddered at the thought of them crawling on her.

Grant lit the stove. At first Bobbie thought that odd. The smoke would lead Jace right to them. Then she realized that's what Grant wanted. He'd already admitted he wanted to kill them both.

He opened the door. "I'm going out to unsaddle the horses. Try not to miss me." The door slammed shut.

She tested the ropes to see if she could get free. If this man didn't kill her, Jace would for disobeying his request not to leave the ranch.

Jace crossed the bridge and rode up toward

the barn. How good it felt to be home. They'd finished checking the property, which meant no more long days in the saddle. The head count of his cattle was better than he expected, but it still fell short of what he figured he would need.

He dismounted and looked around for Bobbie. When he didn't see her, he entered the barn. He didn't find her there either. Something didn't feel right. He headed back out to find Beans.

"Jace!"

He turned to see Sonny hobbling toward him. "Have you seen Bobbie?" The look on Sonny's face didn't ease his worry.

"The stallion's gone. I think she went after it."

"What?"

"I hollered at her to stop. I guess she didn't hear me."

"Which way did she go?"

"Into the mountains."

Jace ran for his horse and climbed into the saddle. *The mountains!* He stared down at Sonny, who turned and pointed.

"Straight across the flat." Sonny looked back up at him. "Take someone with ya, Jace. It's too dangerous out there."

Jace shook his head. "Bobbie's gone and you're laid up. I need some men here to watch the ranch. Send David into town for the sheriff. When they get here, tell Morgan to follow me." He spun his horse around. "But I'm not waiting. Bobbie may need me."

He heeled his horse into a gallop. There was so much territory to cover, and dark would fall before long. He managed to spot some tracks and knew he was still headed in the right direction. Jace sent a steady stream of prayers heavenward, begging God to watch over Bobbie and that he would find her unharmed.

TWENTY-NINE

Uncontrollable shivers woke Bobbie. Her thin coat did little to ward off the chill of the night air. The shack didn't help much, either. Moonlight filtered through the rafters, and broken panes lined the windows. She glanced at the stove giving off very little heat as it coughed and smoldered out thick black smoke. Bobbie struggled to rub her face with her arm. Dirt from the floor clung to her cheek. She couldn't believe she'd fallen asleep.

The lantern still glowed from its perch on the table. Grant Wilcox stood at one of the two windows. He looked at her when she stirred, but turned back to his vigil.

"So, why do you want to kill Jace?"

"You'll learn everything when he gets here. Besides, your nosiness got you into trouble in the first place. Maybe you better shut up before you find yourself worse off."

Bobbie didn't know how it could get

much worse. Her stomach rumbled. She tried to ignore it. "What time is it?"

"The sun will be up soon."

Bits of grit scraped against her teeth. "Can I have some water, Grant?"

"I ain't leaving this spot."

Bobbie stared at Grant's back. He had to want Jace pretty bad to sit perched at a window all night. The fight they'd had the day Jace fired him wouldn't have been enough to cause this kind of wrath. What could have happened between the two of them? She squirmed to find a position to get the blood flowing back into her aching muscles.

"Uh . . . I could really use the privy right now."

Grant growled and approached her. "I don't have a privy. You'll have to use that pot over there." He motioned to a corner with his head as he untied her. He stood and pointed his pistol at her. "Hurry up about it."

Bobbie looked from him to the pot and back again. *He intends to watch me?* "Uh . . ."

"Oh, for pity's sake." He strode to the cot and flipped it on its side. "Squat back there. It's the best you get."

She wasted no time arguing. When she

finished her business, he motioned her back to the pole and tied her to it again. With a tiny bit of wriggling, she managed to position her feet under her — far more comfortable than the hard wooden floor. She said another prayer for Jace's safety.

Outside, the sky grew brighter. Odd that it should dawn another day just like any other. Why had God allowed this to happen? She tried to remember some of the verses she and Annie had memorized together. They weren't coming to her. One said something about God's ways being higher. Was that right?

She had asked Annie how she could trust a God who allowed bad things to happen to His children. Annie grabbed her Bible and showed her a couple verses. Annie did that often. The Bible seemed to have an answer for every one of her questions. Not only did that amaze her, it gave a feeling of peace and security. It was as though God knew all man's questions before they asked and put the answers in His Word.

How did those trust verses go again? She smiled as it came to her. *Trust in the Lord with all thine heart.* She couldn't remember all the middle part, but it ended with something about God directing her path. And He'd sure done that for her. Pastor

Robbins had said something about trouble making some people bitter and others better. She put herself in the latter category since she'd come so far in her battle with distrust. *Okay, Lord. I'm trusting You. Whatever happens, I know Your hand is in it.*

"What're you grinnin' at?"

Bobbie looked at Grant. "I'm smiling because God is so good. Even in tough times, we can feel peace and joy in the knowledge that He loves us."

Grant's nose wrinkled in a sneer. "Don't start preaching to me. I've had a belly full of those lies." He patted the barrel of his rifle. "This is my peacemaker."

The horses snorted, and one of them whinnied. Grant jumped off his chair, causing it to topple, and peered out the window.

"I'm smarter than you, Jace Kincaid," he whispered.

He raised his rifle and aimed it out the window.

Jace spotted the thin trail of smoke as soon as the sun fought off the last bit of gloom. He had searched for Bobbie until it was too dark to see. After spending the night staring at the moon and stars, praying hard, he climbed back onto the saddle as soon as he could see the promise of daylight.

He headed for the smoke. It may or may not lead him to Bobbie, but he had to check it out. Maybe he'd find someone who had seen her. He moved around and through many trees and bushes that slowed him down. Jace jerked the reins back when the smoke led him to a small shack. He couldn't recall it being on his property.

A bullet zipped past him, too far off the mark to be a real threat. He heard it tear through the leaves before it ended with a smack. Laughter followed the sound of the gunshot. He'd heard that same laugh before, and he was tired of being used as a target.

"Come on out, Jace."

Where have I heard that voice before?

"Don't do it!" Bobbie's faint voice reached his ears. "Don't come in here, Jace. He wants to kill you."

"Shut up!" Jace heard the man shout at her, followed by the muffled sound of footsteps.

"It's G—"

Then, sudden silence.

Jace ran toward the shack. He heard the rifle being cocked. He dove for the porch and landed against the shack with a thud. The wood next to him ripped open with the sound of another gunshot. He rolled away.

"I don't know what your plan is, Jace, but

if you want to see this little lady alive, I suggest you give up and come out where I can
see you."

Jace stalled long enough to catch his
breath. "Is that you, Grant?"

Laughter echoed across the small glade.
"Come on out, Jace. You can't win."

Jace heard a pistol being cocked again.

"I'm aiming right at her head, Jace. Show
yourself or she's dead."

Jace slowly stood and moved toward the
window.

"Good choice. Now, open the door."

Jace obeyed. His heart sank to find Bobbie
tied to a post. A rag hung out of her mouth.
Dirt and grime covered her face and clothes.
Grant stood with feet planted wide apart,
both his rifle and a pistol trained on him.
Jace ignored him and moved toward Bobbie.

"Hold it, Jace."

"I just want to take the gag from her
mouth."

"Oh, I don't know. I kinda like the quiet."

Jace sent him a look.

"Go ahead, but not until you put your gun
on the table."

Jace did as told and knelt next to Bobbie.
He pulled a small knife from his boot with
one hand and laid it behind the pole as he
pulled the gag from her mouth with his

other hand.

"Are you all right?"

She nodded as tears pooled in her eyes. "I'm sorry, Jace."

"Shh. It's all right. I'm going to get us out of this." He glanced down at the knife, then back to her eyes.

"Get up, Jace," Grant said.

Jace stood and faced his former hired hand. "What's this all about, Wilcox? Bobbie's not a part of this. You got me. Let her go."

"He's the other bank robber, Jace. He's the one at the celebration." Bobbie's voice sounded tired.

Jace's gaze never wavered from Grant. "You and Coop got together while you worked for me?"

Grant grinned. "It was easy. He still held a bit of a grudge because you didn't make him foreman. I used that against you. And him." He pointed toward a chair with the pistol. "Have a seat."

Jace eyed his gun lying on the table.

"Toss your pistol out the door first. Slow and easy, Jace. Don't make me shoot you . . . yet. Move!"

Jace pitched his pistol out the door and sat on the chair nearest Bobbie. "Now what?"

Grant propped his rifle against the wall. He kept the pistol aimed at Jace's chest and pulled a piece of paper out of his pocket.

"Sign this." He slapped the paper down on the table.

Jace scanned the words. "I can't do that, Grant."

"You always gotta do things the hard way, don't ya, Jace."

"It beats doing things the easy way — like stealing."

Grant pulled his fist back. Jace braced for the blow. It didn't come. Instead, a smirk pulled at the corner of Grant's mouth as the man stepped back and leaned on the door frame.

Grant tapped the barrel of his gun against his chest. "I can't steal something that's already mine. I tried to be nice and just run you off my ranch by taking the cattle, but you wouldn't go."

Jace jumped from his chair, and Grant cocked the pistol and motioned for him to sit. "Let's see. How many head were rustled?" Grant tapped his chin. "Hmm. More than you have left, isn't it? Coop was a big help. He kept me informed as to where you were and what you were doing. He even helped me rob the banks. It's amazing what the man would do for me when I promised

I'd make him foreman." He shook his head. "He actually believed I'd let someone as weak-minded as him have that job."

"Why? Why did you do this?"

"I told you. I want you off my ranch."

"What makes you think this is your ranch?"

The smile disappeared from Grant's face. "I don't *think* it. I *know* it. Couldn't you understand the brands I left on the cows? The ranch will no longer be called the Double K. It's changin' hands . . . to the Double Cross. Pretty clever, don't you think? Considering what your dad did and all." He moved toward the table. "Now, sign that deed and we'll be done."

"What do you mean, what my dad did?"

"Your dad's a thief. My grandfather owned this place before your dad swindled him out of it — out of my inheritance. Now, I want it back."

"Your grandfather?" Jace shook his head. "My dad bought this place from your grandfather. It was all legal."

Grant snorted. "I don't believe that for a minute. My mom told me Granddad was old, senile, half out of his mind when he died."

"My dad took care of him, Grant. He told me Mr. Hillyer and your mom had a fight

369

and she left. She never contacted him again. He loved my dad like a son. That's why Dad got the land."

Grant shook his head. "We have no doubt your dad tricked him in some way to get this place." He rested his hands and the pistol on the table and leaned toward Jace. "But I made sure your dad paid."

The words hit Jace like a fist to the stomach. "You killed them. It was you!"

Grant smirked. Jace lunged for the man's throat, and Grant smashed him in the face with the butt of the pistol. Jace fell to the floor. Grant leaned over him, and Jace kicked his legs out from under him. Grant hit the floor hard, and his pistol skittered through the dirt and stopped next to an overturned cot.

Jace rolled, stood, and lunged at Grant again. The two tumbled against the table, smashing it to pieces. Jace fell on top of Grant. He swung his fists with a vengeance, and Grant grunted as each blow landed. Grant shoved his fist into Jace's stomach and pushed him off. He bolted for the door, and Jace ran after him. The two rolled in the dirt and took turns landing punches.

Jace had to move away when Grant threw dirt in his eyes. He rubbed at them until he could see again. When he looked up, Grant stood in front of him with a knife in his hand and a grin on his face.

"I'm going to kill you, Jace. This place is rightfully mine. But I knew the only way to get it back was to kill your parents and get you out of the way. Once I kill Bobbie, all the evidence against me will be gone."

Grant charged toward Jace. He sliced the blade through the air over and over. Jace jumped back with each attempt.

"You won't get away with this, Wilcox. People are looking for us. They won't stop until they find us."

Grant lunged toward him. Jace jumped back, batted Grant's hand out of the way, and grabbed him around the neck. The two struggled in a death grip until Grant slammed his elbow into Jace's ribs. Jace lost his grip and gasped for breath. Grant spun around, the knife pointed toward Jace's chest.

"Time to die, Jace." An evil grin stretched across his face. "Then I'll have me a little fun with your woman before I kill her."

Grant slammed against Jace, and they fell to the ground together. Jace grabbed Grant's wrist and held the knife away from him while he smashed his fist into Grant's face. He received several blows to the face and neck as the blade inched closer.

Thoughts of Bobbie inside the shack rolled through Jace's mind.

God help me!

THIRTY

Bobbie sawed harder on the rope with the knife Jace placed near the pole. Her sore wrists bled. The knife's awkward position slowed her progress. She spent more time picking it up or readjusting her grip than cutting.

She bore down on the blade with all the strength she had left. The rope finally snapped and fell away. Bobbie scrambled to the cot, grabbed Grant's gun, and ran for the door.

Grant sat on top of Jace, pushing the blade toward his chest. Bobbie pulled the hammer back on the pistol and aimed. She lifted the barrel when the two men rolled over and over. They scrambled to their feet, gasping for breath. Grant still had the knife in his hand. She aimed at him again.

"Hold it, Grant."

Jace looked at her. Grant lunged at Jace. Bobbie pulled the trigger and hit Grant in the right shoulder, knocking him back two steps. He looked down at his shoulder, then up at her. Rage contorted his face. He bellowed and again charged at Jace. His steps faltered and he fell against Jace. The two men toppled to the ground. Red spread across Grant's shoulder and back. He didn't move.

Bobbie ran to Jace's side. They worked together and pushed Grant off to the side. Jace struggled to his feet. He pulled her into his arms and held her. He pressed his lips against her hair.

"Are you all right?"

She nodded. "I'm ready to go home."

He gave a weak laugh. "Me too."

They headed toward the shack but Jace stumbled. After a few more steps, he dropped to his knees.

"Jace?" Bobbie knelt next to him. "What's wrong?"

He held his hands over his stomach and looked up at her. She pulled his coat back. Blood oozed from a slit in his shirt.

"You've been stabbed?" She looked at his face. He was so pale. "Lie down, Jace."

He fell into her arms as she helped him to the ground. She pulled the kerchief from her neck and pressed it against his side. He gasped, and his face gleamed with sweat.

He was losing blood too fast. Panic clawed at her. She pushed it away and tried to think clearly. He couldn't ride a horse. She'd need to find another way to get him home.

Jace groaned. She ran her hand over his forehead and cheek. He felt warm. She fought back her tears, then bent and kissed his forehead.

"Stay with me, Jace."

She dashed into the shack. The cot caught her eye. Bobbie kicked at the legs until they broke off, then dragged it through the doorway and placed it next to Jace. After saddling Mack and leading him to the cot, she tied ropes to the cot and then to the saddle. She knelt next to Jace.

"All right, Jace." He didn't stir. She checked his pulse, found one, and thanked God. "Hang in there. Don't you leave me." *I love you too much to lose you too.*

Tears ran down her cheeks as she grabbed him under the arms and hauled him onto the cot. She covered him with her blanket and moved to Mack's side.

"Bobbie?"

She jumped and pulled out her pistol in one smooth move.

"It's me, Bobbie. It's Sheriff Thomas." He stepped into the clearing.

"Morgan!" She wanted to cry with relief.

"Jace has been hurt. I've got to get him home."

Morgan knelt next to Jace and looked at the wound. "Hang on a minute." He went to his saddlebag and pulled out some cloth. "I want to pack that cut. Maybe it'll slow the bleeding."

Jace moaned as Morgan covered the wound.

"Who did this, Bobbie?"

"Grant Wilcox."

"Wilcox? The wrangler Jace fired?"

Bobbie nodded.

"Where is he?"

Bobbie pointed toward the trees. "Right over th—" Her hand fell to her side. "Where'd he go? He was right there, Morgan. I shot him in the shoulder. I saw the blood."

Morgan stood next to her. "It's all right, Bobbie. If he's hurt, he'll be easy to find. Right now, let's just get off this mountain."

Bobbie pulled herself onto the saddle. "Morgan, you need to look under the table in that shack. I think it might be the evidence you need for all the bank robberies. Maybe even for Jace's stolen cattle."

Momentary indecision flashed across Morgan's face.

"Go on, Morgan. Grab what you can and

then catch up."

He nodded and disappeared inside.

Seeing the stallion and Jace's horse, Bobbie dismounted, grabbed their reins, and climbed back in her saddle. Bobbie nudged Mack with her heels and headed home as fast as she dared.

Morgan caught up with her a short time later. "I don't know how much money he had stashed under the floor, Bobbie, but I got all I could see. He even took notes on how much money they stole from each bank, what he got for Jace's cattle, and how he divided up the cash." Morgan shook his head. "He just put the noose around his, Will's, and Coop's necks."

Bobbie stopped a few times to check on Jace, but she didn't waste any other time getting down the mountain. She and Morgan spent a great deal of time looking for any sign of Wilcox. They didn't want him surprising them. Bobbie prayed most of the ride home for God to keep Jace alive.

When they were close to the ranch, Bobbie fired her gun three times. Dew raced to meet them.

"Bobbie? What happened?" he said as he rode next to Jace.

"Go get the doctor, Dew. It's bad. Hurry!"

Bobbie watched him rush off, praying the

doctor would be in town. They couldn't afford any more delays. She stopped at the kitchen door of Annie's house. David and Beans waited for her. Sonny hobbled as fast as he could to catch up.

"Take him in and put him in my room," she told them.

Bobbie slid from the saddle and dashed forward to hold the door open. Her heart sank when she saw Annie. Every moment her friend had spent worrying could be seen on her face.

"Bobbie!" Annie pulled her into an embrace. "I'm so glad you're all right." Annie stepped back and looked at her. "So, where's Jace?"

David and Beans came in with him at that moment. Annie gasped and followed the men into Bobbie's room.

David and Beans stepped back to let Annie near her brother. Bobbie choked on tears hearing Annie's heart-wrenching cries. She moved into the kitchen and put some water on the stove to boil. She had a feeling the doctor would need it.

Beans moved to her side and put his arm around her. "You all right?"

Bobbie turned to him and sobbed on his shoulder. He patted her back as he held her but didn't say a word. When she calmed, he led her to a chair. She sat even though she wanted to go to Jace.

"Tell me what happened."

Morgan and the others took a seat, and she recounted the entire story.

"It's all my fault," she said at the end. "He wouldn't have gotten hurt if I hadn't run off on my own. Jace told me to stay close, but I didn't listen."

Beans reached for her hands. "Your wrists are bloody. I thought you said you was fine."

"I am."

"Well, from what I know o' that Wilcox fella, and from what all he's done to Jace, I think he'd o' kept on till he killed Jace, regardless o' what you did or didn't do. I don't think you need to go blaming yourself for this."

The other men nodded in agreement.

The doctor arrived, and Bobbie showed him to her room. He turned and stopped her from entering.

"I'm sorry, Bobbie. I'll let you know how he is as soon as I can." He closed the door in her face.

She stood there staring toward the bedroom until Beans took her by the shoulders and led her back to her seat. Bobbie heard the men talking but couldn't absorb a word they said. Her gaze stayed on the door as she counted the minutes. When it finally opened, she jumped up.

The doctor waved her back down. "He's going to be fine. The cut wasn't too deep, but he lost a good amount of blood, so it'll take a while for him to get his strength back. But knowing Jace, he'll be ordering you around again in about a week. Maybe less."

Bobbie laughed through her tears. The men grinned and patted each other on the back before Dew stood and told them it was time to get back to work. Beans didn't move as the others filed out. He took one of Bobbie's forearms in his beefy grasp.

"This little lady needs your attention, Doc." He lifted her wrist for the doctor to see, then sat with her while the doctor cleaned and bandaged her wounds.

"That oughta do it," Doc said as he stood. Morgan followed him out, and they rode off together.

Bobbie could feel Beans staring at her. She couldn't meet his gaze, though she appreciated what he'd said earlier about not blaming herself.

"Ya know, Bobbie," he said in a quiet voice. "If I woulda had a daughter, I'd a wanted her to be just like you."

Bobbie looked up, then wrapped her arms around his neck, and he enveloped her in his. Her tears made a wet spot on his shoulder.

"Thank you, Beans."

He patted her back and cleared his throat. "I . . . uh . . . gotta go cook now."

She leaned away. His eyes were red and damp. He took a step away but turned back. "Make sure you eat something. You look too thin."

She gave him another quick hug before he walked away.

"Bobbie?" Annie stood in the doorway of the bedroom. "Would you like to see him?"

Bobbie's lips trembled as she smiled and nodded.

"Would you mind sitting with him while I check on the kids?"

"Not at all."

Bobbie sat on the chair Annie had positioned beside the bed and took Jace's hand in hers. She stared at his face. She already knew every line, dip, and hollow. She had them memorized. This was the first time she'd ever seen him completely relaxed. He looked too young to have gone through so much.

His hand twitched. She looked down at it. Her hand looked petite next to his. She felt the calluses on the palm as she examined the backside. His knuckles were cut and bruised from the fight. This was the hand that caressed her with tenderness one moment and fought off her captor the next. She lifted it to her cheek as tears slid from her eyes.

"I'm so sorry." She reached up and brushed the hair from his forehead. "I love you, Jace Kincaid."

Bobbie stared at his face until her lids grew heavy. She felt someone touch her shoulders.

"Come on, Bobbie," Annie whispered. "I think it's time we get you cleaned up and put to bed."

She stood and allowed herself to be led from the room. Annie had a hot bath ready. Bobbie stepped into the tub and moaned at how wonderful it felt. What seemed only minutes later, Annie returned to rinse her hair and help her from the tub. When Bobbie finished dressing, Annie led her up the stairs and into a different bedroom. The covers were thrown back and waiting. Bobbie didn't argue as Annie ordered her to bed.

"I'm sorry, Annie."

"For what?" Annie perched on the side of the bed.

"For getting Jace hurt. It's my fault."

Annie clucked her tongue and smiled.

"Now there you go again, taking someone else's sin on your shoulders."

"I didn't stay here like Jace wanted."

Annie raised a hand to stop her flow of words. "I heard you tell the story, Bobbie. I agree with Beans. Grant intended to kill Jace, and he would have tried with or without you."

"But Annie —"

Annie shook her head. "That's the end of it, Bobbie. Jace is home and alive because of you. Thank you for that." Annie leaned down to hug her. "Now, get some sleep."

Annie left with a swish of her skirts. Bobbie was tired but couldn't let herself fall asleep yet. She'd told the Lord that she trusted Him to get them through. She had to thank Him for answering her prayers.

THIRTY-ONE

Jace greeted Cade Ramsey with a grin. With his friend here, maybe Annie would quit hovering. She'd been nursing him for the last three days, and he figured they both could use a break. Jace gestured toward the chair.

"Have a seat. I need the male companionship." He said the last as a jab at Annie as she entered the room.

She made a face. "I just came in to say hello to Cade." Her gaze swung away from Jace and pierced Cade. "You make sure he doesn't overdo."

Cade grinned at her. "Yes, ma'am."

Annie left the room, and Jace scooted up in bed, pulling the covers up over his bandage. "So what's been happening?"

"That's what I was going to ask you." Cade's smile never faded as he tossed his hat on the foot of the bed. His eyes gleamed with mischief. Jace had seen that look many times while they were growing up. He never knew what to expect when Cade wore that expression.

"What?" Jace said.

"Has she confessed her love for you yet?"

Jace laughed. "What makes you think she's in love with me?"

"We've both seen the way she looks at you." He paused, leaned back in his chair, and propped his feet on the bed. "What do you think she's waiting for?"

"Maybe she doesn't realize it yet."

Cade looked skeptical. "So what are you planning to do about that?"

"I'm not sure yet. But if Bobbie loves me, I'll wrangle it out of her some way or another."

Cade sat quiet and thoughtful for a moment, his eyes focused on some distant spot. "Do you remember back when we were both wondering if and when God would bring someone special into our lives? We said that we'd help each other be patient and wait on the timing of Lord. Now, all these years later, the woman God has for you comes riding in on a horse and changes your life."

Jace smiled at the vision.

"I wonder how my future bride will appear," Cade said.

"Probably soaking wet, looking like a drowned rat, and needing to be rescued by a big, dark-haired man with a soft heart."

Cade shook his head. "I'm not all that soft-hearted."

"Ha! You're one of the kindest and most big-hearted men I know. You see some damsel in distress and you're off at a run before anyone else has even given a thought to helping." Jace watched Cade's face show signs of surprise and consternation. "What about Kim? Did that not work out? I know she wondered if you had any interest in her."

"Interest? She's pretty enough to grab my attention, but she's changed some since she lived here. We'll have to get reacquainted."

"So, she plans to stick around for a while?"

"That's the plan. She says she has a few months before she has to make any decisions."

"Decisions about what?"

Cade shrugged. "That will be part of getting reacquainted."

The men talked a little longer before Cade said it was time to head home. He plucked his hat off the blankets and jammed it onto his head.

"The next time you see Bobbie, tell her I'm ready for one of her home-cooked meals again. I want to make sure she stays in practice. Can't have her starving you to death."

A gentle breeze stirred the curtains the next morning. A horse's whinny carried from the corral to mingle with the robins chirping outside Jace's window.

"Annie, you've made me lay here for four days. I need out. I need some fresh air."

His sister stood over him with her hands on her hips. Then she stepped over to the window, threw open the curtains, and turned back to him.

"There's your fresh air. As for getting out of bed, not until Doc says it's all right. Is that clear?" She moved back to the bed and fussed with the covers. "Besides, I think the men enjoy the freedom from having you ordering them around."

Jace saw her lips twitch and could tell she wasn't all that mad at him. He tugged her apron. "I'm sorry I'm such a bear." He lifted the apron and looked at her stomach.

"Jace!" She pulled the apron from his grasp and smoothed it back in place.

"How are you, Annie? You feeling all right?"

"I'm fine. I just have a bigger baby to take care of than I thought I would."

"What!" He reached for her, but she

jumped out of his reach. He flung a small pillow at her. She caught it.

"Well," Doctor Barnes said with a grin as he entered the room, "if you can throw a pillow like that, maybe it's time to let you out of bed."

"That's what I've been trying to tell her," Jace said.

"You're just lucky that cut wasn't any deeper or you'd be in here for a week or more."

After the examination, Doc followed Jace out to the sofa. "Spend a couple days taking it easy, Jace. After that, I don't see why you can't get back to work, as long as it's light. No heavy lifting, breaking horses, or branding cattle."

"Thanks, Doc. Make sure my sister knows that."

"I heard," Annie said behind them. "There goes all my fun of bossing you around."

"Does this mean I get my bed back?"

Bobbie's sweet voice drifted in off the porch. She looked beautiful standing there with the sun resting on her shoulders. She had popped in for a few minutes from time to time to check on him. Minutes weren't nearly enough as far as he was concerned. He wanted hours . . . a lifetime with her.

"Nope," Jace said. "Not yet, but soon."

He held his hand out to her. She came and took it. He felt he could crush her in his arms and never let go, so great was his desire to hold her.

Annie and Doc slipped out of the room and left them staring at each other. Jace motioned for Bobbie to sit. He kept hold of her hand so she had to sit next to him on the sofa.

"Can you stay for a few minutes?"

Bobbie smiled at him. "You're the boss."

"Since when did that stop you from arguing?"

"I haven't been that bad." She looked at his stomach. "I guess you're feeling better?"

"Yep. Doc says I can get up and about again in a couple days. That brings me to a question. I'm riding up to the north pasture day after tomorrow. Will you go with me?"

Bobbie's gaze dropped back to his stomach, concern on her face.

Jace laughed. "In a buggy, of course."

"Oh." Bobbie looked at him and smiled. Then she looked down and tugged her hand free. "Actually, I wanted to ask you for a few days off. The paper has a listing for a nice little ranch. I wanted to ride up and look it over."

Her words hurt more than a hundred stab wounds. "Can it wait? At least for a while

longer? Ride with me, Bobbie. We'll pack
food and have a picnic. If you still want a
few days off after that, I won't stop you."
Please, God, make her say yes.

Bobbie's smile reappeared. "All right. That
sounds nice."

"Jace?"

He looked up to find Sheriff Thomas in
the doorway.

"Ya got a minute?"

"Sure, Morgan. Have a seat."

Morgan glanced from Jace to Bobbie and
back again. "My deputy and I have looked
all over that mountain. We can't find Grant.
At first, we followed the drops of blood, but
they disappeared. So did his footsteps. Once
there was no trail, we didn't know which
way to go. Either he died out there somewhere or he's hiding out again."

"Did you burn down that shack for me?"

"Yes. He can't hide there again."

Jace reclaimed possession of Bobbie's
hand. "He won't get you again, Bobbie.
We'll make sure of that."

"It's not me I'm worried about."

"It's my guess he's dead." Morgan turned
to Bobbie. "With all the blood you said you
saw and with all the drops we followed, I'm
thinking he passed out in some hole and
never woke up."

"We can only hope." Jace squeezed Bobbie's hand. "You still up for that ride, knowing this?"

She gave him a slow smile. "Sure. I'll protect you."

Jace would have tried to kiss her if Morgan hadn't been peering at them from under the rim of his dusty Stetson.

Bobbie awoke and smiled. *One more day until my ride with Jace.* She dressed, skipped down the stairs, and joined Annie in the kitchen. "Can I help with something?"

"Sure. Watch these eggs while I finish these hotcakes."

The two women worked in silence until Annie bumped Bobbie with her hip. "It's about time, you know."

Since Annie whispered, Bobbie assumed she didn't want to awaken Jace. "About time for what?"

"That you fell in love with my brother."

Bobbie's face felt hotter than the flame under her pan. She cleared her throat. "What makes you say that?"

"Well, let's see." Annie put her hand on her hip as she smiled up at her. "Maybe it's the way you look at him. Or maybe it's the way your face seems to glow when he's looking at you. Or —"

"All right. That's enough."

Annie chuckled and turned back to her hotcakes. "So you admit it?"

Bobbie sighed. "Yes."

"Have you told him?"

"No."

Annie looked at her again. "So?"

"So what?"

"Do you plan to tell him?"

Bobbie shrugged.

"I swear you two have harder heads than those horses out there."

Bobbie laughed. "If it's meant to be, it'll happen."

"Oh, it's meant to be all right. You two are perfect for each other."

The conversation ended when Pete and the kids joined them. Jace wandered out from his temporary room minutes later. Bobbie and Annie exchanged several glances as they ate. Bobbie wanted to kick Annie when she saw her staring and grinning at Jace. She would have if she could have reached her.

Jace set down his fork. "What, Annie? Is something stuck to my face?" He wiped his hand across his mouth.

"Nope. You're fine." Annie switched her glance between Bobbie and Jace. She grinned and looked down.

Bobbie avoided his gaze.

"Ben?" Jace turned to his nephew. "Do you know what they're up to?" The boy shook his head. "Well, do me a favor. Keep an eye on them for me. The last time they acted like this, I ended up with a haircut."

Bobbie choked on her hotcake. Annie grabbed a napkin and held it over her mouth. Jace stood and looked at both of them.

"I'll be at my house doing some book work. I can't stay here. You two have me scared half to death."

He walked out of the room. Bobbie and Annie exchanged a look that sent them into gales of laughter.

Bobbie sat in the buggy the next morning tapping her foot on the step. The toe of her scuffed leather boots stuck out from the hem of her new denims. She had contemplated wearing a dress but thought that would be too obvious and settled for her new jeans and shirt instead. She rolled her eyes and groaned as she put her head back. She had looked forward to this ride for two days. Now she couldn't seem to stop her fidgeting.

Mack trotted over to the edge of the corral and looked at her. She felt guilty leaving him behind. As a way of making amends, she put him in the corral rather than leave him in his stall.

Annie stepped out and dumped some dirty water onto the grass. The two women's gazes met.

"Your hair sure looks pretty like that, Bobbie. We need to fix it like that more often."

"Thank you."

She'd asked Annie to help her fix it in something other than the usual braid but still wear her hat. The result was a loose bun at the nape of her neck with soft tendrils outlining her face.

"You two have fun."

"Thank you, Annie, and thanks for fixing our lunch."

Annie waved away the comment. "Enjoy."

She disappeared inside as Jace headed toward the buggy. He'd been walking around the ranch site with Dew. He looked tired. She was about to ask him about it when he held up his hand.

"Don't say it. I'm fine, and there's no way you can stop me from going on this ride."

Bobbie grinned. "I wouldn't dream of it." She handed him the reins. He shook his head.

"You drive."

"Where to?"

He smiled. "I think you know."

She returned his smile and flicked the reins.

They made small talk all the way to her favorite spot overlooking the river. She could feel a certain energy coming from Jace. He placed his arm along the back of the seat and gave her little hugs from time to time. They shared so many funny tales of their youth that Bobbie's sides hurt from all the laughter.

As she told another story from her childhood, he ran his finger from her ear down her jawline and along her bottom lip. Her pulse raced as her mouth went dry. She lost her concentration and almost couldn't finish the story.

Bobbie reined in the horses. "Here we are." Did he notice how squeaky her voice sounded? Heat rose to her cheeks.

When they reached the spot, he helped her carry the picnic basket and blanket. After climbing on top of the boulder, he laid out the blanket and took the basket from her. Then he held his hand out and helped her up. She looked out at the view.

"Beautiful," he said.

"Mmm-hmm. It is, isn't it?"

She looked up at him and found him gazing at her.

He cupped her jaw in his hands. His thumbs rubbed her cheeks in tiny circles. His head dipped toward her. "Do you want to eat or talk first?"

"Ah —" It was difficult to breathe, let alone talk. "I'm not very hungry right now."

Just when she thought Jace would kiss her, he pulled away and motioned to the blanket. "Let's sit down."

Bobbie gladly accepted his offer, her legs too weak to go on. "Are you tired?"

Jace shook his head. "I'm fine." He smiled as he settled next to her. "You make me a little light-headed, and we're up pretty high."

She could feel herself blushing and looked away. He took her by the chin and turned her face toward him. He didn't remove his hand.

"Nothing's changed. I still love you."

She nodded.

"What I want to know is how you feel about me." His intense gaze held hers. "You told me you want to go look at a ranch. That tells me you want to leave the Double K. Yet you've been acting different lately." He smiled. "Less prickly."

Bobbie took a deep breath. "I . . . I've never felt like this about anyone before."

His thumb rubbed below her lip. "Felt like what?"

Bobbie thought she might cry for all the emotions flowing through her. "Disappointment when we have to say good-bye. Looking forward to when we can see each other again. My heart pounding when you look into my eyes or touch me." Her last sentence came out sounding breathless. She took his hand in hers. "I don't want to leave, Jace. I love you. But I need to know that you trust me. That I won't have to continually prove myself."

Jace's lips brushed across hers making her catch her breath. He pulled back and looked into her eyes. He leaned down again. His lips caught hers in a kiss that staggered her senses. They were both gasping when he pulled back. He cupped her cheek in his hand.

"I do trust you, Bobbie. Enough to offer you my heart for the rest of my life."

Happy tears formed. "I accept."

Jace smiled and pulled further away from her. "I'm going to have to watch myself around you, Bobbie. When you look at me like that, I can't resist wanting to kiss you." He took her hand and pressed it to his lips. "I think I'd better settle for this for now."

Bobbie reached inside the basket and

pulled out a sandwich. "Or you can have this."

He laughed as he took it from her.

They finished off the meal and packed up. Jace slid off the boulder. He held out his hand and helped Bobbie down. Instead of releasing it, he held it all the way to the buggy.

She turned the buggy around and headed home, feeling warm inside. Better than that, she felt loved. Months ago, she had come to the Double K with dreams of one day running her own ranch. Instead, she discovered the unconditional love and friendship of God and the Kincaid family. It was better than any dream.

Jace ran the back of his fingers along her cheek. "What are you thinking about to make you look so serene?"

Bobbie smiled. "The blessings God has given me."

"I know the feeling. We've both been through a lot, but knowing God's been walking with us is incredible. He's brought us through it all."

The peaceful feeling lasted until Bobbie broke their staring match and looked away from him.

"Jace."

"Hmm?"

"Look." Bobbie nodded toward home.

Smoke rose into the air in several wispy threads. Jace sat up straight. He snatched the reins from her and slapped them down on the horse's rump.

Bobbie grabbed the seat and said another prayer.

THIRTY-TWO

Jace fought the panic clawing at him. The smoke grew thicker as they neared the ranch. He prayed that Annie and the children were out of the house. Flames licked the air from the bunkhouse and the chow hall as they pulled into the ranch site. They were beyond help.

He drove the buggy past his house, the only building not burning. He stopped at Annie's house and ran toward the kitchen door.

"Annie!"

The piercing scream that came from inside stopped his heart.

He grabbed the doorknob and jerked his hand back, then ran to the front door. Flames licked along the entire porch. A sob of fear escaped his throat. He ran around to the back, grabbed a stick, and broke out a window. He peeled off his coat, laid it over the broken glass, and crawled through.

"Annie!" He moved toward the kitchen. Smoke filled every room. He heard the kids crying. "Annie!" He coughed and dropped to his knees. He crawled toward the stairs. His eyes and lungs burned. "Annie!"

"Jace!"

"Where are you?"

"We're upstairs. I can't see." She started coughing until it sounded like she gagged.

"I'm coming up."

Someone bumped him from behind.

"Jace?"

"Bobbie? Get out of here!"

"No. I can help."

"Get on your hands and knees. Stay by my side."

They crawled to the top of the stairs, then felt their way along the floor. "Annie!" The flames roared below and drowned out his voice. He could hear the kids screaming and gagging up ahead. "Annie?"

"Over here." Her voice was weakening.

"Wait here, Bobbie. I'll bring you the kids, and you get them out of here."

"All right."

He located them within moments. "Give me the kids, Annie."

"No. We stay together," Annie said with determination.

Jace wanted to argue but knew he

wouldn't get anywhere. "Let's go." He grabbed a child under each arm. "Hang on to my shirt, Annie. Whatever happens, don't let go."

All of them were coughing nonstop, but the kids' wheezing scared Jace the most. He had to hurry. They reached the steps.

"Bobbie?"

"Right here."

"Take Ben," he said and felt her pull the boy from his arm. Jace ripped off his kerchief and placed it over Sara's nose and mouth.

"Let's get out of here."

They all scooted down the steps on their bottoms. Halfway down, Bobbie yelled, "Jace! The flames!"

He looked down and saw them creeping toward the stairs.

"Run for it, Bobbie. Go!"

He couldn't see her but heard her footsteps fading.

"Come on, Annie. We gotta hurry."

She scooted past him. He grabbed for her and found a hand. She was headed for the kitchen. He pulled her back.

"We can't go that way. The back window. Go toward the back."

Jace gagged on the words. He was running out of air. He hated to imagine Sara's condition.

They found the window. Bobbie stood waiting for them. Jace handed Sara to her.

"Come on, Annie. You're next."

The maneuver was difficult because of her pregnancy. Bobbie assisted from outside while Jace helped Annie keep her balance. Annie's feet touched the ground, and she ran to her children. Jace crawled through and joined them.

The children were coughing to the point of throwing up. Sara cried and gagged again. Jace pulled Ben into his arms. He seemed to be breathing easier. Tears ran down Ben's face and left trails through the soot. Jace kissed them away and thanked God in his heart they all made it out of the house.

The sound of shrieking pierced the air. Bobbie looked up, her eyes wide with fear. "Mack!"

"No, Bobbie. Stay here."

Jace's breath was wasted. She sprinted around the house and disappeared.

Bobbie raced toward the barn. Flames devoured the entire front side. Movement to her left caught her attention. She looked and saw Mack in the corral, rearing in fear. Relief rushed through her.

More shrieks came from the barn. The stallion and wagon team were still inside. She ran to the side and peeked in one of the windows. The flames were mostly to the front of the barn. With all the dry straw inside, it wouldn't be long before it sped through the entire structure.

She looked around. *Where are all the men?* She heard a loud crash. The roof of the bunkhouse collapsed. *Oh, no, Lord. Please don't let them be in there.* Another shriek from one of the horses sounded like a child's scream. The cry sent shivers down her spine. She peeked in the barn window again. The flames were moving toward the back in a hurry.

Bobbie ran to the back of the barn. Thumping came from the other side of the door. Her heart pounded right along with each bump.

"Help!" The voice sounded raspy.

"I'm here." She tugged on the latch. It wouldn't budge. She examined it and found a piece of wood jammed near the hinge. She tried prying it out, but it wouldn't move. Bobbie wanted to scream with frustration. She took off her boot and hammered on it till it fell free.

She flipped the latch and pulled the door open. Smoke billowed toward her as Beans fell through the doorway. He coughed and gagged, then turned back into the barn. Bobbie pulled her boot on.

"Beans? What are you doing?"

She grabbed at him but missed. Smoke burned her eyes. Beans backed into her, dragging a limp body through the doorway. She grabbed an arm and helped pull him to safety. That's when she saw the man's face.

"Grant?"

Beans coughed and spat. "Yeah. He attacked me in there."

"Is he dead?"

"I don't know."

"Is anyone else in there?"

Beans shook his head.

"I'm going in after the horses." She jumped to her feet, took a deep breath, and ran into the barn.

"Bobbie! No!"

The desperation in Jace's voice didn't stop her from dashing back inside. She ran to the farthest stall. The flames were mere feet away, and the horses reared and banged against the stalls. Bobbie's eyes and throat burned.

She grabbed a sack, stood with her back toward the flames, and flung the gate open. She waved the sack at the horse as he came out of the stall, and he ran off toward the door. She prayed he made it out as she moved to the next stall and sent the next horse out toward the door.

The stallion was farthest from the flames but acted the wildest of the three. Bobbie dropped to her knees as she tried to catch her breath. She struggled to her feet, reached for the latch to the gate, and flung it open. The stallion ran right toward her. Bobbie waved the sack in his eyes. He bumped her as he raced away from the flames, throwing her back. She landed hard.

Bobbie rolled to her side. Her chest burned as she fought to get air and found nothing but smoke. She held her sleeve over her nose. The front of the barn was collapsing. She couldn't find the strength to get up.

She rose to her knees and then to her feet and stumbled toward the door. She started falling and put her hands out. They met a pair of strong arms. Bobbie felt herself being lifted. In a matter of moments, she was breathing in fresh air. She choked and gagged for several minutes. She looked up into Jace's concerned face staring down at her. He pulled her against him.

"Don't you ever do something like that again," he rasped in her ear.

"Where are the others?" Her voice came

in a choked whisper.

"Others? You mean Dew and David?"

"And Sonny and Adam."

Jace looked around. "Dew and David are off checking on some breeding mares for me. I sent Adam to town."

"And Sonny?"

Jace stood. "I don't know. He was to stay here and keep an eye on the place."

He headed toward the still smoldering remains of the bunkhouse. Beans and Bobbie followed. Sonny lay face down several feet from the bunkhouse. Bobbie ran toward him and dropped to her knees. Jace knelt next to her. Together, they turned him over. Bobbie gasped.

Sonny's eyes and nose were swollen and blackened. A large piece of wood lay nearby. Jace felt for a pulse.

"He's alive." Jace lifted him into his arms and carried him to the buggy. "We've got to get everyone to town."

Bobbie nodded and headed toward what was left of the house to retrieve Annie and the kids. She heard some shouts and turned. Her heart lifted. The town was coming to them. Pete led the way.

As the sun prepared to greet the mountain crests, Jace and Bobbie stood next to Beans near the ruins of the barn. Some men from town were busy wrapping Grant's body in a blanket. They lifted him into the back of a wagon, then climbed onto the seat and headed the horses toward the bridge. Pete and the doctor had taken Annie, the children, and Sonny into town. Matt and Rebecca Cromwell invited Pete and his family to stay with them as long as necessary. They wanted Bobbie to join them. She shook her head and insisted on staying a while longer, as did the rest of his wranglers. Jace appreciated their support, but his insides were as charred as the remains of his barn and Annie's house.

Beans gestured toward the departing wagon. "I didn't mean to kill him, Jace."

Jace turned and met Beans's gaze. "I know." Jace clapped him on the back. "Tell me what happened."

"I was in the barn getting some eggs. The buzzard ran in with a torch. He told me he just wanted the stallion and he'd leave. Said something about needing a good stud for his new ranch." He looked at Jace. "My guess is he planned to burn the barn once he got what he wanted."

"You're probably right. Tell me about the fight."

"Weren't much of a fight. He didn't seem

to have much spunk. Bobbie's bullet musta weakened him. He swung the torch at me to keep me back. I smacked him in the jaw when I had the chance. He threw the torch down and came at me. The barn lit up like kindling. I hit him as hard as I could. He fell back an' almost landed in the fire." Beans scuffed his boot in the dirt. "I felt I had to help him. So I grabbed him and that's when I saw the branding iron stuck in his back. I dragged him to the door. I didn't know he was already dead."

Jace squeezed his arm. "You did fine."

"I couldn't get the door open. I thought I was gonna die. Bobbie saved my life."

Jace patted his back one more time. He'd heard all he could stand and craved some time alone. He wandered off toward Annie's house and stepped into the ashes. Some pieces of wood still smoldered. He kicked at them. There was nothing left. Nothing had survived but his own house. He looked up at it and shook his head. The only reason he could figure that Grant didn't burn it too was that he didn't have time to get to it. Either that or he wanted a place to live once he took the ranch from him.

Jace walked through what used to be the living room. He heard something crunch under his boot. He looked down and found one of Annie's porcelain dolls. He grieved for all that had been lost at the hands of an evil and selfish man. Jace and Annie lost their parents. Annie lost her home and belongings, and he lost his ranch.

I'm beaten. An evil man set out to destroy me and won. Why, Lord? Why did this have to happen? What good could possibly come out of this? He stifled a sigh. *Lord, I'm trying to trust that You have a perfect plan, but I'm struggling with doubts right now.*

He looked around the ranch. Bobbie stood watching him. His heart broke completely. He planned to marry her, to have his children with her. He had dreams of running the ranch and riding over the range with her by his side for the rest of his life. Those dreams were dead — burned up with everything else. He had nothing to offer. He couldn't ask her to marry a poor man. He dropped his gaze from hers. He'd lost her too.

The sound of a fast-approaching horse jerked him from his thoughts. His heart sank even further at the look of concern on Cade's face as his horse raced toward him. He stopped at the edge of the ashes. "Annie's having her baby!"

Jace ran toward the corral, but Cade

stopped him. "Take my horse. I'll get yours and follow."

Jace jumped onto the saddle and heeled the horse into a gallop. He prayed the whole three miles into town that Annie and her baby were all right. With all the smoke she had inhaled, he feared for them both. This was too soon. She still had a few weeks before the baby was due. Sweat drizzled down his back as he ran into Matt and Rebecca's house. Silence met him. His fears increased.

He moved to the kitchen and found Matt and Mandy, Matt's daughter, trying to feed Ben and Sara. The children ran to him. He scooped them in his arms and pressed his face into their hair. They smelled like soap. Where had they gotten the clothes they were wearing? They looked wonderful, as though they had never fought for their very lives earlier.

Jace looked up.

Matt met his gaze and shook his head. "I haven't heard anything yet."

Matt motioned to a chair, and Jace sat but waved away the plate Matt offered. His stomach wouldn't hold it down. He set Ben and Sara on the floor.

"Why don't you two finish eating before your food gets cold?" They picked at the food. They didn't look any hungrier than he felt.

A scream from up the stairs set his hair on end. Jace jumped from the chair and ran up the steps. He skidded to a stop when he heard the wail of a newborn, then leaned against the wall and slid to the floor. With both hands over his face, Jace broke down and wept.

THIRTY-THREE

Jace sat in the office of his house waiting for all of his wranglers to arrive. He had managed to avoid Bobbie for two days, even when she came to the Cromwells to visit Annie and the baby. Bobbie finally accepted the pastor and his wife's invitation to stay with them. Jace stayed by himself on the ranch. Staying alone made eluding her easy, but he wouldn't be able to avoid her forever. Today, he had to face her — and all his other ranch hands.

He felt better after getting some sleep. Better, but not great. The bitterness was gone. Someday, he'd get to the point where he could forgive Grant. That ability could only come from God. The sense of defeat and failure lingered over him like a dingy gray cloud. He'd been beaten. He couldn't shake the feeling that he'd let down his dad. Dad had been proud of this place. He'd taken the small ranch Mr. Hillyer had sold him and built it into something grand. Over the years, he'd added more acreage and increased the herd. In less than two years, Jace let it all slip away.

The sound of voices brought his mind back to what he had to do. He stood as the door opened. Dew allowed Bobbie to enter first, and the rest of the men followed. Jace met Bobbie's gaze for a moment. Pain and questions lingered in her eyes.

He turned away and looked at Sonny's face for the first time since the fire. He had since learned that Sonny didn't have any idea what had happened that day. Sonny had stepped out of the bunkhouse and something slammed him in the head. He didn't remember anything else until he awoke to find Doc Barnes stitching up his face.

Jace pulled him into his arms and patted him on the back. "You look terrible," he said with a grin.

"Well, thank you, Jace. Yer not so pretty yerself."

Jace clapped him on the back again. He would miss these men. He motioned for them to take a seat and chose a spot against his desk for himself. He took a deep breath and let it out slowly.

"What I have to tell you isn't good news."

He took another breath. This was harder than he had thought. "I'm selling the ranch. I'm going to have to let you all go."

Dew rose to his feet. "No, Jace." He looked at the others, then back at Jace. "We had a feeling you might decide to do this. We all talked, and we decided we'd work for you for free till you get back on your feet."

Jace's eyes burned. He rubbed a hand over his face and shook his head.

"I appreciate your offer, but it won't help. I don't have the funds to rebuild. Not even with the money Sheriff Thomas found in the shack. Only a small portion of it came my way." He rubbed the back of his neck, but the ache of disappointment remained. "I've figured it every way there is. All I have is the land, a few head of cattle, my stallion, and a small bank account. I could sell the horses and cattle and rebuild all the structures, but that would leave nothing for the following year."

He looked at his desk and fiddled with some papers. "At least if I sell the land, I'll have a little money to get by." He scanned their faces. "You've all been great. Hard workers with a big heart. I wish I had a dozen more like you."

Not a word was spoken. He hated the

silence. He stood and moved behind his desk. Several sheets of paper lay inside one of the drawers. He pulled them out and cleared his throat. "There's some money waiting for each of you at the bank. I talked to Pete. He'll have it ready for you. I've also written up letters for you. Maybe it'll help you land a job on a good ranch."

"This *is* a good ranch," Sonny said.

Jace looked at him and noted the red-rimmed eyes. "It *was* a good ranch. It can be again in the hands of a good rancher."

"*You're* a good rancher."

All eyes swung to rest on Bobbie. The men nodded in agreement. Jace could see in her eyes her love for him, and he ached to hold her. He looked away, thankful he was behind the desk. He handed each of them a letter.

"I'll be praying all of you find a job soon. It's my hope you hire on at a successful ranch with a good and honest boss."

Dew stepped up to take his paper. "Where will you go, Jace?"

He shrugged. "I'll be looking for a place just like you, I guess. I don't think I could stay here and work for the new owner."

"I can understand that. You had anyone come asking for the place?"

"I haven't announced it yet. I wanted to talk to all of you first."

"I appreciate that, Jace." He held out his hand. Jace took it in a firm grasp. "You take care of yourself, you hear? You ever need another foreman, look me up."

"You'd be the first I'd ask, Dew. Keep in touch. Pete and Annie plan to stay in Rockdale. You'll be able to reach me through them."

They shook again before Dew left. The other men filed past Jace and said their good-byes. Bobbie still sat in her chair. Her stare bore straight through him. He sighed. He hated to hurt her but saw no other way.

She gestured toward his stomach. "How's your wound?"

He looked down and patted it. "It's fine. I'd actually forgotten all about it. Doc says it looks good."

"*You* look good."

He met her gaze and tried to smile. "Thank you." Except for the sadness in her eyes, she looked wonderful — too wonderful for him to say the words. She stood and walked toward him.

"What about us, Jace? You said you loved me. Now you're letting me go like the other wranglers, like there was nothing between us." She choked on the words.

"I'm sorry, Bobbie. I didn't want it to be this way."

"Do you still love me?" Tears glistened in her eyes.

"Yes!" The word ripped from his throat. His eyes burned. "I'll always love you."

"Then why, Jace? I don't understand."

"I can't ask you to go through this hardship with me. I want better for you than that."

"I've been through the hardship with you. We survived. Our love survived."

"But I still had something to offer you then. Now I have nothing."

"You have me."

He looked down and shook his head again. "I can't. Don't you see?"

Bobbie choked on a sob. "I see your pride keeping us apart."

"I'm sorry, Bobbie." He wanted to reach out to her. He gripped the edge of the desk. "I hope you'll go back to Roy. At least then I'll know someone's taking care of you. Do you think you might do that?"

She sniffled. "I don't know right now. I haven't given it any thought."

Jace leaned toward her. "Will you let me know?"

Bobbie started crying in earnest. She nodded and turned to leave.

"Bobbie?"

She stopped.

"I —" The clock on the mantel ticked by the seconds. "Be careful."

She stepped through the door and closed it behind her. He slammed his fist onto the desk and fell onto his chair.

Help me, Lord. I don't know how much more I can take.

Beans had waited for Bobbie. She didn't think she'd ever been so glad to see him. She stepped from the porch into his waiting arms. She vented all her pain and frustration into his shoulder. Beans didn't say a word. He didn't have to. His comforting presence and his arms were what she needed.

When her cries turned to hiccups, he handed her his kerchief. She took it and tried to smile. "Thank you."

He put his arm around her shoulders and led her toward Mack. "Don't give up yet, Bobbie. It's all still new. Give him time. He'll come around."

She shook her head. "I don't know, Beans."

He grunted. She smiled.

"I'm going to miss your grunts, Beans."

He grunted again and she laughed.

"That's better. Nothing brighter than your smile."

Beans rode with her all the way to Pastor Robbins's house. They said their good-byes with a long embrace. He touched her cheek.

"You take care o' yourself, little lady."

She nodded, too emotional to speak.

Bobbie sat through the evening meal, toying with her food while she listened to Pastor and Garnett chat. She didn't join in unless they asked her a question. Afterward they prepared for their evening Bible study and asked her to join them. Her Bible had burned in the fire and she hadn't attempted to purchase another one. Maybe some Scripture was just what she needed to perk her up.

The pastor led the group in prayer, and then he asked them for examples of what happens when God's people lack faith. After several in the group spoke, he described the wonders God performed for the Israelites in order to free them from slavery in Egypt — the plagues on the Egyptians, parting a sea, providing water and food in the wilderness. The Israelites witnessed an abundance of God's power and provision. Yet when they were to take possession of the land He had prepared for them, they refused to enter because they feared the people living there.

"Because of their lack of faith," the pastor said, "most of them didn't get to see the land God promised them. They lived in the desert for forty years. Without faith, it is impossible to please God." Pastor Robbins closed his Bible. "We should try to look back and remember all the wonderful things God has done. The Bible records so many examples of His faithfulness, as do our lives. I think we should each sit down some time this next week and make a list of all the wonderful things He's done for us. Once we see them, how can we not be thankful and trust Him in return?"

Bobbie marveled at the study of faith. Did the pastor realize her need and prepare the message just for her? She went to her room, readied for bed, and climbed under the covers. With all her tossing from side to side, it didn't take long for the covers to come loose.

Bobbie sighed and sat up. She lit the lantern and fixed her bed before moving to the chair by the window. The stars were out in force. She pulled her feet up under her, wrapped her arms around her legs, and rested her chin on her knees.

The stars confirmed God's power. The sun, moon, and every living creature spoke of His strength and sovereignty. Annie's new baby boy that Bobbie held in her arms earlier that day was another example of

God's miracles, as was the change He had produced in her own life. She didn't have to look far to find proof of His love and faithfulness.

The pastor's words echoed in her mind. *How can we not trust Him?*

"Trust in the Lord with all thine heart," she said against her knees, "and . . . and . . ." *What was that part about our paths?* She jumped from the chair and moved to the dresser. She opened the drawers one by one. Nothing. Her gaze moved to the small table beside the bed. She pulled the top drawer open and smiled. She had a feeling Garnett would have a Bible in every room of the house.

Bobbie sat on the side of the bed and turned the flame of the lamp higher. She flipped to Proverbs for the verse that eluded her. Her finger trailed down the page. "There!" *Trust in the Lord with all thine heart; and lean not on thine own understanding. In all thy ways acknowledge Him, and He shall direct thy paths.*

"Direct my paths. That's exactly what I need," she said.

Show me the way I should go, Lord. I feel so lost right now. Help me know what I'm supposed to do.

Her thoughts moved to Jace. She prayed

the Lord would help him too. He seemed just as lost as she felt.

The pastor and Garnett were already in the kitchen chatting when she joined them the next morning. She felt better, rested. Seeing the newspaper lying on the table, she poured herself a cup of coffee and began reading. Maybe she should take Jace's advice and go back to Roy. For some reason, that idea didn't appeal to her. She checked the ads. Maybe some rancher was looking for help. She had a feeling the other wranglers were doing the same thing this morning.

"Maybe we could have a bake sale or something to help raise money," Garnett said. "There's got to be some way we can help."

Bobbie continued to scan the paper as she listened to the couple talking. They had her attention, but she didn't interrupt.

"I know if we could raise the funds, most of the men in town would help him rebuild." The pastor tapped the table. "It's been a while since I've swung a hammer, but I'd sure be out there helping."

"And I'd be there with the bandages for your thumbs," Garnett said.

The pastor chuckled, but then grew serious. "I don't know. It may take something big to make it work, something like a partner. Jace would probably hate the idea at first, but someone might be able to talk him into it. It sure beats losing the ranch entirely. At least I would think so."

Bobbie sipped at her coffee. Her gaze was on the newspaper, but she was no longer reading. Her mind raced with plans. She stood and headed for the door.

"Bobbie?"

She turned and saw the questioning look on Garnett's face.

"Are you all right?"

Bobbie smiled. "All right and getting better by the minute." She slipped into her coat. "Um, I'm going to run an errand. If all goes well, I may be out of town for a while. I'll let you know one way or the other."

She moved back to the table to wrap her arms around Garnett's neck and kiss her cheek. She moved to the pastor. He stood and accepted her hug.

"I appreciate you two more than you know."

She dashed for the door, praying Dew hadn't left town yet.

THIRTY-FOUR

Once finished with the few chores Jace had to do each day, all that was left was to feed the stallion. Jace propped one foot on the bottom rung of the corral and rested his arms on the top rung as the black moved the few steps to greet him. His quiet nicker produced a smile from Jace, the first in many days. He reached out and caressed the stallion's head, amazed at the horse it had become under Bobbie's firm but tender care.

Bobbie's face came to mind, something that had happened quite often since she left. He knew letting her go would always rate near the top of difficult things he endured. He snorted. *I didn't let her go. I pushed her away.*

Someone rode across the ranch toward Jace. He cringed when he recognized Hank Willett. *Why am I not surprised he's the first to respond?*

Posting the notice of his need to sell the ranch took more than a week. He wanted to delay the inevitable as long as he could.

"Hello, Jace," Hank said as he dismounted. The man's grin was a little too wide for Jace's liking.

"Hank." Jace shook the hand extended. "What brings you by this afternoon?"

"Well, I believe you know what I want. I think I've made it clear over the past year. Don't play d—" He cleared his throat. "I want to buy your ranch."

Jace bit back his smile. Being nice must really hurt this man.

"What's your price?"

Jace quoted an amount. Hank cursed and spat on the ground.

"You aren't getting that price from any man." Hank pointed at the ruins. "You've got no barn. You've got no bunkhouse."

"Why would you need a bunkhouse, Hank? You already have one at your place."

"You're asking too much."

Jace shrugged again. "That's my right."

Hank cursed at him. "I know you're only doing this to keep me from getting the ranch."

Hank continued haranguing him, but the words didn't register. His gaze moved beyond his angry neighbor.

Hank thumped him on the chest. "Listen to me, you young pup! I —"

Jace shoved past him and moved past the corrals. Cattle were running down the slope toward his ranch. His mouth dropped wide when Dew opened the gate. David chased several horses into the corral. Sonny, Adam, and two others herded the cattle out toward the prairie.

There must be close to 300 head.

Wagon wheels rumbled over his bridge. He turned back. Bobbie sat on her horse near a corral. She gave him a timid smile as she dismounted, melting his heart. He moved toward her, stopping mere inches from her. He thought he'd never see her again.

The wagons pulled up next to them. Cade sat on one with Beans driving the other. They were laden with new lumber. All the men rode up behind Bobbie. The two became the center of attention. Jace looked at Bobbie for an explanation.

"There's more lumber on the way," she said.

Jace had to swallow to make his voice work. "Why?"

Bobbie's gaze dropped from his. He willed her to look at him.

"After I left here the other day, I did a lot

of praying and thinking."

He saw her throat working to swallow. Why did she appear nervous? What was she about to say?

"Jace, what do you think about a partnership — between you and me? I've got the money. You've got the land. We could make it work." She looked around. "You don't want to lose this place. I know you don't." Her gaze went back to his. "I don't either. I've dreamed of owning a ranch, and I think this arrangement could be the answer to both of our prayers."

Jace thought his legs would buckle. He wished he could sit down. His brain struggled to comprehend all that she'd said.

"Jace?" Dew dismounted and stood next to him. "I think she'd make an excellent partner. She approached me the other day with her ideas. They were sound. I agreed with everything she presented." He motioned to all the other men around them. "As you can see, they all agreed. They rode to Pueblo with us."

Dew placed his hand on Jace's shoulder. "We found some of your cattle in Pueblo, Jace. About eighty head. They bore an altered brand, but they were definitely yours. Bobbie went to work proving it and won. She's quite a businesswoman, Jace. I wish you could have seen her in action. It was a sight to behold." He chuckled. "I would have hated to be the man trying to say no to her."

Jace looked at Bobbie. Pink tinged her cheeks.

Dew pointed toward the prairie. "There's almost three hundred head of cattle. She also bought more horses, including two good breeding mares. She's got the best eye for horses I've ever seen."

She's got the best eyes I've ever seen. Jace couldn't look away from them.

"We also have two young men looking for jobs. They're willing to learn all there is to know about wrangling." Dew bumped him. "Jace?"

Jace looked at Dew and saw the mirth on his face.

Dew gestured. "Two new men."

Jace saw the boys from the cattle drive. Excitement stirred within him. The vision for the new beginning Bobbie presented came to life before his eyes. He saw the ranch flourishing with new cattle and horses. He pictured new buildings gleaming in the sun. He saw Bobbie standing next to him as they enjoyed God's blessings.

"Jace?" Bobbie's soft voice brought him back to earth.

He reached for her hand, but someone grabbed his arm from behind. Jace spun around.

"I'm buying this ranch!" Hank's eyes burned with fury. "We were making a deal."

Jace removed Hank's hand from his arm. "Sorry, Hank. You didn't meet my requirements." He turned and put his arm around Bobbie. "I've been made a better offer."

"Why, you —"

Hank's fist drew back. Dew grabbed him by the elbow and turned him around.

"I think you've been given your answer, Willett. Time for you to move on."

Hank yanked his arm free. He sent Jace one last glare before he turned and walked to his horse. He left without another word.

Dew faced Jace. "Did that mean what I think it did?"

Jace smiled as he turned to Bobbie. "Under one condition. If it's not met, the deal is off."

Bobbie's eyes looked hopeful. "What is it? What's the condition?"

Jace took her hands in his. "We have to be life partners. I love you, Bobbie. I can't work beside you any longer unless you're my wife."

They stared at each other in silence. Bobbie's tear-filled eyes did all the talking for her Still, he wanted to hear the words.

"So whadaya say, Bobbie?" Dew said.

Bobbie laughed and wiped her eyes. "I say you men better get to work on that bunkhouse if you want a roof over your heads before the first snowfall."

The men whooped and tossed their hats into the air. Jace pulled Bobbie into his arms and swung her around. She hugged his neck. He set her back on her feet but kept her in his arms, never wanting to let her go again. He leaned close, his lips near hers.

"So do we have a deal?" he whispered.

She leaned back and held out her hand. He took it and placed it around his neck.

"I had something different in mind to seal the deal." He leaned down and kissed her.

Jace pulled back, and a smile spread over Bobbie's face.

"I like the way you do business," she said with a saucy wink.

Jace laughed and gave her another quick kiss.

They turned and watched the men unload the wagons. The sun setting behind them caressed the top of the mountains. The pink blended into orange and then yellow. The scene was breathtaking.

Jace smiled. Dawn lingered only hours

away. He knew it would be brighter than
ever with Bobbie by his side.

ABOUT THE AUTHOR

Janelle Mowery is the author of several novels, including *Where the Truth Lies.* When not writing, reading, and researching, she is active in her church. Born and raised in Minnesota, Janelle now resides in Texas with her husband and two sons, where she and her family have the opportunity to raise orphaned raccoons, look at beautiful deer, and make friends with curious armadillos.